SPECIAL DELIVERY

Ted Lowenstein, a new member of the team, returned to tell her that the package was addressed specifically to Inspector Donna Thorpe.

Donna went down the long corridor to the steel-reinforced room where the package had first been taken. It was Ted's job to pry open tricky packages, and he just stood there shaking his head.

"This is not a bomb. We peeled away the outer layers and the dog doesn't respond to anything he's trained on."

"So, what's the odor?" Donna asked, without really needing an answer. The stench of human decay was familiar to her now.

"I think you know."

Thorpe came closer to the table where the package rested. The contents were fully exposed, and she stared rigidly at the sight of the pulpy human tissue resting neatly on a white napkin. On the outside were the words: WASHINGTON APPLES ARE BEST.

"He's been busy again."

DR. O

ROBERT W. WALKER

ZEBRA BOOKS
KENSINGTON PUBLISHING CORP.

*This book of horror and mayhem, written by a crazy is affec-
tionately dedicated to a co-crazy, the good person who got me
this job, Adele Leone, for whom such cliches as thanks, thanks
and thanks just don't suffice to cut, carve or dice it . . .*

ZEBRA BOOKS

are published by

Kensington Publishing Corp.
475 Park Avenue South
New York, NY 10016

Copyright © 1991 by Robert W. Walker

First printing: August, 1991

Printed in the United States of America

Book One

The soul of man does violence to itself . . . when it becomes an abcess and . . . tumor on the universe. . . .

> Marcus Aurelius, Meditations

Every one is a moon, and has a dark side which he never shows to anybody.

> Mark Twain

Chapter One

FBI Chief Inspector Donna Thorpe flinched at each sudden crack of the twenty-one gun salute in honor of her closest friend in the agency, Tom Sykes. It was an old ritual, a gesture toward the dead from those left behind to wonder what might have been . . . those left to second guess not only the actions of the deceased, but their own actions as well. Doubts filled Donna Thorpe's mind; her thoughts ran like quicksilver, one moment obvious, the next moment unclear. The same thoughts sent sparklers of electricity through her every nerve as she stood amid the agency's top men and women and felt like a failure.

Tom had died at the hands of a maniac who enjoyed games and who enjoyed calling himself "Dr. O."

Case file number 87133 was not like any other problem she had ever faced; Maurice Ovierto was like no killer she had ever known. He was a highly intelligent meglomaniac and sociopath who felt nothing for anyone but himself, nothing but his desire to do evil and bodily injury to others. He enjoyed torturing not only his victims but Donna Thorpe, to whom he "reported" in one form or another his every foul deed.

She did not know why he had targeted her as the recipient of all his ugly gifts, such as Tom Sykes's body, telling her alone where it could be located, or why he had made her the privileged audience to his macabre killing spree. But he was no ordinary psychopath or serial killer with a demented set of parents and a brutal childhood. On the contrary, he'd had a sterling upbringing in a well-to-do family. He was a medical doctor and had once lived a routine, normal life. Something had changed him; something had occurred which turned him from an M.D. to a maniac M.D.

Dr. Maurice Ovierto had brought her to this: to stand before an open grave into which Tom Sykes's remains—at least those parts finally released by Dr. Samuel Boas's forensics labs—were now being lowered into the earth.

She thought of Ovierto's taunting letters, which proclaimed him the "Picasso" of cutters, an artist with a scalpel. Tom's body had been almost unrecognizable. Dr. Boas's crime lab had had to call in a dental pathologist to be certain it was Sykes.

Donna Thorpe had never known Boas to go white and shaken, but Sykes's body had had that effect on anyone who viewed it. Donna Thorpe, too, had stood there shaking.

Ovierto could be anywhere at the moment, while Donna Thorpe's best friend was seeing Arlington National Cemetery from a special perspective, a view none of the camera-snapping news people would ever know.

The gesture of the twenty-one guns—of burial for that matter—seemed useless, and yet it was only proper for Tom to be brought home. Ovierto had buried him once before, buried him with crushed bones and severed arteries while he was yet alive, or so Boas had led her to believe. Such a

8

nightmare . . . poor Tom.

She desperately needed a drink. *I like high stakes, but this is too high, and too damned painful,* she told herself. They'd come up together; they had been friends when they attended the academy at Quantico. They'd continued their friendship, despite her having risen in rank faster than he. They had shared weekend hunting trips, watched ballgames together, shared family together. . . .

Tom's crippled family was this moment being held up by her own.

Tom had liked high stakes too. His backup, Bateman, ought to have slowed him down, for Christ's sake. Bateman was the junior partner, though, and so far, his body hadn't surfaced. No doubt Dr. Ovierto was experimenting still.

For the moment, it seemed the mad genius of Dr. Ovierto would continue and continue like a series of cheap sequels to a bad horror film. For all anyone knew, the "Dr. O" was some kind of wolfman or vampire, indestructible by common means; maybe he carried the genes of Jack the Ripper.

No, no! She forced back the thought of Ovierto as some supernatural power or fantastic Devil's agent, just as she always did. *Ovierto is flesh and blood, a man, and in the end he'll be stopped,* she told herself. *He must be stopped . . . must be. At any cost,* she promised Tom as she stepped beside the coffin and tossed in a flower as a final useless gesture.

She knew that Tom's soul would not rest easy until Ovierto was punished.

Her husband, Jim, held her shoulders. She'd begun to cry again and to quake. Jim was now the strong one. And she was Auntie to Tom's two boys and his girl. Together with her own kids, they made for the black limo in a flurry of sniffles and bawling, the very littlest ones playing tag, not understanding that they couldn't play here. Their last memory of D.C. would be a dismal one. The limo driver had orders: straight to the airport. Bags would follow. Today they had a date with Delta Flight 132 bound for Lincoln, Nebraska by way of Chicago.

Out of the Virginia-Washington area, perhaps for good.

The ride in the plush red velvet limo was confining, coffinlike, and quiet. Everyone—Brucie, Jim Jr., Kay and their father—each had his or her own thoughts. Donna Thorpe felt the familiar tight scars across her abdomen where Dr. Ovierto had once cut her so badly that she'd only stayed alive by holding onto her insides. The scars seemed now to want to burst, and a fiery itching traced the long stitch lines. This was true although they were years old. She'd been the only agent ever to bring Ovierto in. Too bad she hadn't killed the bastard when she had had the chance. There was no asylum or prison in the country that could hold Ovierto.

After his escape, no one had come close to catching him again. Donna now felt her husband's hand firmly squeeze her own. The silent gesture told her how concerned he was for her. She needn't say a word, but the silence was too much for him: "It isn't your fault, Donnie. . . . Donna, maybe Nebraska's not such a bad idea. . . . Perhaps we can be a real . . . a real family and life will be closer to . . . to . . ."

"To normal?" she finished. She stared into the eyes of her children. "I could use a little normal. How about it, guys? You want to show me some normal, huh?"

10

Jim Jr. worked up a sad little smile. "Uncle Thomas, Mom, he should've waited for backup, and if he had—"

"Son, your uncle was the best, I don't care what else you hear. . . . Remember, he was the best."

Brucie chimed in. "You're the best, too, Mom."

"Yeah . . . that's why we're going to Nebraska."

The kids were sullen about uprooting on top of the death of their loved one. Like her little girl, the two boys fell silent once more. Jim just squeezed her hand even more tightly.

She thought about Dr. Ovierto and just how the man managed to elude the most sophisticated police network in the world. Primarily it was accounted for in the evil genius of the man and in his gifts of charm and gab and disguise. His life was a sleight-of-hand performance. The man had an amazing ability to make use of simple distraction, but he was helped by the amazing gullibility and stupidity of people around him. His impostures were so good that people helped him escape, helped hide him, in fact—and often died for the privilege. When he was in custody, seeing he was a madman, guards, shrinks, and others had underestimated him.

When the case fell to Tom Sykes, she had repeatedly warned Tom about the insidious and devious nature of the beast. But Sykes thought he knew Ovierto's every alias, his every disguise and M.O. Tom had been with her in Houston when they'd nailed the human aberration, Thorpe almost losing her life in the bargain. They'd been canvassing St. Stephen's Hospital on a tip when she came eye-to-eye with Ovierto and something in the moment of knowing clicked along with the knife he suddenly rammed into her, pulling her into a stairwell, racing away and leaving her to bleed to death. Had Tom not found her there . . .

11

An APB was immediately put out, and Ovierto was surrounded in the plaza, where he stabbed to death his own hostage, tore out a policeman's eyes, and managed to scar several others before he was subdued. It had been only sheer, dumb luck that several units had been available for backup on what everyone thought would be a routine call.

She had warned Tom again anyway, repeatedly reminding him of how sudden the viper turns and strikes. To no avail, it would appear. She wondered where Tom had slipped up, and recalled once more that her own mistake with Ovierto had been so sudden and startling that there hadn't been time to draw her weapon.

She had lost the right to hunt Ovierto down and feed him his own pound of flesh. Along with Tom's life, her *team* had lost credibility. A big loss of prestige with the department converted into a major loss of monies, manpower, equipment, and the confidence of her superiors. But it was losing Tom Sykes that made Donna Thorpe feel like a washed-up, useless member of the department. Had it not been for this devastation, maybe she'd have stood up to Jennings and pushed his crap back down his throat. But there was no bringing Tom back, and so maybe Inspector Thorpe deserved what she got.

"You're only as good as your last job, Donnie," she said, reminding herself and her family what Tom would say of the circumstances, *if he were here*. It was a phrase Tom used over and again since their training days together. It was a phrase their training officer, McEachern, used a lot. McEachern, too, was gone, killed years before in the field by a crazed bastard with less than a tenth of Dr. Maurice Ovierto's brains.

McEachern had been good. Sykes, over the years, had become the best; and yet he was found twenty feet

12

under the earth where Ovierto had instructed the FBI to dig in the loose, sandy soil of a resort village in the Florida Keys, near a pier two weeks before. Forensics, Boas's team, had finally released Tom's remains for burial after their intensive examinations. The coroner's results would ordinarily have come to Donna, who, as Sykes's commanding officer, would oversee the manhunt, but not now. She had been yanked from the case, reassigned to nowhere by the idiots in charge. Still, she wanted very much to see Boas's findings. Sam was the best in the country. She knew she could learn more about Ovierto from the reports. She also knew that the reports would sicken her to no end. Still, the inspector in her knew that she must get a copy and read every bloody word and view, every photo and slide depicting the new Tom Sykes—*persona non living*. What choice did she have? She must do it for Tom, just as she'd stood there the whole time Tom's putrid remains were laid out on a table like the seemingly unrelated pottery and stone pieces of an archeological dig. She'd gone to get Tom's body in the morgue in Miami, to see it returned to Quantico, Virginia, where it had been flown, encased in ice.

She had called in markers in order to get a copy of Boas's final report. She had Dr. Lee Rogman working on it. But Rogman was blubbering fearfully about losing his job if he did so. Word was out on Donna. Word had it that she was too close to the case and that, as good a chief as she was, she was slipping where Ovierto, and now Tom Sykes, were concerned.

Inspector Thorpe didn't know what mistake or mistakes Tom Sykes had made, only that his body was riddled with torture marks and his insides burned out by the detergents and bleach he'd been forced to swallow. The body had been wrapped in Handi-Wrap and chains. The purpose of the chains—or the "meaning" of them—remained a mystery.

Inspector Thorpe had stood over what was left of Sykes's worm-eaten form at the autopsy, praying over it for the least clue to Ovierto. If Sykes could have, he would have etched a message in his own skin with his teeth to tip Thorpe off to Dr. Ovierto operation—*operation;* sick term for what the mad M.D. did. He'd sometimes take a portion of his untold fortune to set up shop in a storefront as a caring, ghetto doctor (once in Cincinnati, once in San Diego). Other times he'd served on staff at a hospital or a university medical complex (Chicago, Portland, Atlanta, and even D.C.—under their noses!).

There was a long, long list of his "cures." Only trouble was that Dr. O's cures usually led to an agonizing death; only if the patient died did he feel himself a "successful surgeon." Lately, too, he had begun playing with poisons. In fact, he had sent in a request to the U.S. Patent Office to patent one of his poison concoctions, labeling it: *Euphamirine.* He was a card . . . a deadly, wild card. He'd adminster/test his concoction and sign a death certificate all in the same hour.

At the autopsy, there wasn't enough left of Sykes to be of any apparent use to either the FBI or anyone else. All that was left was a pale, pulpy shell of the man, his physical ghost. Donna Thorpe would never forget the sight of her friend and partner on the slab. In fact, she'd begun to have nightmares about Sykes and the way he had died.

For this reason she was never alone. She had Jim in bed with her, and the kids were never far away. Weekends now she'd have to cultivate new ties, new networks, including those personal ones with the local folk of Lincoln, that's all—join the bloody club, get some golf or tennis in, keep busy, forge useful contacts with local cops, attorneys, judges, and medical experts.

The alternatives were pretty near as bleak: let the mind fester until it boiled over with guilt and impotence and rage, compliments of Dr. Ovierto. Or quit, turn in her badge, walk out. Some people would applaud that.

She was goddamned forty this month. She ought to have kept Tom on a tighter rein, ought maybe to have been right beside him on this one, ought maybe to be wherever Bateman might now be. Barring that, maybe her superiors were right. Maybe Inspector Donna Thorpe ought to be in Nebraska.

They arrived at Washington National Airport, where Dr. Samuel Boas joined them to wish them well. Boas was a lanky, gray-haired man with probing eyes and a Germanic demeanor that gave very little away. Just before she stepped onto the plane he said to her, "It's no longer your problem now, Donna. Let it go and reclaim your life. You have so much else to turn to. Let it go."

She hadn't been able to respond to Sam. If there was anyone on the planet who should understand that she could not possibly let it go, it was him. She gripped his hands in hers. "Sam," she began slowly, "get the results of Tom's autopsy to me, whatever it takes."

"Or else you use your information against me? You've become that obsessed, haven't you?" His eyes covered over with a terrible sadness.

"Just do it." She stalked down the empty gangway to the plane, the last to board, fighting her own steps.

Chapter Two

Dr. Maurice Ovierto believed that it would be great fun to keep Bateman for a while.

The safe-keeping of an imprisoned man — an FBI agent at that — was no simple matter. Still, before leaving for Europe, he had made arrangements, leaving the man enough food to sustain himself — if he stretched it. As for water, the bottom of the mine shaft that Bateman lay in was always wet. Ovierto had had to find just the right place, and he had. It was actually the most perfect place for his needs with regard to Bateman. No one around for miles. A rat hole from which escape was impossible, especially for a man with two severed Achilles tendons.

The location had also served well as prison to Tom Sykes for a while, before he became more trouble than he was worth, attempting an escape. Sykes had been tough and shrewd, and starvation had had little effect on the man's will to fight back.

Dr. O. now weaved through the curtain-network of chains dripping with condensation in the old foundry, a dark place thousands of miles from where Thorpe's old friend, Tommy Sykes had been buried alive. He'd

16

begun to bore Maurice. He was just barely able to lift a finger anymore, much less present a threat or be of use in any entertaining way. So, Ovierto buried him near his precious love, the sea.

Donna Thorpe would find that out in due time: that Sykes was alive when Maurice had decided to cover him over in the dunes of a deserted stretch of Florida beach. She'd learn the truth from Boas, when the autopsy report came in, if the autopsiest stayed off the booze.

Boy, Thorpe was going to be pissed.

Ovierto snickered at this. Good and holy bitch, Donna just didn't know what to make of him, sending her letters to tell her where to go and what to look for, providing her with clues so the game might continue, telling her what it was she was looking for and who was responsible. If the public only knew! One day, maybe he would tell the world just what a bunch of screw-ups the FBI was made up of. Without directions they'd be unable to find their way to the john. Was it any surprise they could get nowhere near him? He was that good. . . .

They were so fucking stupid they'd have trouble following a monopoly board. He was so far ahead of them that they were only now dispatching a team to the site of the killings in England.

And the idiots had busted Thorpe, burying her in a Nebraska bureau! No matter, he could do business with Donna in Nebraska. It all made for a kind of Wizard-of-Oz logic, except that Dorothy hailed from Kansas, and now Donna hailed from Nebraska. Close enough. Might even be fun getting out of D.C. Certainly was closer to Bateman than Virginia . . . *getting warmer*, Donna . . . *hotter, hotter!* The thought made him chuckle. He got so little out of life, a good laugh was the least he might take, he told himself.

He'd have to remember to share this one with Donna soon . . . give the poor girl a call, for old time's sake.

He plied his way through the dangerous sections of the ancient foundry here amid a Colorado backwash, miles from the nearest town. The rental car was outside, but would draw no attention from the road because he'd pulled it around back. One thing he knew, aside from how best to practice bad medicine: how to really get around. He owned a "doctor killer", the latest in private jets made by Beechcraft—owned it outright, registered under an assumed name. So far, they had not traced this alias.

He heard a noise and at first believed it was Bateman in agony. He'd have to be in agony now, left alone in that craggy hole all these weeks without a scrap beyond the raw chunks of meat tossed down to him before Ovierto left. Bateman's ankle tendons had been surgically severed. He could neither stand nor walk, even if he could escape the dungeon into which he had been thrown. Bateman's suffering had been long and gratifying, and the thought that it would continue gave Dr. Ovierto a contented feeling. But the noise was not human; it was rather a scurrying sound, and Dr. O saw a rat race across a girder, onto a pillar, and up and away.

He reached Bateman only to find a corpse. He'd come all this way for nothing.

"Damn . . . damn," he cursed his luck. He'd been looking forward to watching Bateman's last breath. Maybe he could do something yet with the body, he thought. Maybe Donna'd be interested in chasing it, as she had in chasing Sykes's. Death may come, he thought, but it was never too late for fun.

Below the glare of his flashlight, Bateman's lifeless male form was not entirely useless if he were to enjoy

18

himself; had Bateman been a female agent . . . well . . . no use in wishing. He'd just go out and get one.

The place was already rank from Bateman's remains. Rats were feeding on him down in the darkness. Dr. Ovierto wondered if he wanted to fight the rats off for any of the man's parts. It again occurred to him that Donna might like to have a part of Bateman sent her, something she could stew over. He chuckled quietly to himself.

"All right, you!" came a voice disrupting the stillness, military and aggressive, yet female in timbre. "I want you to come straight out into the light, *now!*"

It was a gift, a police officer by her uniform, come to him like a conch washed ashore at his feet. He could use a woman in the experiment he had in mind.

"Right away, officer," he called back, looking about to ascertain whether she was alone or with a partner.

"What are you doing in here?" she asked as he came closer to the light, grinning at her like a death mask.

"My property, officer. Just purchased it."

"March out into the light where I can have a look at you," she ordered.

He did so with aplomb, saying, "I assure you, officer . . ."

"Whatever you want to buy this old place for?" she asked.

"Plans . . . big plans for it."

She was alone except for the voices coming over the radio in her car. He reached into his breast pocket.

"Hold it, right there!" she ordered, bringing up her weapon.

"Please, I only want to show you the papers. I only just signed them."

She relaxed. She was a smooth, black woman, with a fine buxom shape. He spread the papers on the hood of her squad car. She leaned in closer to see, un-

19

aware that the breath-spray container he lifted toward himself was actually pointed at her face. The spray instantly blinded her, sending her reeling while, at the same instant, Dr. O grabbed the .38 special from her hand.

"I want you to spend a little time with Death, sweetheart." He spoke into her ear where she lay on the ground, tossing her head from side to side before the blow from his massive fist knocked her unconscious.

Now he had his hands full. The radio in her car was crackling with static and a dispatcher's voice. He'd have to get rid of the car, but he must first secure her.

He took hold of her and she lashed out at him, beating with her fists, kicking, trying to bite. He pummeled her again, causing bruises and bleeding about the face, shouting, "Stop it, now! Stop it!" He only quit hitting her when she slumped unconscious again.

He then dragged her inside.

There he began stripping away her clothes, finding the heavy belt with night stick, the uniform and badge an additional kick as he ripped them all off. This done, he lashed her body with chains, pinning her to the darkness of the concrete wall down which dripped water and which rats curiously crawled.

Bateman had disappointed him. . . .

Reading her badge plate, he rolled her name off his lips: "Roshwanda Farris. You won't disappoint me, will you, Roshwanda? You like going to the doctor's office, don't you? I got my medical in my car."

She screamed and pulled away from his touch when she awoke to find his hands rushing over her nude form. But she could not see. She felt the warmth of blood in her eyes and streaming down her face where he had slit each pupil. Blind and helpless, she presented an alluring target for Dr. O.

"As for your eyes, I've done you a kindness—a thing

20

Dr. O is not known for. Who knows, I might even let you live to tell your friends and family about me, about *us* . . . about this night. And if you just can't tell it to anyone else, you can tell it to yourself and the walls of your asylum, over and over." He shrieked the laugh of the mad, blotting out her scream.

"You know, darling," he left spit in her ears where he spoke into them, "I've sent a lot of people to asylums across the country. It's either that or death. Which do you prefer?"

Chapter Three

Lincoln, Nebraska

Two days later H.Q. knew nothing more about Bateman's whereabouts than did Donna Thorpe in Nebraska, and the fact that they had heard nothing from Dr. Ovierto had everyone imagining the worst. Bateman was only twenty-seven years old.

Donna Thorpe was firmly in place, in charge of the Nebraska Divison of Criminal Operations on the seventh floor of the Nebraska Federal Bureau of Investigation, in a building that wheat had built in Lincoln, Nebraska. She was still uneasy in her reassignment, still resisting it, still thinking always of Dr. Maurice Ovierto. The Ovierto operation had cost the Bureau hundreds of thousands of dollars, while it had a bottom line of zero.

She somehow must now roll the dice with a sure hand to regain her former status, to gain reassignment to D.C., and to get even with Ovierto.

But Thorpe was off the case. Her only hope of getting back to D.C., of being returned to her former status and demanding Ovierto, was to make a big score from Lincoln, Nebraska. As unlikely as that had seemed the first day of her reassignment, she was sniffing out something big; the smell was so strong it followed her home, to the shower, and into bed with Jim. She was afire with the idea.

Donna had every right to now reopen an old case, a murder that occurred in Nebraska, one of Dr. O's earliest victims. Some still argued that contention, but she and Tom were sure it was the dire work of the doctor. She had every right to reassess the case that had been forgotten over time. In so doing, she had every right to the recent forensics reports on Dr. O's latest victim, to compare. She felt a twinge of guilt about the Nebraska victim, knowing that she didn't acutally care about the ancient history in which a woman had had spleen and pancreas had been removed with the skill of a surgeon.

The woman had undergone the operation without anesthesia. A self-professed killer had taken responsibility for the slaying before taking his own life, and the case had been dropped, but Tom had stumbled on it during his research years later. At the time they'd had enough to deal with, and the information on the Nebraska case was let go—until now.

Now, it would enable Donna to keep her foot in the Dr. O affair—to provide her a smokescreen, if not unofficial sanction.

She had a list of possible, future victims of the madman, and their addresses. For Thorpe's money, Ovierto had been responsible for a number of deaths abroad, and if his threats were to be taken seriously, Ovierto was racing toward several key scientists who'd done governmental research at Fermilab, just outside of Chicago, Illinois.

The men and women killed abroad in various mysterious accidents were all scientists working toward a common goal and a common good via a NASA project. Ovierto had made his first mistake, showing a pattern—victims all in a row. But no one was willing to take Donna Thorpe seriously on this, not yet. A number of *somebodies* of importance must die here in the Americas first, she sadly thought. In two, maybe three days, yet another scientist would be dead. Thorpe was so certain of it that she had gone on record about it.

"Damn, damn, damn!" she cursed loud enough for her operatives to know of her frustration. She wondered how long she could afford to wait around for the next murder. Without true sanction, her hands were tied, and so far the Bureau wasn't responding to her telexes, the material she had amassed and faxed to them, *nothing*.

"Who do we know outside the agency in Chicago who owes us big?" she suddenly asked the people in the debriefing room.

"Remember that hot-headed bastard?" asked Pyles.

"Cop there by the name of Swisher, remember him?" asked Perry Shoup.

"Real pistol—"

"Decoy operative, reckless as hell."

"Wasn't he the guy that shut down that doctor that was mudering people for AIDS-free blood a year or so ago?"

The banter went about the room. There were a few people who hadn't a clue about Lieutenant Joe Swisher, but as these men were filled in by others, Donna Thorpe leaned back in her chair and recalled the tough, cynical Chicago undercover cop with a mixture of admiration and dislike. Admiration because he did his job so very well, as when he cornered the infamous Widow-maker a few months back, a whacko who had killed eighteen men by firing a high-powered rifle into windows from great distances for reasons the killing mind alone understood. She de-

24

tested Swisher for the methods he reputedly used, for instance, torturing a man for information leading to someone that Swisher had been chasing for years in some ongoing vendetta. It had been to this vendetta that she and Tom had once played Swisher.

At that time, Lieutenant Joe Swisher had been chasing down a small-time creep named Camera, beating heads together for any information he might gain concerning the drug lord who dared work Swisher's territory. She and Tom had stepped in with a deal, seeing to it that the game plan went another way, intercepting Swisher, snatching up Camera as well. Camera was wired and returned to the streets to do a bigger job for the Feds. Camera walked as part of the deal. They had had to squeeze Joe Swisher pretty hard, using some old files from a police shrink against him. After it was over, Swisher torched the files and the Feds told him that he owed them.

Camera was relocated, given a new identity, the whole package, but someone managed to get to him anyway—a large .44 through the skull at close range. Detective Joe Swisher was at the top of the list of suspects.

Time was just right to pick some fruit from that tree again. Since Sykes's brutal death, Thorpe had come to believe that she understood Joe Swisher's unquenchable thirst for violent revenge.

Another of Joe Swisher's supposed victims had been a child-porn filmmaker and child-brutalizer by the name of Julio Zaragoza. Zaragoza had died of drowning, found head-down in a toilet bowl, his feet in the air. His head and face had been battered and he'd been knocked unconscious before he drowned.

Dr. Maurice Ovierto would have approved, no doubt. Ovierto had made brutality a way of life; it seemed that Swisher had also. Ovierto was a raging psychotic who coolly masked his psychosis; so was Swisher. It takes a thief . . .

At the moment they were swamped with missing persons believed to be kidnapped, some taken across state lines. These kinds of cases seemed on the rise and typically turned into murder.

Thorpe got on her phone, called Chicago, Precinct Thirty-one, and asked for Lieutenant Joe Swisher. Told the lieutenant was indisposed at the moment, she persisted.

"Indisposed?"

"Out on duty."

Thorpe wondered what mayhem the lieutenant was into.

"This is urgent. Could you patch me through to his vehicle?"

"Who is calling, ma'am?" asked the female dispatcher.

"FBI."

"I see," she said with a mind full of doubt. "I'll need a name, ma'am."

"Hoover, godamnit! J. Edgar."

"Thank you Ms. Hoover, and please hold."

"No, thank you, dear," she said with mock politeness.

"I'll try to hail his frequency, ma'am, but he's on a ten eighteen."

"Ten eighteen, that's suspect injured, isn't it?"

But she was off the line, trying to get through to Swisher. It took more time than she had patience for. She was about to slam down the receiver, when static struck and was replaced by the sound of another female voice. "This is Sergeant Muro."

"Who?"

"Joe's partner . . . in the field . . . can this wait?"

"No, it can't."

"You're not going to come back at him with all that phony crap about knockin' off your witness, again, are you?"

"I have Swisher's best interest at heart, ahh . . . Muro."

She laughed. "Sure you do, you FBI bitches are all alike."

"Hey, Muro, I'm just trying to alert him to a danger in your sector."

"What danger?"

"Serial killer who seems to like high-powered scientists as targets. You read about the three in England? Everybody's read about that. Now it's starting here, and if our information is correct, Chicago and Dr. Ibi Oliguerre is next, along with a possible second physicist working out at your Fermilab. Is that reason enough to alert Swisher? I'd like him *in* but it's completely unofficial."

Muro hesitated a moment before saying, "Why should Joe want anything to do with you? You break into his shrink's office, lift his file, use it against him—"

"Muro! This is bigger than us, or old sores!"

"Why does it sound like a set-up to me? Unofficial?"

"I can't explain it over the phone. Will Swisher meet with me if I fly there? Tonight?"

"You nuts? He wouldn't give you the time of day."

"Put him on! This is too damned important, Muro."

There was more static and some commotion on Muro's end. Joe Swisher came on. "Thorpe, sweety, how's D.C. this time of year?"

Donna knew now that Swisher knew about her demotion. She chose to ignore the barb. "Your partner fill you in on the situation? Will you meet with me tonight?"

"Why're you asking, Thorpe? Why didn't you just

bust in and cuff me? Drag me in before your holier-than-thou presence and just explain things to me? Like you did when you got Camera and those three women killed so you could get your man. Oh, by the way, tough luck about your partner . . . ahh, Sykes? But what's a few bodies along the way to a gal like Donna Thorpe, huh?"

Donna recalled having said the exact same words to Swisher once. She almost told him to fuck off. Instead, she swallowed it and calmly replied, "Hey, mister, I'm the one saw that your unsavory file and your unsavory ass came out of that one intact and alive, or did you forget that? As for your file, you got it back, remember?"

Swisher hesitated on the other end. "My problem is you, Thorpe. I just don't like you or your methods."

"Then we agree to disagree, because I don't like your methods either."

"You call me out of the blue, sic me onto some poor slob like you've got me on a leash. Then maybe I blow your problem away, and then I'm carted off for it, shut away tight; end of Donna Thorpe's backside itch. Great."

"No, no . . . Lieutenant, it's not like that."

"Then why aren't you going through my captain?"

"It's not officially my case. I can't go through channels, and I can't order anyone on or off it, you understand?"

"Until it becomes your case, I'll say no thanks and *hasta luego*."

"Suppose I told you I know who did Stavros?"

"Bullshit," he replied and promptly hung up on her. In Nebraska, she said, "Damn that man." She then called for the helicopter to be readied, and she made a few preparatory calls for her visit. She'd go to the Windy City with what she had on Ovierto, lay it all out for Swisher, and take her chances. She knew just where to locate Swisher. He'd be at a watering hole, a bar and grill called *Transfusions,* on Kedzie near Damon Avenue.

Swisher had his own agenda: people he wanted to put away forever. There wasn't a murder in the country reported that Donna Thorpe didn't know about; she'd read with great interest the news of a man named Stavros who'd ostensibly bled to death from a wound in a nasty place, a wound a man needn't die from, unless the killer had also grotesquely arranged for the victim not to get medical attention. The case smacked of Dr. Ovierto's handiwork, and she believed it could be a *decoy* killing—one of Dr. O's endless red herrings, to lead police in one direction while he sought out another.

One phone call and the Stavros thing would be turned over to Lieutenant Joseph Swisher. The ties that bind, thought Thorpe.

She got Swisher's captain on the line, a man that she had made use of before many times. Brian Noone was physically one of the biggest men she had ever encountered, but his bull shoulders and huge middle belied his intellect. He was shrewd. Even more than shrewd, he was ambitious. He was what was fast becoming a rare breed: an inner city police captain who welcomed FBI involvement on a case. Not that he actually believed that the FBI knew what they were doing.

After the initial amenities, including a few remarks about how sorry Noone was to hear about Tom Sykes, Thorpe told him, "I'd like you to put Joe Swisher on the Stavros case."

"Is that a request?"

"It is."

Noone was assessing her tone. "Brian, it's important. Can't give you all the details, but—"

"That's all right. I love being in the dark," he replied with what amounted to a lot of sarcasm for Noone.

She cleared her throat. Brian. I've got reason to believe Stavros may be connected to one of our *most wanted.*"

"Ovierto, huh?"

"This stays between us. Okay, Brian?"

"Swisher's got a full docket."

"You can loosen that up, a little juggling."

"Just snatch it from the dicks that're on it now and dump it in Joe's lap, just like that. Tell me, Inspector, what does my department get for our trouble?"

"Things work out, you and your man will get plenty of press, I can guarantee that."

"Press . . . I give a shit about press."

"I'll see that you get citations of—"

"How about a word to my chief . . . I'm up for promo soon."

"I can't make any promises on that score . . . but I'll make a call."

"Maybe you haven't heard, Donna, but a lot of people these days aren't taking your calls."

She stewed a moment over this. "I'm coming back, Brian, so don't put all your eggs into one basket."

Noone chewed on this thought before saying, "All right, you'll have Swisher on Stavros."

Thorpe knew that Stavros must be upsetting for Swisher; that it would be the impetus for driving "Swish" straight into her hands. Noone didn't know it, but Donna Thorpe knew more about motivating Joe Swisher than his captain ever dreamed of. She had had an FBI psychological workup done on Swisher before using the files stolen from Swisher's shrink. She knew what made Joey tick, what made him run, what pissed him off, and what made him vomit.

In some ways, she knew, she was a lot like Swisher and getting closer by the day. Both of them skirted the letter of the law. Catching and punishing the guilty was uppermost in both their minds.

Her fingers sought the small, neatly wrapped box on her desk, and, using a pair of tweezers, she removed the portion of male genitals sent her by Dr. Ovierto only recently. Even Dr. O knew that she was now in Nebraska. He would continue sending his disgusting gifts not to the Bureau, but to her, to Donna Thorpe. She lifted the desiccated, bad-smelling penis mailed to her and postmarked Elmhurst, Illinois, a Chicago suburb. The note was as nasty as the contents: *Fuck yourself, Donna, honey. Tommy boy would want it that way. It's his thing.*

But she knew it wasn't part of Tom Sykes. She'd have the lab verify this fact, but somehow she knew it was not part of Tom.

She looked again at the signature. Ovierto had used his penname: Dr. O.

Chapter Four

Chicago, Illinois

Joe Swisher looked like a professional linebacker and he stood half a head taller than Captain Noone. Noone knew that he was also sharp-witted and streetwise. Joe smelled something wrong in Noone's suddenly reassigning a case—*any case*—to him.

He'd grown up on the North side of Chicago. He was thirty-seven years old. He detested being treated like a fool.

Why did Noone really want him to handle the one case Swisher had done his very best to avoid? Officially the case was known by the victim's name: Stavros. It was more than just the nightmarish, bizarre nature of the killing, which the newspapers had leapt on, that troubled Swisher. It was the resurgence of the old horrors that he'd fought back for so many years.

Mutilation killings disturbed him to his core. Having remained in vice for so long before taking over a homicide detail had shielded him somewhat from the ugliest of crimes. Big man on the force—afraid of nasty, splatter pictures and crime scenes that made him throw up, scenes that reminded him of Jerri's death.

Lieutenant First Class Joseph Swisher of the Chicago Police Force paced tiger fashion before simply saying, "I don't have the experience with mutilation cases to start now."

"Got to start somewhere."

"Besides, I've got enough headaches! I don't need or want Stavros. Currently my team of only three are juggling some twenty-seven investigations ranging from vice to murder and back again."

As he argued with Noone he saw Jerri's ghost over Noone's shoulder. She'd only been fifteen, his big sister. He had come home from school that day to find her dead in a grotesque pose at the end of the bannister where the killer had tied her distorted remains. Later, a neighbor's kid, aged nineteen, was arrested for Jerri's murder. It was a boy she'd known casually almost all her life.

Back at his desk, he now could barely bring himself to glance at the details of how a little old man's life had been disrupted. The cryptic report did not begin to describe the terrible way in which the sixty-year-old Stavros, owner of a pet shop and supply store, had succumbed. He'd bled to death on the removal of an organ not vital to life, his penis.

The object of the killer's apparent affection was not found at the scene of the man's death, but had been carried away by his attacker.

The newsmen were having a field day with it.

So were some rank cops in the locker room.

Swisher was no prude; he was a Vietnam vet and a former VA Hospital resident, but this Stavros business grossed him out.

Try as they might, the detectives on the case, Paul Doley and Frank Lefever, could not long contain the awful story. The cause of death was listed by the coroner as loss of blood. Stavros, relieved of his genitals like a Texas steer, had been held in place by the killer, who remained to watch as he bled and bled until he was too weak to help himself.

The Stavros "thing" — as it was being called by the working stiffs in the department — had effectively opened old wounds in Swisher, wounds no shrink could heal. The hideous case sent him back along a timeline that placed him in that fiery hot foyer where he'd gaped at Jerri's disgorged remains, some of which lay on the floor, some of which ran along the railing, some of which had been slung about, staining the walls and carpeting. Jerri's carcass looked as though it had come out of the discard basket beside the butcher's block. Only her eyes, wide and staring back at him, had been left intact.

Stavros . . . Jerri . . . the helpless, cornered victim.

And him nowhere in sight; no way to help, to draw off the pain.

Shattered nights, days, months, years.

The killer had been caught burying his bloody clothing in a wooded area back of the houses. Young Joe Swisher found himself trembling but concentrating on what the policemen were doing, the methodical, plodding steps they took to uncover the killer in a matter of hours. He was fascinated, and in that fascination he kept his mind intact.

It took almost two years to convict the killer. Joe, at fifteen, testified to what he knew of his sister's killer, how his sister had fended off his lewd advances more than once. He'd put it behind him; had gone into the service and had wandered aimlessly for a time before becoming a cop. He never examined why he became a cop, except that he felt lost after returning from the war; something solid, something smacking of the military life, was attractive at the time. He'd never married, but he enjoyed a tumultuous, romantic relationship with his female partner, Robyn Muro. As for Jerri's killer, he was up for parole at the end of the month.

Robyn had, for some time now, become a sweet distraction from his sister's ghost. Jerri haunted him, hounding him to avenge her.

He tried recalling how he'd met Robyn. They didn't at first like one another. They'd been assigned as a team in an undercover sting operation in Burnham Park. K & J's Laundromat was a natural front for the operation that had burned a consortium of gangs in the Burnham Park District. The thugs had begun to convince small businessmen in the area that they needed "insurance" against bad people. People were being bullied and pressured into taking out a "policy" with the gang to protect them from other gangs. Gangs on both sides of the street were cleaning up and sharing the profits—a fine example of "gang co-oping" which the police department had been pushing on the punks for a year now, except the police were talking about legitimate ventures such as staging a block party.

Early on police were called in, but there was no evidence, and the handful of people willing to testify had soon changed their minds. To gather the evidence, Joe and Robyn had volunteered to open up shop in the aged neighborhood. Working as operators of the poorly lit, poorly equipped laundromat had only one up side, so far as Joe Swisher was concerned that first night: he got his laundry done for free. They had sat up with the churning machines for four weeks now, photographing each night. They got some pretty weird people in off the street, but no sign of the Bone Breaker's Insurance salesmen. Until the night all hell broke loose, and Robyn earned Joe's undying respect. The place was littered with the street scum before the two of them were through—some twelve collars, several wounded.

He and Robyn had come out unscratched. Unfortunately, the washers and dryers hadn't a chance.

Even so, like a married couple, they had their differences, as in the child abuse Hampton case, on which she had once again wanted him to slow down.

Noone handed him a file. "You're on the case, Joe. Give it your best."

In the squad room, he ran into Robyn Muro, who pushed coffee his way. Their two desks faced one another. "Face it, Joe, you're working for the Feds again."

"So I noticed. Damn that Thorpe."

"Swartze—*guy you shot this morning?*"

"What about the little weasel?"

"Already made bail."

"What!"

"Easy, Lieutenant, remember your image."

"Already made bail! Christ, guy's a known offender, his third robbery, and he walks?"

"Well, no . . . he's not walking. That slug you put in him left him paralyzed, Joe. He won't be robbing any more liquor stores, but he's suing you, and the department, Joe."

"Best news I've heard all day."

She lifted the Stavros file from where he'd tossed it and began to sift through it. "Dick-gusting," she said.

He frowned, and replied, "Goddamnit, Robyn, just because the *Times* and the *Tribune* and the nightly news are all making sick jokes over this, doesn't mean we have to follow suit. Got that?"

"Sure, sure boss."

"Jesus, I'd exected better from you."

"Why, because I'm a woman?" She raised her shoulders, bouncing her blonde hair, a look of surprise coming over her. "Hey, who's made more damned 'penal' jokes over this case than you? Were you so bashed last night that you forgot?"

He squinted at her. "Hey, what goes on at the bar, off the job, that's one thing."

"Hell, you were *on* the bar, reciting this long diatribe about pricks. You even had a name for it: prickology; remember?"

He did half-remember, and now it bothered him. He had had quite a few drinks, but he had also seen Stavros's body at his shop; he'd been in the vicinity when the call came over. Later, he'd seen some vivid Kodacolors that Lefever had pushed under his nose when the other man thought Swisher would be interested. At the time, in front of Frank and Paul, he'd pretended the shots had no effect on him. They had talked around him about the scene at the city morgue. It was enough to drive anyone to drink, cop or no.

He'd gone from Lefever's pictures to the bar. He'd had the good sense to at least steer clear of the morgue on this one.

When he'd gotten to the bar, Robyn was waiting for him, along with some other friends, also cops. Other cops were the only people foolish enough to hang out with cops.

As the night wore on, Swisher got drunk. Robyn tried to steer the conversation off work, especially away from the Stavros case. She tried desperately to match him drink for drink, but she soon gave that up. Remarking on the awful scene at the pet shop, he'd confided that the incident had deeply disturbed him, but he wouldn't say anything else about it after that. He just kept belting down drinks.

About then Robyn had had enough. She coaxed him, in the expectation they were leaving.

All the night long he'd heard little snickers and jokes and off-color stories from cops at the watering hole, where they let off steam in an atmosphere where others understood the need. He climbed up on the bar and called for everyone's "goddamned" attention. He then told them that he had done extensive research in the field of Prickology. That brought a round of laughs. He then told them all that he knew about the penis, aka the "thing."

He next shouted, "The given names for the virile manly member are, and I quote: bone, cock, cod, dick, ding, horn, knob, prick, prong, prod, rod, root, wick—"

Robyn was tugging at him and shouting, "Get down, Joe! Come down from there, Joe! Joe!"

But he was on a roll. "—privates, genitals, one-eyed, short arm, middle leg, snake, yo-yo, junior, silent flute—my personal favorite—night stick, joy stick, lady's lollipop, Old Slimy, Cupid's torch, root of evil! Hammer, pole, hose, handle, and let us not forget *tree of life*."

He had run out of names and energy, and so had then allowed himself to be talked down amid the laughter, tears and applause.

"Tell you another thing," he shouted to the assembled men and women in the bar. "Compared to a horse, or even a boar, men have proportionately very small ones. Two and a half feet for a stallion! One and a half for a boar!"

"Stop it, now! Joe! Damn you!"

"And another thing," he continued. "I have it on good authority—the cadaver man himself—that when you die, they're all the same size; nobody wins any prize."

Now, in the squad room, the day nearing an end, Swisher half-blushed at the memory of his drunken antics, but he would not admit as much.

"It was kinda funny," she said.

Don Mallory shouted across at them. "Kinda funny? I was in tears! Swish, you're one of a kind, man!"

"Yeah, right . . . I really had the audience in the *palm* of my hand . . . get it?"

"Playing to the lowest common denominator," she said.

"Touché."

"So, you going to be okay with Stavros?"

"It's mine now."

"I don't get Thorpe's involvement."

"She'll let me know when she's moved to do so. Bitch . . ."

"You really hate her, don't you?"

"Does a snake have fangs?"

"How's Frank and Paul going to take this?" She shook her head. "It was their case. Kinda looks bad. Kinda unusual, isn't it?"

"Hey, it's not like it's gone sour. Hell, the coroner's report isn't even in, yet."

"Joe, I know you; I also know that this case isn't . . . *right* for you."

He had told her once about his sister's death. He met her stare, but said firmly, "If we nail the bastard, the case'll be right for me."

"And if we don't?"

"Negativism."

"Your sister Jerrie."

He flinched, his big form contracting at the sound of Jerrie's name.

She said, "You didn't tell me all of it, did you?"

"She—she was cut *everywhere*." He inhaled so deeply it made a scuba diver's noise. He then rushed out to the men's room.

Chapter Five

Sergeant Robyn Muro felt that she was as close to Joe Swisher as the man would allow anyone. He'd close down faster and tighter than a bear trap if he felt threatened on an emotional level, and yet he was dangerously fearless of any mortal wound. She began to worry about Joe when she got a second call from Inspector Donna Thorpe, the FBI vamp who'd used and hurt Joe before. The woman simply would not take no for an answer, it appeared. First she had arranged for Stavros to be dumped on Joe, and now she was hounding him for a meeting tonight.

She chose not to tell Joe when he returned. She leaned back in the cushion of her chair and watched him as he went about the business of checking his calendar and rummaging through a desk drawer. He acted as if everything was normal, and as if their earlier conversation had not taken place.

"Look, I'm sorry if I spoke out of turn, partner."

"Don't mention it." She took the double entendre as it was meant.

"Quittin' time."

"My feelings exactly."

"Well, then . . . you want to have dinner with me tonight?"

"Sure, if you're up to it."

"We can then take in the Black Hawk's game, whata-ya' say?"

"Sounds great."

"This twenty-four hours a policeman crap is getting too much for me."

"Nice to hear you admit it. Yeah, the Hawks . . . sounds great."

She went back to the report she'd been writing.

"Robyn, thanks."

"For what?"

"For being here . . . and on my side."

"Joe, you have more friends and more admirers 'round here than you know."

"Is that right?"

"Wouldn't be surprised if Thorpe didn't kinda' like you."

"Rather bet on the Black Hawks! It's a safer bet."

"Don't sell yourself short, handsome. I'll just tidy up a few loose ends and meet you later."

He watched her go, thinking how much help she'd been in both his personal and professional life, and how little he'd given her in return. He wondered why she stayed with him.

Robyn Muro often worried about the man she loved. Swisher was both enigmatic and disturbing, as well as quite easily the kindest "tough guy" she knew. He might be a "blue knight" in many respects, but he was also a *black knight*, doling out death to those he felt deserved death. An inner turmoil of grief, guilt, and anger had eaten away at his humanity for years now. What such emotions did to the psyche no one knew. Had such an experiment in terror and loss, depression and a life of seeking revenge ever been conducted at a university or in a laboratory? Joe

41

Swisher's life on the edge had taken its toll.

Joe's insomnia had led to more drink, and his drink had led to more confusion and internal struggle. He had turned away from her for support from Hiram's Old World Whiskey. And she didn't like the storm signs.

They'd talked about it, and he had made promises. But she didn't know if they were promises he could keep.

Joe was not easily understood. Yet he had no secrets from her anymore, and his motivations were straightforward enough that she should be able to help him. She saw his life as an interrupted journey. He might've done anything in life with his Michael Douglas smile, full baritone voice, and rugged good looks. But all that went by the wayside when Jerrie was so brutally killed. It made for a twisted ending to his life as a boy, and a corrupt beginning to his life as a young man. Now his every action was predicated upon that horrifying event, a multilation killing. And now Thorpe was knowingly rubbing his face in it, not allowing him to flee, forcing him to obsess on it and confront the ugliness. What would that do to Joe? Robyn feared it might become a sickness, become like carrion to feed upon continuously for the rest of his life. . . .

Maybe . . . just maybe she could help him, and maybe not.

The warm shower water soothed her nerves. She always washed the cop off her before leaving the precinct each evening.

"He'll bounce back. This thing with Stavros has just got to him," Peggy Olson, a fellow policewoman and friend, assured her. They stepped from the shower, draping themselves in towels and heading toward their lockers. "We've all hated people we've gone after.

Doesn't mean anything."

"Yeah, true. But with Joe, it runs deep," she said.

"It's just not like any other job."

"The adrenaline high, I know."

"Adrenaline and hatred can keep you alive, kiddo."

She rushed to finish. She was meeting Swisher outside in her civies in five minutes. She'd do a makeover at her place, later. Something had occurred to her as she'd spoken with Peggy "Peg-leg" Olson, three years a sergeant detective herself. She wanted to share her idea with Swish, but she wasn't certain how to approach him with it.

During the drive to her place, he was silent when she brought up the issue with him, saying, "Joe, you know, whoever did Stavros has nothing to do with—*you know*—what happened to your sister twenty-four years ago."

"I don't know," Joe replied. "Maybe all hate and all killing is linked somehow, like a virus that goes from one to another of us."

"But Joe," she tried to continue with her concern, "maybe you're too close to this kind of a case; maybe so close that it'll just ball you up in knots. Hell, Noone doesn't know what it's doing to you—"

"Not a word to him, Robyn!"

"All right, don't shout."

"I mean it."

She nodded. "Just because we're cops, that doesn't exclude us from having feelings," she said tentatively. "All I'm saying is that in some cases, strong emotions like . . . like this . . . can cloud judgement, cause more harm than we know."

"What're you getting at?"

He was always abrupt when angered.

43

"When judgment is clouded, procedure is forgotten, a guy like Hampton has his precious rights stepped on, and *poof!* he's given an open door."

"To go and sin some more."

"This Stavros case, Joe—"

"What about it?"

"Maybe . . . I was thinking maybe you ought to hand it over to someone less . . . less emotionally involved."

He looked across at her to determine if she were serious or not. "Who might that be?"

"Me."

"You?"

"Yes, me."

"And you see yourself as less emotionally involved?"

"Hey, for one thing I'm a woman and—"

"*Whoa up,* there! What's being a woman got to do with it?"

"Well, I don't have a penis."

"Only penis envy, huh?"

She shook her head and frowned. "Joe, it stands to reason. You see what I'm getting at?"

"No, I don't."

"Damnit, Joe, you know you do. Already, you're thinking Stavros was killed *for* his penis and that the killer had some perverse reason for keeping it, and—"

"That hasn't been ruled out of my thinking, no."

"But you *started* with that assumption!"

"Christ, why not start with that assumption?"

"Because, you're going about it sloppily. It's not textbook."

He stopped the car, biting into the curb before her apartment complex, shaking her up. Here they continued what was fast becoming an argument. "The crime is not exactly textbook either; nor is it an Agatha Christie whodunit!"

44

"You're not going by the book, Joe!" she continued. "You're so bent on *how* Stavros died that you haven't even considered the obvious!"

"And you're going to tell me what's obvious?"

"I will if you'll calm down. God, you men. You think the world begins and ends at the head in your pants."

"All right . . . okay, supposing I am missing something on the Stavros case. You can fill me in over dinner. For now, I could use that cold beer you promised, or is that too much to ask?"

She knew he wanted time to fathom the meaning behind her use of the words *textbook* and *obvious* in relation to Stavros. She now wanted to throw it in his maddeningly smug face, but she resisted the urge.

At the very least, she had gotten him to give thought to her proposal. It would be an easy out for him, to spare himself all the hurt and grief, and no one but they would know. He'd routinely handed her other cases down the chain of command. Why not Stavros?

Swisher hadn't said another word about her proposal until much later in the evening when they were having dinner, after his third drink. She wondered how much weight she could give to what he had to say, under the circumstances.

"Who'd you have in mind to work with, Robyn?"

"What?"

"On the Stavros case."

"Peg-leg, maybe . . . and maybe Carter. We've got to bring her along, and there's no one better at talking to people."

"Peggy Olson and Melody Carter, sure . . . all

women, you think?"

"Give us a chance! You might be pleasantly surprised."

"You and Peg've proven yourselves. Want to indoctrinate Carter, huh?" The thought of unloading Stavros on her and the all-girl cast seemed suddenly good, like a weight lifted off his shoulders. The proposal was, in some respects, quite appealing.

"It's bloody, you know that."

"We can handle it."

"I mean very, *very* bad, Robyn."

"Swish—" She had reached out, putting her hand on his, when he looked up, eyeing two men walking in at the front door. Their light-weight trench coats weren't meant for Chicago in November, a telltale sign they'd just come off a flight. Guns bulged beneath their clothes. Swisher didn't recognize either man, but he also didn't like the way they hovered near the door without coming straight into the place for a table or to the bar for a drink. He saw that they were searching the darkness for someone. The dark interior hid Joe and Robyn for the moment as his eyes and mind played over the strangers. In the past few years he had made so many enemies, both on and off the force, that he no longer took anything for granted. Too many assumptions had killed friends and partners, filling the neighborhood cemeteries with good men like Jeff Cox, Dave Veck, Mike Ward, and others. He feared one day Robyn might be too close when *he* was meant to be the target.

"Hold on here," he told her. "I'm going for another drink."

She knew this was a lie.

The kitchen door at Swisher's back came open just as he was slipping from the booth. Robyn saw the two men pushing through, but not their faces, since Joe's massive form blocked her view. She responded to the fact they'd come in through the rear, again in summery trench coats. She shouted a warning to Joe and raised her gun to fire at the same instant that Joe wheeled with his weapon, the barrel finding Donna Thorpe's form. Thorpe's people shouted FBI as they, too, whipped out weapons, the triggers cocked.

"Son of a bitch, Swisher!" shouted Thorpe. "Put that horse pistol away! Christ, you still carrying a .357?" She ordered her men to stand down. Cops at every table in Transfusions had dived below tables, turning them over, their weapons trained on the unfamiliar G-men. "I just want to talk to you, damnit!" finished Donna Thorpe.

The standoff was complete; the room in deathly silence. They could hear the sweat trickling down their faces.

"What the hell's the idea sneakin' up on me like that? You're lucky your face isn't in the kitchen right now," shouted Swisher in return. "I thought you were in Virginia!"

Thorpe took the dig without a word. She'd just flown in from Lincoln. "I helicoptered here. These are my men. I didn't know you were so goddamned jumpy, and I'm not thrilled at the idea my people knowing I'm asking favors of . . . of *you*. This must be Sergeant Muro. Oh, yes, now I recall." Her gaze lingered over Robyn. Robyn returned the cold stare.

"Is this Dick Tracy shit necessary?" Robyn asked.

Thorpe ignored this. "Can we talk somewhere, private, Swisher? If it weren't important —"

"Upstairs, my place, come on."

Thorpe addressed her three traveling companions. "You men, have a drink . . . relax."

"Swish," said Robyn, staring hard at him. "Watch your back with this woman. Last time she used you, remember?"

Swisher recalled the first time he'd ever laid eyes on Donna Thorpe. It had been at Cook County Hospital over the body of an earlier partner who'd died because Joe had not gotten to a backup position seconds sooner. By that time Thorpe had already had her boys break into Dr. Harrelson's office to steal Swisher's file. Thorpe had displayed the file there at the hospital. She had read from it and Joe had wanted to kill her; she was setting Joe up to do a little job for her or suffer the consequences. FBI blackmail, the surest kind.

"Why don't you join us, Robyn?" Joe asked now.

She was taken by surprise. "Sure."

"No," said Thorpe. "This is strictly between us. A need-to-know basis on—"

"Stuff your need-to-know shit. We know how you play."

"This is highly sensitive infor—"

"Hey, Thorpe, I have no secrets from my partner, not even about you."

Swisher took Robyn by the arm and they started down the corridor to the stairwell that would take them to Swisher's place over the bar and grill. Thorpe, fingering the small plastic box she'd held since entering, said, "Fine, enchanting."

Chapter Six

Donna Thorpe laid out all the information she said she had on Dr. Maurice Ovierto, interchanging the name with his aliases. The information had been assembled, she said, by top agents at Quantico, but since Ovierto's whereabouts were now suspected to be the Chicago area, it was out of her "sector." This meant if she were to go through proper channels she'd be dealing with a man named Gerald Wymes, Chicago Field Office of the FBI. "A complete ass."

She went on to plead for Swisher's help. Swisher glanced at Dr. O's file. It was subcategorized five ways, by those victims of Ovierto's "rampage" who were caretakers, such as wardens, doctors, nurses; by random victims suspected or known to be the work of Ovierto; by police and FBI agents who'd succumbed to Dr. O's web of terror; by an emerging fourth category of highly placed scientists killed by the maniac.

The final category was a list of child victims that the madman had conducted "experiments" upon.

"Some kinda freak," said Swisher, handing the file to Robyn. He felt quite ill on seeing a photo of one of Dr. O's recent victims, a man Swisher had met, Tom Sykes.

"Unofficially, the man has a contract on his head—

shoot to kill. He's too cunning and dangerous to fuck with, you understand? Trouble is, he's never the same man twice, and he's fast, lightning fast, and as thorough as — well, as God."

"What do these categories represent . . . to him, I mean . . . killing all the scientists, for instance?" asked Robyn.

"Wish we knew. Some master plan, Perhaps. Others, as with the children . . . we figure, just jollies. He's as mad as the mad get, you see, but he can function as one of us — as a normal human being."

"Then how do we know you're not him?" asked Swisher, half-kidding.

"You don't. That's how good he is."

"And your people, with all you've got in the way of technological toys, still don't know why he does what he does?" Robyn was intrigued.

"Not really. Other than to say he has some notion that he serves the *god* of insanity."

"Why here, now? What makes you believe he's in Chicago."

"He's here."

"How do you know that for certain?"

"This." She handed the white box, the size of a Q-tip box to Swisher.

"What's this?"

"Part of your man, Stavros. Understand the case is yours now."

The two of them stared across at one another. Swisher wiped at his brow and opened the box to reveal the organ missing from Stavros. "How the hell do you know this . . ." he began shakily, "that this is Stavros's?"

"That's for your crime lab to find out, isn't it? It was a . . . gift . . . from Dr. O. Stands to reason, the pattern . . . likes innocent people as his victims."

"And this guy, this Ovierto, he's not contacted any-one with a list of demands? And he just, what, talks to you?"

"Talks . . . no, he doesn't talk . . ."

"Sends you disgusting things through the mail, then — federal offense, isn't it? Bitches the Feds off, doesn't it?"

"You're damned straight it does!" Thorpe shouted and then found an edge of the couch to rest on. "Christ, Swisher, the man's an animal in every sense of the word, but he's as cunning an animal as . . . as a cougar. He's a medical doctor, and when he's not em-ploying surgery, for Christ's sake, he's employing drugs and poisons. He's left bodies in almost every state in the goddamned Union!"

"If that's true, this ahh . . . body part . . . could've come from any number of bodies."

"Don't you think I've thought of that? Hell, man, we have a missing agent named Bateman we believe is in his hands. He was working with Sykes and —"

"— And if Sykes is dead, yeah . . . see, what you mean," said Swisher, calming a bit.

"This man sounds like a lunatic we dealt with once before," said Robyn.

"No, no . . . he's not like anyone else. He's as close to Satan as the human mind can get. He enjoys watching people die; enjoys experimenting to prolong death. Nothing like anything you've ever known, Ser-geant, believe me."

Swisher found some glasses and a bottle and rattled out some ice from his freezer, asking the others if they wanted any of his Scotch. Robyn declined, but Donna Thorpe called out, "With a little water and ice, thanks."

Swisher busied himself with the drinks as Thorpe roamed about his place — like a thief canvassing a store, Robyn thought. She took an immediate dislike to Donna Thorpe, colored mostly by what she knew of the woman from Joe's previous dealings with her. But Joe had said nothing about how pretty—no, beautiful—she was, what a stylish dresser she was, or the fact she moved with a Lauren Bacall grace that made Robyn feel self-conscious in her presence. She didn't look anything like the middle-aged bag with three kids that Joe had painted her.

Thorpe had taken in the room quickly, and now she caught Robyn staring at her. Their eyes flashed like two swords, but Joe, sauntering back in with the drinks, hadn't seen a thing.

"You two gettin' acquainted?" he asked.

"As a matter of fact, we are," offered Thorpe.

"Why do you suppose he's here?" asked Robyn.

"Pattern. Ovierto will follow through with his pattern, and the next two on his list are near here, at Argonne, at Fermilab in—"

"You're certain?"

"It's the way the man works."

"Meaning what exactly?" pressed Swisher.

"He's a real smooth operator, crazy or not. Takes time to really get to know the habits of those he kills. Kind of a thing with him. He learns the names of their damned pets before he kills them; where they jog and how far; who they speak to and who they sleep with. The guy is a professional killer and he's a psycho, a neat-as-a-pin psycho. I came here to tell you about this man and to warn you that he's about to become a Chicago problem, unless you can stop him."

"Do you have a picture of him?" asked Robyn.

"Here," she said, spreading out three different pictures of the killer. Each one looked like a different person. "He's a chameleon, Swisher, not unlike yourself.

That's why I thought of you when I determined he was heading for Chicago next."

Robyn and Swisher studied the pictures. Ovierto had piercing, mad eyes. Swisher had seen eyes like that in a preCivil War picture of the madman John Brown, taken days before he stormed a U.S. Arsenal at Harper's Ferry with a contingent of eleven men. Maybe this Dr. Ovierto was simply a madman on a self-appointed holy mission to save the Earth from physicists and NASA and the CIA. In one picture Ovierto was seen in a front view, the skin pulled tightly about the protruding portions of his face. He was thin, angular, starved-looking. He was very pale in this picture, looking somewhat like an East European prisoner of war.

"Is this his true likeness?" asked Swisher, lifting the full face picture of a man dressed in the clothing of a servant or waiter, a dull expression on his face.

"Affirmative," she said, falling back on her FBI lingo.

The second shot was of a man in a Marine uniform. He was heavier about the jowls and fleshy ears jutted out. The nose was fuller and the hair dark where the other was an Andy Warhol white. "Doesn't look like the same man. Was he ever a Marine?"

"Yes, but here he's using a disguise. He uses many disguises. He is a capable makeup artist, as you can see."

"Can't do much with these eyes, though," said Robyn.

Swisher agreed. "Strange look deep inside there."

"He'll change his eyes with contacts. He could be anyone you meet. You'll have to see him before he sees you."

"Some decoy set up, huh, Swish?" asked Robyn.

They studied the third glossy photo of Dr. M.

Ovierto. Once again, the eyes shimmered out of the flat photo at them. In this picture Ovierto was using one of his favorite disguises, according to Thorpe. He was dressed as a woman, and he looked quite convincing.

"As it turns out he's a cross-dresser."

"Transsexual, maybe?" asked Swisher.

"Very sharp, Lieutenant."

"You were going to hold that little smidge of info for later, maybe?"

Donna Thorpe ignored this and continued. "Be a woman any time he chooses. Helps him get in close, if you know what I mean."

"I do."

"Men are easily beguiled by women; easily overtaken. He knows this. Knows a great deal about human nature. At any rate, he knows how to walk in heels and hoisery. His heels are deadly, however. He's been known to ram them through a man. He's versed in the martial arts, and if you can imagine a jujitsu kick with those heels making contact against your head, well . . ."

"Tough and mad," said Swisher.

"Dangerous, no doubt about it. Well-versed in all forms of armament as well."

Swisher nodded and said, "Of course."

"But according to these files he's not killed any of the victims with a gun," said Robyn, confused.

Thorpe got up from the chair she sat in and rocked on her feet a bit. "Yeah, Dr. Ovierto is funny that way."

Swisher stared into Thorpe's eyes; the woman was pushing hard, and she was weary. The eyes told Swisher of the awful wear on a person who has lost a partner. He understood this.

Swisher took the photo from Robyn again and

stared into the egg-like eyes that bulged there. In the full-faced picture, the one that most closely resembled the real Dr. Ovierto, Swisher saw something flash like the taunting flicker of the Devil himself. It was as if the photo eyes had turned up, or down. It shook Swisher where he didn't like to be shaken.

To hide his inner trembling, Joseph Swisher quickly asked, "This file for me to keep? You got copies, I presume."

"You've got a complete background file here, Joe. It's all yours."

"Swish," said Robyn, "you can't seriously be thinking—"

"If this nut's running around Chicago; if he's the guy that did Stavros—"

"We don't have any proof of that," replied Robyn.

But Joe, for the first time, was giving it very serious consideration. He lifted and quickly put down the box with the severed penis inside it, saying, "I'll get this typed; determine if it is Stavros. Meantime, I want something for our trouble in return for Ovierto, should we get him."

"Name it."

"Alpha status with the company."

"What?" asked Thorpe.

"You heard me."

"I don't know if I can—"

"If you and I bring in Ovierto, you can write any ticket, Thorpe. I know how things work in D.C."

"All right," she replied. "You've got it."

Alpha status meant free access to all FBI files, including those considered top secret.

"Something stinks in all this," said Robyn. "She's just interested in getting you killed, Joe."

"I'll admit people have died around me, and sometimes because of me," Thorpe said, "but Joe, you know that you and I are not so different. I see an ends, I make a means, same as you. I see a wrong, I make it right. This wrong can best be righted here and now, by you."

"I don't like it, Joe," Robyn said in his ear.

"Complete access to the files?" he asked Thorpe.

"My own terminal."

"In Lincoln?"

"In D.C."

This made Joe laugh. "No horshittin' with partitioning programs to keep me out?"

"My word on it."

"I want more than your word."

"Anything."

"I want it in writing, a contract."

Thorpe hesitated.

Robyn shook her head in disbelief. "How're you going to trust her, Joe?"

"Well?" pressed Swisher.

"All right. I'll have the papers drawn up."

"A contract to kill Maurice Ovierto at your request, for payment in information retrieval from the central computer at Virginia's FBI headquarters to search for two men. I want the names in the contract."

"Done."

"Shit," moaned Robyn.

"Done," said Joe. "And Robyn, Stavros is yours if this—" he held up the box again, "turns out to belong to someone else."

"Thanks for the crumbs." She suddenly stormed out and down the corridor and stairs. Maybe it was for the better, he thought. Maybe he should have spoken to Donna Thorpe alone in the first place. He slammed the door hard on returning to Thorpe, who'd once again made herself comfortable in the sparsely furnished room that sported glistening, well-kept wood flooring, and paneled walls hung with citations and guns.

"Good riddance," Thorpe mumbled. Swisher made no reply to the remark, but simply paced before her before suddenly taking her in his arms and kissing her.

"Lieutenant, you do have a great deal of work to do." She pointed to the file. "Study it carefully. You must understand Ovierto. He's like no other adversary you have faced. He's diabolical, far more so than either you or I. The first man he killed, Dr. Coleman, you can read about it. He was skewered in ten places by a falling chandelier in his ancestral home. It's postulated that Ovierto got to him by becoming an electrician. He so timed the fall of the chandelier that Coleman was sitting under it having his brunch when it crushed him, a mammoth piece of metal and crystal. He was killed on impact."

"Tricky."

"Like you," she said, pulling away from him.

He moved to kiss her again, but she put him off. "Strictly business partners."

"Why is that? Was it that way with you and Tom Sykes?"

He knew he had struck a sensitive cord when she darted for the door. "I'll be in touch."

Chapter Seven

"You're going to do it? After what that bitch did to you?" Robyn was furious as she stormed about her apartment the next day. "You poor, dumb bastard."

"Look at it this way, sweetheart," he said with a casualness that she found attractive. "I bag this guy and the sky's the limit for my career. This guy's big time bad, baby."

"I smell something; something's just not right. And that Thorpe woman!"

"Woman's intutition doesn't change the fact this filth, Ovierto, is out there cutting people up, dicing guys who work for NASA and that not even the FBI's been able to stop him. Suppose a Chicago cop did the job for them? How's that going to look on Thorpe's record, huh?"

"Is that your plan? Embarrass her? Burn her?"

He raised his shoulders. "Why not."

"You're playing with fire, Joe. That woman is a forest fire."

"Come on, Robyn, I'm a big boy. I can take care of myself."

"Think so, Joe? She's capable of using you, Joe. You should know that by now."

He put both hands on his head, nursing a hangover, saying nothing.

"Where is she now?"

"Flew back to Nebraska where she's headquartered now. How do you like that? She was booted from Quantico over this Ovierto business."

"What'd she promise you, Joe? What?"

"Will you get off it, Robyn? Christ, I don't owe you any explanations."

"No . . . no, I suppose not. What am I to you anyway?"

"Come on, Robyn . . . Robyn, don't—"

She pulled away from him. "What are your plans?"

"Plans?"

"For Ovierto. For the operation."

"Going to wait for him to show up."

"She seemed to think he already has."

"No, I mean I'm going out there today, to Fermilab, set myself up as a janitor, keep watch."

"Backup?"

"This guy would smell backup a mile away."

He'd done it before, and they had argued over the chances Swisher took. Now they stared across the room at one another, and he finally said, "You just get busy on that Stavros thing—I mean, case."

"Sure . . . sure. Now, if you don't mind, Joe, I'd like to get dressed. Maybe I'll see you later."

"Yeah, later, much later, and stop worrying." He kissed her at the door.

"Joe, be careful. This guy's a real nut case."

She closed the door on him without returning his kiss.

Dr. Ovierto, dressed in a drab coat and tie with wire-rim glasses, looked bookish and priggish as he moved down the crowded corridors of O'Hare International Airport. He found the necessary doorway, marked Airport Security, and, readying his badge, wandered through. On the inside a pair of uniformed guards were having coffee at an urn, laughing over some recent incident at the airport. It sounded as if it had something to do with a dog and an old lady, Ovierto only caught snatches of the tale. The uniformed men barely gave him a glance, continuing with their socializing until one was beeped and had to answer the call, saying goodby to his friend. Behind a desk a clerk with glasses too large for her face squinted up at him.

"Can I help you?"

"FBI," he said, "Inspector Bateman." He flashed the ID and badge, and she became nervous.

"Can, can I help you," she repeated.

"I need to know if an Inspector Thorpe has arrived in Chicago. She would likely have used an FBI helicopter. Now, I've checked with Mid-Way and they've had no contact with her. Inspector Donna Thorpe."

"When would this have been, sir? I mean, we have a lot of small traffic."

"Yesterday some time."

She frowned. "It will take some time to—"

"Please, can I just come around. I believe I could bring up that information, if you don't mind, in just a moment, using the call numbers of the helicopter. It's most important, vital even."

"Vital?"

"National security, you might say."

The uniformed officer had moved over, curious. Dr. Ovierto felt the scalpel in his breast pocket as if it were enlarging there. He'd have to use it if they began to suspect anything. "What's the problem, Molly?"

"Special agent Bateman," he said, turning and tak-

60

ing the other man's hand, spilling some of his coffee. "FBI. Just a routine check on another agent's arrival."

"Molly, can you get that information?"

"Sure, Mr. Banks. What are those call numbers?"

"HL-705."

Banks hung close by, sipping his coffee, watching. He had heard that some FBI chopper had flown in and out the previous day. He wondered why this fool didn't know that it had already left O'Hare, if he was one of them. He was about to ask when Molly declared that the flight had arrived at 11:09 the previous night and had left at 2 AM.

"Damn, then I did miss Inspector Thorpe . . . shame, a real shame. We've worked together for many years, but it has always been long-distance — fax machines, telephone, wires, you see. No one told me she'd be in town. Ah, well . . . thank you . . . thank you both for your time."

"Sorry we couldn't be of more help," said Banks.

"Yeah," agreed Molly.

Both of them went back to work as Ovierto darted a glance back at them, wondering if he wouldn't like to turn around and kill them both, wondering if doing so would serve his purpose or not. He quickly decided that it would not. He'd let them live, as he had let the girl in Colorado live. He had set her free in the wilderness, blind and naked, to wander wherever she liked. He would not be returning to Colorado.

Molly gave him a perfunctory, kind smile, without any special twinkle in her eye, without any real feeling. He thought she was rather plain and unappealing and his look may have conveyed this, for suddenly she dropped her eyes, turning a bit pink in the cheeks with a blush, pretending to work. Ovierto smiled and gave her a little wave as he slipped through the heavy door. Outside the door the rush of the river of people in the corridor swept him up.

"Oh, shit," said Molly at the desk the other side of the door.

Banks stepped again to her desk, asking what now was the problem.

"That guy left his pen—an expensive one, too." She held up a Cross pen and it sparkled beneath the florescent lights here.

"Maybe I can catch him," said Banks. "Give it here."

"Oh, can you try?"

"Give it a shot." He placed the pen in his own pocket and went for the door.

Molly returned to some filing that was piling up beside her. She was angry with her sister, Nan, who had gotten ill and left her responsible for getting her kids off to school that morning—for the fourth such morning in what was getting to be a tiring routine—and her work had been suffering as a result. Along with my looks, she told herself as she glanced at her reflection in a strip of metal that ran across the top of the filing cabinet.

Her desk was cluttered with items that needed typing, duplicating and filing. She dug in, her mind going back to the FBI man who had seemed such a gentleman. Most men in police work, even the stiffs in uniforms about the airport, like Banks, were usually so concerned about being macho that they didn't know how to be a gentleman. Bateman seemed an exception.

While she shuffled the papers on her desk, one flew out at her and wafted to the floor. It was a report from the FBI, the very woman that Bateman had been asking about, Thorpe. She hadn't seen it before and imagined it had been given to the night girl. She saw that copies were attached and a message said, "Distribute to all airport security. Urgent request from FBI."

This made her frown. Why hadn't Cathy simply done the job? Why make the copies and stop at that? What was the bitch trying to prove? Then she looked at the bulletin board in the security guards' coffee room, finding a copy tacked up there. That was Cathy's idea of distribution, all right.

Sighing, she decided she'd have to get the copies around, but she'd have to wait until Banks or someone else came in to hold the fort, catch the phone, and such. Then she noticed one of the names on the list she held in her hand. It was *Bateman*.

She decided that perhaps she ought to read the memo. It said that the FBI's most wanted could be coming through the airport, and that he frequently used the aliases attached:

Dr. Richard Armour
Dr. David Samson
Wolfgang Meir
Thomas or Tom Sykes
David Bateman

The last two names, the memo informed her, might be used in connection with an FBI badge. An accompanying photo of the real Bateman didn't look at all like the man.

Her first thought was for Banks and his safety. She shakily rushed for the door, looking both ways for Banks, unable to find him. She cursed and raced back to her desk and the PA system, trying to clear it, to override flight deputies and information and people being paged, calling her need Priority One, an emergency. She feared she'd be too late, or that she'd say the wrong thing and place Banks in worse danger than he already was in or that Banks would mistake her call—or, worse, not hear the message at all if he were himself radioing other security to help locate the supposed FBI man to return his Cross pen.

She feared what the man would do to Banks if he felt suddenly threatened.

Hesitantly, she first tried buzzing Banks via his radio, but he wasn't responding. He was likely sending.

She spoke into the PA, using Banks's security number. "311, please return to airport security, 311 . . . 311 . . . respond if you hear . . . 311 . . . 311 . . ."

An overwhelming fear engulfed her and she immediately radioed other guards, telling them that Banks was in danger and that the man the FBI wanted was in the airport at this moment.

She was immediately cut off by a woman's voice, a woman who said she was Inspector Donna Thorpe, FBI.

"You? It was you that he was looking for."

"Where is your location?"

Someone beside Thorpe told her where the security offices were.

"Is Banks following the suspect?" she asked Molly.

"Yes, but Banks doesn't know who he is! He's trying to—" she was cut off "—give him back his pen."

He was truly sorry that he had missed Thorpe. He would like to see her again, face to face. But he didn't know that he could end her life. He had come to the realization of late that he needed someone like Thorpe, someone who paid particular attention to his whereabouts, his comings and goings, and, most importantly, his deeds. *For it is through deeds and acts that ye shall be judged,* he told himself wryly now.

She had come in to warn the good doctors at Fermilab about his imminent arrival. Guards would be doubled, and perhaps there'd be police staked out all around. It only made the challenge more enticing for the killer. She knew that . . . knew that he'd respond like a titillated child with a dare in his face.

He looked over his shoulder to see that Banks, the security guy, was carefully following, keeping him in sight. He saw other men who looked like plainclothes cops all around. He realized it was a trap, a setup, and his options were limited. He jumped onto a down escalator, pushing people aside as he rushed onward. He saw Banks taking the stairs, calling out to him. At the foot of the escalator he dodged around a corner and stepped into a men's room, hoping the airport cop would continue past. In the meantime, he fought with a quarter to step into one of the stalls. He worked free of his disguise, casting off the suit to create a more leisurely look, and had tossed away the glasses when he heard Banks rapping on the stall door, saying, "Mr. Bateman. Inspector!"

Ovierto tore out the scalpel from the coat he'd hung on the stall door, yanked the door open and lunged at Banks, driving the scalpel into and across the stout man's throat. Banks caromed off the wall and into the row of sinks, holding himself before the mirror, staring for a moment at his own death before he slid to the floor in a pool of blood where the shimmering Cross pen that Ovierto had left behind now swam.

Another man stepped from a stall, saw what was going on, and locked himself back in. Ovierto rushed from the men's room and back into the teeming life-pool of the airport.

In another part of the airport, Donna Thorpe got word of the airport guard's slaying. She rushed to the scene with a handful of men working in the Chicago

65

Bureau. She'd sent the helicopter out of the airport the night before for Ovierto's benefit, knowing he was quite capable of learning her whereabouts. When she got to the men's room, finding Banks dead of blood loss and shock, she pounded her fists into one of the stall doors. It rattled under the pressure and a sport coat fell onto the floor. She found the glasses beside the coat.

"It was him," she said.

One of the Chicago men said, "How can you tell?"

"I can smell the bastard. Get a forensics man down here to take charge of the coat and glasses," she said as she rifled through the pockets. She found wadded bubble gum papers, a pack of cigarettes with only a few missing. She found a locker key which made her eyes light up. She pocketed the key and asked one of the airport security men to take her to the locker number she wanted.

Ten minutes later she carefully opened the locker, fearing a bomb might greet her. But there was no explosion, only a package, carefully wrapped, about the size of a bread box. It smelled, and she knew that it was some part of Bateman. The package had a carrier stamp on it: DV.

"Denver," said the airport guy.

"Go back to my men. Tell them I need an E.T. team over here."

"E.T.?"

"Evidence techs. *Now.*"

"Yes, ma'am, yes ma'am!"

There was also a small envelope with her name on it. Thorpe swallowed hard, lifted it with a pair of tweezers, and opened it, flattening it out against locker, reading his words:

Glad you could make it to Chicago, Donna.

Sorry I missed you, but maybe this will make up
for your bad luck. . . .

"Bastard! Bastard!" she said, gritting her teeth,
making a lady with several children cringe and move
her children away. She didn't see the man behind the
newspaper, sitting amid the crowd across from
the locker, grinning like a jackal over her distress. She
didn't see Ovierto enjoying himself to the fullest. She
just wondered how he knew that she'd be here to find
his crumb-trail of bodies.

Chapter Eight

Later, with a Chicago coroner named Jeremy Likes, who worked for the FBI—a huge, red-headed, dapper man who didn't look as if he'd care to get his hands dirty—Thorpe unwrapped the package. It was Bateman's decaying head.

It made everyone, including Likes, tremble. Thorpe could hardly swallow, and her knees had gone weak. She found a place to sit down. One of the others brought her a coffee. She felt, for a moment, that she was the cause of Bateman's mutilation, that Ovierto was doing these unspeakable acts just for her, as a kind of sick floor show. She had never hated anyone so much as she hated Maurice Ovierto.

He knew she was here. He knew she would be at Fermilab. And still he'd come to play the game. It was all a game to him, a deadly game.

She worried that she would lose her wild card, Swisher, if he learned about the recent turn of events. "I want this kept absolutely quiet," she told the others.

"Within reason, sure," said Special Agent Jack Harris, who had been assigned to give her any and all help she requested. Harris hadn't liked his assignment as yet, and he had done his work in a sullen, joyless silence. Now he wanted some answers.

"How did he know you were here?"

"How the hell should I know? We sent the chopper out with my look-alike aboard. Everything that could be done—"

"And now a man dead and another man's head is left for you like a goddamned valentine."

"Macabre son of a bitch," said the coroner.

"Get what you can from the . . . from Bateman's head," she told Likes.

"Sure, sure Inspector."

She walked out on her confused collaborators, going for a room where she could get some sleep. She wanted to be ready for tonight.

Sleep, however, was short-lived, troubled, and disturbing. She almost welcomed the interruption from a courier who brought word from Nebraska. It was information rerouted from D.C., from Boas—the final autopsy report on Tom Sykes. Her hands shook when she signed for it.

She took the brown, clasped envelope to a coffee table in the suite provided at the Bureau. The place gave one the impression she was actually in a room at the Hilton or the Marriott. There was even room service, which she called now, laying the report aside.

She asked that fresh coffee and toast be sent in. She then went to the telephone and rang her husband at home.

"Donna, how are you? How is everything there?"

"Just wanted to hear your voice, Jim. Everything is . . . fine . . . everything here is . . . fine," she lied. "Are the kids home from school yet?"

"Just arrived."

"I need to talk to them."

"Sure, sure, honey. You sound tired."

"Very."

"And depressed."

"Don't worry. I'm not suicidal . . . not yet."

"This case is driving you too hard, Donnie."

She wiped a tear from her eye. "The kids, Jim . . . the kids."

Talking with her children was like a balm, a way to keep sane. She listened to their petty squabbles, to their news of school. Brucie was trying out for baseball while Jim Jr. was writing for the school newspaper and planning his future down to the last detail, which included a Pulitzer someday. Kay was having difficulties with her girlfriends at school, something about her nose being too large, and the fact she did not own a Billabong jacket.

For a few minutes, she forgot about Dr. Maurice Ovierto and what he was doing to her insides.

Then Jim got back on the phone and wanted to know exactly what the kids wanted to know. When are you coming home?"

"When it's finished here."

"You really think you guys'll get the bastard there?"

"It's our best shot . . . best we've had in a long time."

"Then you know for sure he is there?"

"Yes . . . quite sure." She thought of the head in the locker stinking up the airport.

"Honey," he said, "please, please come home safely." In one piece, he meant. "I will. I will."

"God, I hate this."

"Jim . . . Jim, I love you."

"But you put me and the kids through hell, Donnie . . . you do."

"It's my work, Jim." She thought he had no idea of true hell.

"Your work is here, in Nebraska. You didn't have to go to Chicago, and you don't have to be in the bloody lion's den when—"

"Yes, I do. I have to see that this man is stopped, Jim."

"Why you, babe? Why?"

"We've been through this before and—"

His tone changed. "Want to know the truth, kid?"

"Jim . . ."

"Truth is, you're tied to this guy at the fuckin' hip, like Ahab to the goddamned whale."

"Jim."

"*I've got to go!* Thought I'd say it this time!" He hung up.

"Jim, Jim . . . I need you."

But he was gone and she was alone in the empty room with the report on Sykes which she had all but blackmailed Boas for. Her coffee and toast arrived and she was grateful for the new interruption. It would take a certain amount of bolstering and posturing in front of the screaming brown envelope before she could open it. She thought of the times she and Tom Sykes, alone and far from home, had found comfort in one another's arms. She sensed that Jim knew about it, but she was uncertain. Tom's wife most certainly had known . . . no secrets there. Donna hadn't loved Tom passionately, but she and Tom had loved one another's company, loved working together, loved the danger and the wonderful sweet experience of *closure* when a case was resolved to her satisfaction. On occasion, amid week-long stakeouts, amid the joy of success, she and Tom had fallen into one another's arms. But she loved Jim, and he knew this. . . .

She filled her stomach with toast, drank the coffee, and when she had no further excuses she went in and took a shower. In her robe a few minutes later, she did her hair and watched the clock tick away. It was nearing three. In a few hours she'd be out at Fermilab, preparing to kill Ovierto once and for all.

The phone rang and she went for it, her eyes still avoiding the report on Sykes. She had fought so hard for the report, and now she was beginning to wish she'd lost the battle. "Hello, this is Thorpe."

"I thought you were in Nebraska," said Robyn Muro on the other end.

"Who is this?"

"Sergeant Muro, as if you didn't know."

"Why are you calling me, Sergeant? And how did you get this number?"

"Let's just say I'm a resourceful cop."

"What is it you want?"

"I want Joe to stay alive, and around you I'm sure that's not possible."

"Someone's told you about the airport?"

"Things like that have a way of spreading."

"Listen, Sergeant, we are involved in the biggest manhunt of the decade, and Joe is a big boy."

"Yeah, well that's the problem. Joe is just a *big boy.*"

"He was given a choice, and he made his choice. A man like him, I suggest you back off and let him do his job."

"Do you intend telling him about the airport?"

"I already have," she lied.

"You've talked to Joe today?"

"He came by my place . . . we talked . . . yes."

There was a long silence at Robyn's end. "I see. I . . . don't think Joe cares to work blind. You should know—"

"We discussed everything in detail . . . every little thing."

"If Joe is hurt in all this—"

"What? You're coming after me?"

"Something like that, yeah."

"I hope it doesn't come to that, Robyn. I like you."

"And I like snakes, Inspector, but I'm not crazy about rats." She hung up.

"Just don't get in the way," she said to the dead phone.

Now there were no more excuses. She grabbed the autopsy report on Sykes and began scanning it.

Sykes had been alive when he was intered in the sandy earth in Florida. He had not died of his wounds or scars or torture, but through suffocation. Ovierto had buried him alive. She gasped at the thought, her trembling hand going to her face as she fought back her emotions.

She scanned past the cause of death to information on Sykes's shoes, which had been embedded with a layer of mineral-rich earth that did not match with the soil where he was buried. The minute earth sample corresponded with the alkaline-rich deposits of the western United States. Boas matched it to Utah, Colorado, or Nevada.

Bateman's severed head had come by way of Denver, Colorado. What was Ovierto doing out that way? Had he held Sykes there? Did he have a hideout there?

She got on the phone and called HQ in Nebraska. She identified herself, giving her code name and number, and then she told her people to scan the news coming out of Denver for anything remotely smacking of Ovierto's work. She was assured that such information would be scrutinized and that she would be apprised.

She went back to the report on Tom Sykes. *Ankles were cut at the tendons . . . impressions on the skin had been from chains . . . heated chains . . . some evidence of having been force-fed cleansing fluid of an undetermined nature . . .*

She stopped, unable to go on.

"Tonight, you lousy bastard . . . tonight . . ."

Chapter Nine

The hard FBI woman had left Joe Swisher a lot of
data to read, mull over, and scan through, and he
had scanned a good deal of it, finding the information on Sykes's death especially revealing. Now he
was working a mop at the Fermilab, and he found
himself trying to recall all that Donna Thorpe had
said as well as what she had only half-said the night
before when she had surprised him with a second
visit. He had learned from the files just what a nasty
piece of work she had put him on to. This guy
Ovierto was very bloody, very deranged, and filled
with rage, a real maniac's maniac. And she had lost
a partner in the most gruesome way imaginable.

Donna Thorpe had sauntered back in looking like
Lauren Bacall in Key Largo. Her sultriest look came
when she suddenly lifted one of Swisher's guns from
the wall of his apartment, shouldering the weapon,
which had been his father's M-16. It had been a
heavy rifle to carry all over Europe.

"Government issue," she had said.

He asked her why she'd returned.

"Your father's, right? World War Two? I know all
about you, Swisher."

"You think so?"

"And, in many ways, I understand and sympathize with you."

Swisher gave her a skeptical look, wondering what she was getting at, but he said nothing.

She continued to fondle the M-16 and talk. "I've lost people close to me. I know how badly you feel. I know how guilty you feel."

"Guilty? Not me, lady."

"Yes, guilty. Any cop who loses a partner wonders why it wasn't him . . . or her, that got it."

He frowned. "Maybe."

"I know how the hate takes hold."

"Don't expect me to bow and scrape shit off your shoes, Thorpe."

"I know, you've got your own shit to clean up."

"So, what're you saying? That we're alike? Not in your wildest dreams, Thorpe."

"Just wanted to leave you with another file."

"What's this?" he asked, taking it and the heavy rifle from her. He put the M-16 back in its place, realizing that the barrel now smelled like her, as did the file. He lingered over the odor a moment.

"All I have on what happened to my partner at the hands of this maniac we're after."

"All right. I'll look it over."

"This man is more than just a maniac, he's a cunning maniac. Listen, despite what your partner thinks—"

"Leave Robyn out of this. *I* have."

"Despite what she thinks, I didn't come here to see you killed."

"But you won't shed too many tears if I am."

She stared at him. "I only want to bury Ovierto." She turned from him and walked away, speaking. "Just a bit of advice from someone who knows what

Maurice Ovierto is capable of. You read about the death of Lady Hugh Cartier? The English scientist who died in England a week ago?"

"I seem to recall something about it; reported as an accident."

"Read the Scotland Yard report in your files. They figure he spent some time before he pushed her over into that ravine, just to watch her scream and beg mercy before he turned her and her lawyer into ashes. He's a psycho, and to get him, everything you need will be placed at your disposal. I have a chopper on standby at O'Hare for you, and a mobile unit with communications equipment parked outside right this moment."

"I see you've thought of everything. You *are* worried about me, aren't you?" he replied in a flippant tone, going to the window that overlooked Kedzie, where he stared down at the unmarked van across the street.

"Get familiar with the two scientists at risk."

"Which one do you figure to be next?"

"Oliguerri."

"What is that, Italian?"

"Ibi Oliguerri is Nigerian."

"Look for a black guy in a white lab coat, huh?"

"Picture is in the file, and please take care of those records."

Swisher shrugged, poured himself another drink and said, "Hey, unless some overachiever with too much time on his—or her—hands *steals* them, they're in good hands. Besides, you must have copies."

"Joe—can I call you, Joe?"

"Make it Swish."

"All right, Swish, this is all hush-hush; a leak in

77

the wrong dike and we all drown, you understand?"

She wheeled at the door, staring back at him, her eyes boring into his. "Swish, let's try to put the past behind us."

"You're just trying to play me for a fool, *Donna*."

"I only have one aim in all this, Joe."

He smirked. "Yeah, to get me into bed."

"To get Ovierto in the neck."

He rushed at her, his eyes blazing. "No matter how you do it? No matter who gets killed, like your pal, Sykes? Or me?"

"You've got all the answers, or so you think. Get your head out of that bottle long enough to smell the blood! This guy's a psycho and he will leave a trail of bodies in your city that—"

"Really?"

"Yes, damnit."

"Is that right?"

"Bank on it. Anyone who gets in his way, anyone he must use he'll kill. Hell, he'll kill for the use of a ballpoint pen if it helps him achieve his ends. You may think you are ruthless in your desire to see an end to these two men you've hounded through the years, Swisher, but beside Maurice Ovierto you're a charitable and good citizen of the realm."

"Compliments?"

"Get to Oliguerri as soon as you can."

"Is he on the run?"

"No. He's shaken, but he doesn't know the extent of the danger he is in. Oliguerri, like the other American scientist on Ovierto's hit list, believes it has to do with the Major Government, or possibly the KGB, and that it will not cross the ocean."

He stared, sizing her up. "But it has, hasn't it?"

"The two others—"

"Two others?"

"—met with *accidental* deaths in the States, but they were Canadian citizens on holiday. Good friends, they were traveling together when they got botulism—or so the death certificates read."

"What did they die of?"

"Rare poison extracted from a mushroom. Very painful death. Seems their waiter was an *imposter*."

Swisher considered this for a moment. "Maybe it is just coincidence. How do you know otherwise?"

"They were fed poisonous mushrooms. Found on autopsy."

Swisher paced about the room in a small circle, thinking. "So, I'll be as much a surprise to this guy, Oliguerri, as this doctor character?"

"Not quite, but close. We've contacted Oliguerri discreetly to tell him we were taking precautions, just in case."

"I'm to approach him as a Fed?"

"Any way you like. It's Ovierto we're after. Any way that ensures we get Ovierto."

"Hold on. Are you asking me to distance myself and wait for Ovierto to strike this Nigerian guy before I should step in?"

"Your prerogative entirely, Swish."

"Christ, and I thought I was a cold bastard."

"I'd trade six Oliguerris for Ovierto's fuckin' head, you'd—"

"How many Swishers would you trade?"

She slowed down. "All I'm saying is that if you spook Ovierto, we've lost him. Simple as that. And if we lose him, his killing spree will continue."

"Better choice of words, huh?"

She had a look on her face that said slap, but she was too strong for that. She took a deep breath and matched his stare with her own. "Ovierto will smell you, and he will kill you along with Oliguerri if you go near Oliguerri."

"So, bait him with the scientist, bring the bird out in the open, and after Oliguerri is dead, get Ovierto, a nice slug for his brain?"

"However you can get Ovierto, get him."

"Christ, lady, are you as cold as you act?"

"I can be very warm."

"I'll bet you can."

He went to her, unashamedly attracted to her despite his words, attracted to her callous exterior, wishing to scrape it down, find out what was beneath. He embraced her and she returned his passion with passion, but suddenly she put him off. "Get Ovierto for me, and then . . . and then I'll come to you."

He smiled wide at this. "It's a deal . . . a solid deal."

"No one but you and I know about this operation until I can make it stick as official, Joe . . ."

"Sounds fine to me."

Despite herself, she became angry with him. "Damnit, you don't get it, do you?"

"Get what?"

"Anything happens to you, and we never heard of you." She closed the door on him.

"Standard operating procedure," he had said through the door.

Now here he was, in what amounted to a sterile environment surrounded by pencil-toting, white-coated people with enough optical wear to open a booming franchise. He had learned as subtly as possible where Oliguerri operated, since the building was enormous, going up and up as far as the eye

80

could see. He had stood in the brightly lit lobby, looking up to the pinnacle of the building, a sleek, tall, pyramid. Each floor was littered with greenery in the form of live trees and shrubs which required watering. He had been put to this task as well.

He was looking forward to a break. He was beginning to wonder if Thorpe's information on Ovierto was accurate or not. He had been told that a Sergeant Muro had been trying to get in touch with him, but he wasn't ready to deal with Robyn just yet.

A couple of cleaned floors later, Joe Swisher was beginning to wonder if it hadn't all been a wild goose chase. Thorpe had been known to be wrong in the past. Then someone's footfalls began to approach in the quiet, upper corridors here, where the serious lab work was done and where Ibi Oliguerri and Elena Hogarth were working on something to do with macro-strings and curls in space, which meant absolutely nothing to Swisher. He thought it sounded something like Chef Boyardee microwave-able spaghetti.

He had met Oliguerri only briefly, telling the self-assured black man who he was and why he was here, mainly because it was exactly what Thorpe didn't want him to do. Oliguerri wasn't in the least concerned, but Hogarth had become jumpy at the notion the police were in the building. Oliguerri said they had too much work to concern themselves with such nonsense. Dr. Elena Hogarth reminded him of the deaths of their colleagues in Atlanta. Swisher had wondered why Ovierto had targeted these people and asked them if they knew.

"We can tell you nothing of what goes on in a madman's head," said the African. "It is like the villager who has all good shiny teeth, another villager will want the same teeth, even if he cannot possibly fit them into his head."

Swisher frowned at the little parable, wondering if that was all there was to it, that Ovierto was simply jealous. "Men seem to be killing one another for less and less these days," he had said.

Hogarth was shaken by the talk. "If we're going to work, doctor," she said to Oliguerri, "then let's have at it."

"Is there any other exit from your lab?" he asked.

"There is a freight elevator at the back for samples," she said.

Swisher thought she was pretty, in a pale, fragile way, but not at all his type. She realized he was staring, pushed her glasses up and dropped her own eyes. "Are you alone, or do you have help, officer?"

"I've got the FBI behind me," he told her as much to reassure himself as her.

"Then he is coming, isn't he?"

"Like a train, ma'am, ahh, Doctor."

"Thank you for your honesty. Until now, no one would answer my calls."

"What about Donna Thorpe?"

"I've been unable to get through to her."

"In Nebraska, you know."

"No, they said she was here, in Chicago. I thought you knew."

"Sonofa—sorry, Dr. Hogarth. No, I didn't know." He had had to admit. They then closed their door on him, looking like a pair of animals hiding in a cave.

And now footsteps were coming toward him, while

he pretended to mop the floor, just below the lab where Hogarth and Oliguerri had remained for hours. He looked up, giving his broadest, dumbest smile to the guy in the Commonwealth Edison uniform. The badge said James Early, Electrical Engineer, CEC, but it could just as well be the man of a thousand disguises, Ovierto.

He watched Early's eyes as he opened his mouth to speak. "You Joe Swisher?"

"Who wants to know?"

"Special Agent Jack Harris, FBI—"

"Jesus."

"—Chicago Bureau."

"You guys crawling around the building now, too?"

"I got a call earlier from a friend of yours."

"Is that right? Thorpe send you?"

"No, Thorpe did not send us."

"Who called you then?"

"Your partner."

"Robyn Muro?"

"That's right. Seems Thorpe isn't telling you everything she knows about Ovierto."

"Hell, I knew that from the beginning."

"I mean about the airport incident earlier today."

"Airport incident?"

"O'Hara, one security guard killed and a package left in a locker for Thorpe."

"A package?"

"Another agent, guy named Bateman. It was his head."

"Christ. So, we know for sure he's here, in Chicago."

"Now, I don't think Thorpe's thinking clearly anymore about this maniac, and she's not exactly being

. . . ahhh . . ."

"Straight with either of us?" Swisher was trying to determine if this guy was interested in moving up a peg on the old FBI ladder, or if he was for real.

"That's it as I see it. She thinks this creep's some kinda superman or something, that he can smell us before he sees us. Anyway, there're four of us in the building and we're using these. Take one." He held out a two-way radio. "Just to keep in touch. Big place we have to cover here."

"You've got to know that he's watching the place, if he's not already inside. He see you come in?"

"Me and another guy came in a Comm Ed truck; two others came in a Coca-Cola truck, uniforms and all."

"Well, thanks for filling me in, and thanks for the backup. What about Inspector Thorpe? Where's she?"

"So far as I know she's back at HQ catching some sleep."

"Sleeps like a baby, I'm sure."

"Cold one, that's for sure."

"Maybe she has to be."

Harris bit his cheek and nodded, "Yeah, maybe. But I was a cop before I was FBI, and in my book, you don't keep secrets from your partners."

Bucking for a promotion, Swisher decided, realizing the "partners" speech was bullshit with this guy. If he were involved in taking Dr. Maurice Ovierto out, Harris would get some gold stars stuck to his forehead. "Look, Swisher, I brought you up some coffee, too." He handed him a small coffee thermos, the remnants of the label still clinging to it.

"Fresh, huh?" he asked.

"I'm covering the East entranceway and the back

84

stairways there. My other guys have the lower floors and the docks. You need anything, just buzz me, pal."

"Sure, sure . . ."

Swisher watched the tall, good-looking Jack Harris disappear. "Robyn, why am I blessed with you?" he asked the empty corridor, opening the coffee and pouring the hot liquid into the lid. From across the causeway, through the open space that would be a sheer fall of near fifty feet to the lobby, Harris waved from the elevator that took him away.

Swisher was more grateful for the elevator than the coffee.

Chapter Ten

Argonne National Laboratories, Eola, Illinois

Dr. Maurice Ovierto entered the front door of Fermilab with the guided tour, doing so for the second time, dressed now as a woman. He had taken great pains to locate Oliguerri and Hogarth, his two intended targets for this evening. The last tour began at five-thirty and ended at six-fifteen. He had taken great caution in putting his plan into effect. In the tour also was Deter Fomichs. Deter was a former asylum patient and a friend. He made eye contact with Deter to register how the other man was doing. He seemed calm and capable, but who knew for sure with a man like Deter. Ovierto had worked hard on the other man all day long, explaining to him how he could become a national hero if he could stop the infiltration of the giant Fermilab by an agent of a foreign government, a spy.

The tour guide's voice droned on about how the space program at NASA had given Americans far-reaching, important discoveries about the atom and atom smashing.

"If you would care to sit here, there will be a short film, explaining what exactly our scientists do here," said the guide.

Ovierto had earlier taken note of all key exits, stairwells, and elevators, as well as doors closed to the public; he had watched the approach and entry of the trucks and deliveries made, and he had noted their schedules. On his previous visit he had remained for hours, just watching. He had particularly liked the timing of the Coca-Cola truck and had since learned that it arrived promptly at six o'clock and was gone by six-thirty-five. It might be useful.

As the others viewed the film, Ovierto quietly left the little movie theater, leaving Deter on his own with orders to shoot anyone who came at him in any threatening way. He would be fine for at least the length of the film, Ovierto believed, some ten minutes, enough time to get to Oliguerri.

Earlier he had seen a Commonwealth Edison representative with uniform and hard hat, blueprints in his hands and a truck parked out back of the enormous facility. With those layouts of the building, Ovierto could gain even more information about the building. With a badge proclaiming that he was a man named James Early, he'd have no opposition. He went directly for a door marked Employees Only, where the Edison electrician had gone.

The man on the other side looked over his specs rather casually when he saw who it was.

"Lady, you can't come through this way . . . lady . . . you okay?"

Ovierto, in wig and makeup, appeared to be faint and suddenly went to one knee. Early rushed to what he thought was a woman in distress when a screwdriver-sized hypodermic was suddenly twisting in his stomach. Snatched out, with Early staring at his attacker, the bloody tool suddenly bored into the electrical engineer's throat, cutting off his scream, toppling him over a catwalk. His body plummeted to the ground floor and was hidden among boilers that sent up a terrible racket.

Ovierto was pleased. He'd have the uniform, badge, and keys without getting the clothing sullied. He climbed down the metal stairs toward the dead man, who had ingested enough poison to kill ten men. He tossed away his wig as he climbed down and tore at a handkerchief to wipe away his eye shadow, rouge and lipstick. This done, he bent over Early and began to strip him. It was going so well.

Then he discovered the small two-way radio on Early's belt. It was not sending. Early was FBI. The building was crawling with FBI, alerted by Thorpe. Maybe even the Coca-Cola guys were FBI.

"Well, now the wolf's in the fold," he said to Early, snatching his gun from inside his uniform. He searched for and found Jack Harris's ID and FBI badge as well. He then picked up the radio so as to better monitor the movements of the others. He wondered if Deter had gone nuts yet. It didn't seem so, not with the radio quiet.

It would come soon, drawing them like flies to Deter. Poor Deter.

He climbed back up to where Harris was, reading the building specs, and he studied them for some moments, memorizing what he needed and moving on.

Inspector Donna Thorpe's helicopter flew over Fermilab, and she studied the details on the ground. The cars in the lot thinned out quickly now. The enormous Fermilab was a monument to nuclear physics, built by the U.S. Government; all its research was government-funded. From it had come an array of nuclear physics by-products and a better understanding of space and the universe. The huge circle at the rear of the building, the length of several football fields, appeared to be a giant racetrack; in fact it was the world's first nuclear "loop." Inside the accelerator loop, atoms were bombarded against one another and "smashed" to create infinitely smaller pieces of matter, the behavior and nature of which was carefully scrutinized and monitored by the sophisticated computers and analyzed by the geniuses employed here.

From where she sat she could see both the industrial area and, in the distance, Fermilab Village, with its empty farmhouses and a grazing herd of protected buffalos milling about. She could see the Geodesic Dome, the Proton Area, the Master Substation, and the Meson Detector Building. She saw all roads leading in and out of Argonne National Laboratories, which was bordered by Kirk and Butterfield roads. All those entrances were now being blocked on orders.

She had been unable to stop Harris and his three friends from interfering with Swisher and Ovierto, but she had him in the net now and that was what counted.

She stared again at the accelerator, imagining the speed with which the atoms flew through the concrete-lined tunnel—the speed of light. For a moment she wondered if Dr. Maurice Ovierto's brain did not work like the atom smasher, ever moving in heats to destroy and reduce and reduce and reduce. It might be a fitting place to see him reduced to a sniveling, pleading pulp of flesh.

The atom smasher was so large that it could not be seen in its entirety except from the air. Like her plan, she thought. So far, nothing untoward had happened.

She tried to raise Harris again, but the man seemed to be deliberately ignoring her calls. He'd pay for his insubordination. She cursed him for his arrogance.

"Take me to the top of the building," she ordered the pilot.

"Yes, ma'am."

Despite herself, she had to get inside . . . had to get close. She could smell Ovierto, another and even more arrogant bastard. He was here. So close it gave her goose bumps.

The specs had shown the service elevator which he now approached. He had hoped to kidnap Oliguerri and Hogarth, string out their deaths, enjoy them. If he killed them here, it would be too quick, too painless. But the place was filthy with FBI agents. He may not have any choice in the matter. Still, the acid he'd brought for the pair to swallow would disintegrate their insides.

He rode the elevator up and up to where Oliguerri's offices and lab could be found. He was grateful to Special Agent Jack Harris for having provided the specs.

The elevator door opened on a lab, and from across the room they stared at him. He lifted a calming hand, telling them, "I'm Special Agent Jack Harris." He flashed the badge and ID, coming closer. "Just checking out this avenue . . . making sure . . . can't be too safe with this sicko, Ovierto."

Something shaky in the woman's eye, he could see but not quite make out. She began backing toward the front offices. "You want to talk to Officer Swisher?" she was asking, going for the door.

"No, no, that's all right."

But it was too late. She was outside in the hallway. Oliguerri stood his ground, watching Ovierto smile and ask dumb questions. "What are you working on? High-level stuff, huh? Something to insure world peace, huh?"

"Something of that nature, yes," said Oliguerri who didn't even see the capsule that Ovierto shoved down his throat, holding him like a vet holding a cat, rubbing his Adam's apple, making him swallow. He kicked Oliguerri viciously in the groin, doubling him over and then went for the woman, Hogarth.

Swisher had let the buzz of the radio he'd put aside continue a third time before he picked it up and almost dropped it into the pail of water at his feet. He pressed the button and asked, "What is it?"

"Harris has been killed, stripped of his clothes!"

"Who is this?"

"Dunbar, damnit. The killer's got Harris's clothes on!"

At the same instant, Elena Hogarth came rushing toward Swisher, saying, "There is an agent Harris in the lab who wants to see you."

Swisher's eyes must have told her the truth when he grabbed her roughly and pushed her to the ground, ripping out his .38 Police Special, and saying, "Stay down, stay down."

"But Dr. Oliguerri is in there!"

"Get to the elevator. Get as far from here as you can," he instructed her.

She slithered along the freshly cleaned floor,

reaching for the elevator button when she heard shots behind her, making her scream. She got up and raced for the stairwell. A bullet followed her through but missed her. She panted and started down when she heard a woman's voice call out, "This way!"

In the lobby, on the main floor, there was more gunfire. Elena looked down through the maze of open concrete to see a pair of dead security guards. More shots were fired. She looked up at the woman who waved her toward the roof. "Dr. Hogarth, it's me, Donna Thorpe! I have a helicopter on the roof."

She raced to join her on the roof. Thorpe settled her into the helicopter and ordered them to wait. She went back into the building and down the same steps. Someone was coming through the door. She steadied herself, taking her stance, holding her gun out firmly with both hands, ready to fire.

Joe Swisher hardly had the strength to push through the heavy door, using his body weight to do so. He was a bloody mess, having taken two bullets, one in the chest and one in the face. He looked up at her, their eyes meeting moments before Swisher fell over the railing and to the lobby below, leaving a trail of blood along the concrete facings.

"Bastard! Bastard!" she screamed and raced for the door, tearing it open onto a dark, empty hallway. In the middle of the floor was a mop and an overturned water bucket. She scanned the dark shadows for any movement. Closer, closer, she moved, toward Oliguerri's lab. She yanked open a closet door, sending junk tumbling across the wet floor. Silence reigned again, when suddenly the elevator door across from her dinged and an overhead light went on. She aimed for the occupant.

The doors opened on Robyn Muro who stared across at her. "Where's Joe?"

She hadn't time to explain Swisher's whereabouts or his condition now. She turned and silently rushed toward the lab.

"Where's Joe, damnit? They've got the maniac downstairs. He's dead."

Thorpe turned and in the dark her face was creased down the middle with light, dividing her features like a mask. "No, Ovierto is up here. And . . . and he just killed your partner."

"No! No!" Robyn was unwilling to believe it.

"The stairs, through there," she indicated and moved away from Muro for the interior of the lab. Her eyes instantly went to Oliguerri, who was choking and spewing forth blood from his mouth. The man's huge, white eyes seemed to be popping from their sockets. He was in a bad way, but his wild eyes followed her, pleading for her to help him. He appeared to be paralyzed.

She scanned the offices and the labs, looking through rows and rows of glass.

Nothing. Silence and emptiness save for the pitiful leavings of a dying Oliguerri who begged in gibberish for help. Her eyes fell on the elevator doors. The light indicated it was at the basement. She had to get to a radio—the chopper.

As she made her way back, passing Dr. Oliguerri, the dying man lunged toward her and trapped her ankle, pulling her to the floor, tugging and straining at her. She kicked out to free herself, shouting, "I'm going for help!"

"Dow-leaf-me . . . dow . . ." He could not speak clearly. She shouted to Muro as loudly as she could, "Get medics up here, now! Now!"

93

But she knew it was too late for Oliguerri . . . had known it when she entered the room. Dr. Ovierto left nothing halfway done . . . left no one half-dead. Whatever he'd done to Oliguerri, it was lethal. Still, she screamed for Muro's help.

But Robyn Muro remained frozen over the sight of Joe Swisher's body, which looked as if it were in a deep well filled with his blood.

All of Oliguerri's remaining strength seemed to be in his hands as he held tight to her ankle. She had to break free, if she was to catch Ovierto, *and it must stop here*. Then she saw the communicator awash in the water out in the hallway. She used her gun to break free of Oliguerri, hammering his hands until he let go. She then rushed to the communicator and picked it up. It was almost covered with water and Swisher's blood. She pressed a button and shouted into it. "All agents, stop Ovierto, service elevator, east side of the building!"

"He's dead, Inspector!" shouted one respondent.

"Took him out at the lobby."

She was confused. Then she remebered the shots welling up from the stairwell at the same time that Swisher was taking two bullets.

"You assholes are looking at Joe Swisher's body."

"No, damn, he come out of the rafters, but we got the looney down here, twenty-five or thirty slugs in him."

"No, no! It's a decoy."

"Decoy?"

"A duck . . . damnit, a stooge! He's gotten a stooge to divert attention. Where's Harris! Damnit, Harris! Get your men deployed at the service exits on the east side of the—"

"Harris is dead!"

"Dead?"

"Dead and stripped of his clothes earlier."

"What kind of clothes?"

"Same as I got on, Commonwealth Edison uniform. We came in a truck."

"You fools! Damned fools! He's getting away in that van!"

She threw down the static-filled radio and started to rush for the helicopter when suddenly she realized that Robyn Muro held her in her gun sights. "Robyn . . . you don't want to do this."

"I kill you and it's chalked up to Ovierto's doing. Righteous payback for Joe. I knew you'd get him killed."

"You don't want to do this, Robyn. His murderer is getting away at this very minute and together we can still catch the bastard. Ovierto killed your partner, not—"

"You killed him, you bitch! You and your obsession. Lying to him."

"Lying to him?"

"You left out too much about Ovierto."

"Not so! I gave Joe everything I had on Ovierto . . . everything."

"No, there's more . . . more to Ovierto, more to this whole damned business."

"I gave Joe every file—"

"Shut up! Just—"

The elevator doors opened and both women wheeled and aimed. It was Harris's men.

"I'm out of here!" shouted Donna Thorpe, rushing for the roof and the helicopter.

"Not without me," said Robyn.

They sized one another up for a moment, before Thorpe said, "We're wasting time here."

They raced up to the helicopter, Thorpe asking her pilot where Elena Hogarth had gone—for she was missing.

He merely shrugged. "Ran back down."

"She'll be all right. Come on. Get in!"

The helicopter lifted off while Thorpe shouted for the guards to detain a Commonwealth Edison truck that would be speeding their way.

"Have you seen any sign of the truck?"

"No, nothing like that," reported one guard.

"Sorry," agreed the other.

"Where the hell is he then?" she pleaded. "Hit your searchlights, Tim," she told the pilot who responded like his machine. The lights cast an eerie glow along their path but just outside it all was blackness. November night in Chicago.

"Have any—repeat—any trucks gone through your sector?" asked Thorpe.

"Just the Coca-Cola guy," said one.

"Damnit, that's him! Turn this thing around, Tim, head for Eola and 56!"

Robyn Muro snatched on a pair of the headphones at the same time that Thorpe did, monitoring every word. Now she said, "Put out an APB on a red Cola truck going east on Butterfield Road."

"How do you know he'll go east?"

"Airport."

"But he's got a private plane. It could be at any airport in the area, including small municipal airports."

"Then which way do we go?"

"Damn, damn!" moaned Thorpe. "That close . . ."

"He hasn't gotten away yet."

"Yes he has. Look down there."

It was the Cola truck. Dr. Ovierto had already

made a switch.

"All right, all right," said Robyn. "Then we put out a call to every airport in the vicinity to shut down all traffic."

"And we hit the closest ones in succession, until we get him?"

"That's our best shot."

"We'll do it." Donna Thorpe put out the call. She then turned to Robyn and asked, "What's your best guess?"

"Dupage Airport. Recently put in a new landing strip that will handle private jets, and it's the closest of the larger strips."

"These airport people won't cooperate for long. Tim, you heard it, Dupage Airport."

The pilot brought the helicopter around for a north heading.

"Why didn't that Hogarth woman stay put?" Thorpe asked aloud, expecting no answer.

"She's running scared. She saw what happened to Oliguerri."

"No, *I* saw what happened to Oliguerri."

Chapter Eleven

Dupage, Illinois Airport

"I'm telling you, he went up without a clearance or so much as a how-do-you-do," said the controller at the airport.

"I want a full description of the plane."

"It was a Mooney."

"No," said a second man, "it was a Doctor killer."

"Beechcraft, you mean?"

"Yeah."

"You're sure."

"Yes, certain."

"Did you get the call numbers?"

"We've got 'em here."

"Great, let's have them."

Thorpe copied the numbers in a notebook she carried. "Send these out. Anyone seeing this plane is to alert the FBI."

"Yes, ma'am."

"Bastard's gotten away."

"And Joe's dead because of you," said Robyn.

"Robyn, you pinpointed Ovierto's point of departure like a pro—"

"Don't try to change the subject, you bitch."

"Joe died in the line of duty. I don't feel any better about that than you, but—"

"You cold, calculating cat, you used him and you lied to him."

"Look here—"

"No, you look here!" She tore open a folded copy of a fax, sent to the Chicago coroner's office from Nebraska FBI, that told her that the penis sent to her in Nebraska had no relationship whatever to the Stavros case in Chicago. "You used us all."

"All right, that's right . . . and I'd do it over again."

Robyn's right fist came up and bloodied her mouth, sending Thorpe reeling. The helicopter pilot grabbed Robyn, pulling her away, trying to soothe her.

"I don't have any choice, Muro. I've got to get Ovierto at any cost, *any cost!*" For the first time Robyn saw the flash of madness in Thorpe's eyes which had been so controlled a moment before. It was a look that came over Joe whenever he talked revenge.

"You're as bad as Ovierto . . . you're just as bad."

"No . . . nothing on this Earth is as bad as Ovierto."

"Then you run a close second."

She stormed out, the chopper pilot following her, leaving Robyn with her bruised knuckles and an emptiness inside that was close to overwhelming her.

Robyn telephoned Peggy Olson, telling her to get over to Joe's place and to use her badge if necessary to get into his apartment.

"What's this all about, Robyn?"

99

"Joe's . . . Joe has been killed."

"Oh, Christ, no! Oh, Robyn, I can't . . . can't tell you—"

"Peg, the best thing you can do for me right now is to follow my instructions."

"Whatever you want, Robyn, name it."

"Get over to Joe's, above Transfusions—you know the place. Bartender is also Joe's landlord. Get him to open Joe's place for you."

"For what?"

"Files . . . I want any files you find. I'd do it myself, but I'm the hell out in Dupage."

"Dupage?"

"Don't worry about that. Just get the files before that Thorpe woman does. I want that information."

"FBI files? Hey, kid, what're you getting me into?"

"Peggy, it's for Joe."

"All right . . . all right."

"Get there before Thorpe's people do."

"I'm on my way." She hung up, and Robyn wished her luck as she dialed for Melody Carter to come and get her. She and Melody took turns crying over Joe Swisher's death for some time before Robyn said, "I need you to come get me. I'm out at the Dupage Airport."

"I'll be there in half an hour. Poor kid, you shouldn't be alone. Should be among friends, home."

"Hurry, Mel."

But when Melody arrived, Robyn didn't want to go home. She wanted her to take her back to Fermilab. Melody gave her no argument, taking her to Joe, tears in her eyes as she drove.

Fermilab was lit as if by a bonfire from all the police cars and floodlights. It looked like a drive-in on Saturday night. Inside, where everything was being cleaned up, including Joe's crushed body, detectives, and cops milled about like so many construction workers puzzling over a problem. She was unable to go to Joe, unable to look into the body bag.

Melody stared at her dumbly, not knowing what to do with her.

"I'll be upstairs," she told Melody, who was now holding firm to her arm. "Want a look at Oliguerri."

The local FBI and police were all around now and she was stopped at the elevator by a man in a suit. She flashed her badge and he let her pass.

Robyn went directly for the lab, where she could see that snapshots were being taken. Another guard at the door made her show her badge. "I'm sorry, only FBI inside," he replied to the badge.

"Get the hell out of my way," she said.

"Now listen, cunt."

"What's going on here?" It was Captain Brian Noone.

"This prick won't let me pass," she said angrily.

"Haven't you taken enough of a beating for one night, Sergeant Muro?" asked Noone, genuinely concerned. "I'm . . . I'm real sorry about Joe. He'll be missed . . . God, all I can think to say is one long cliché. Joe was a *good* man, *good* cop, despite his rough edges."

"Can you get me inside, Captain?"

"This is an FBI matter, Robyn."

"This was Joe's matter! FBI matter? FBI? Hell, Cap, don't you think I know that?" She bored into his eyes with the fire in her. "We cooperate with Thorpe, she'll wipe our asses, right?"

"Stow that kind of talk with me, Muro."

101

"Stavros had *nothing* to do with Ovierto, *nothing*. That's what I came to tell Joe, but it is too late. Why didn't he answer my calls?" Her voice cracked and tears threatened to well up before she caught herself, steeling herself once more. "Now, damnit—"

"You're sure, about Stavros, I mean?"

"Absolutely. I had the coroner obtain tissue reports from Nebraska to make a match. No match."

"So, appears that we've all been fucked over by Thorpe."

"You're fucked. I'm fucked, but Joe's dead."

"Nobody could have predicted that Joe'd be killed. Hell, the man thought he was bulletproof, and he had convinced just about everyone else of that, including Thorpe."

"There's no excuse for that woman, and there's no telling what other threads of the web she has managed to keep from you and me."

He frowned and gave her a guilty look just before his voice took on an angry edge. "All right, damnit, if it'll make you feel any better, come on inside and have a look . . . have a good look at Oliguerri over there."

The FBI had wasted no time with Oliguerri. The men circled the body like flies. Their chatter was a guarded whisper, not so much in respect for the dead as in respect for the fact that the CPD was on hand. These men were trying desperately to find some trace fibre or dust particle that might help lead them to Ovierto. Oliguerri was being airbrushed for such details, while his eyes remained wide open, his teeth set into his tongue so deeply that uppers and lowers were touching where he had nearly bitten it off. He'd obviously died a cruel, painful death.

"Poison of some sort," said Captain Noone. "I've

102

seen enough. Wait for you outside."

She glanced from Oliguerri's sad carcass to the room itself. She roamed toward his office when an FBI voice said, "We figure Ovierto entered through the elevator and exited the same way. Service elevator for transporting scientific equipment, experimental stuff."

"Yeah, experimental stuff," she replied, continuing to look around. She knew the FBI guy had been put on her to watch her every move.

As she passed Oliguerri's lab table she saw some paperwork there, just some scribblings in a foreign hand, German, or perhaps his tribal Ibo. She turned and pretended a sudden surge of warmth as if she might faint.

"Are you all right, officer?" he asked.

"Suddenly feel . . . oh, I don't . . . water? Is there any water?"

"Cooler over there. Just take a seat, and I'll get it for you."

"Thank you so much."

She snatched the papers and placed them into her purse as quickly as possible. He was still pressing for the water when she straightened and looked back at him, the papers secure. She drained the water, took great breaths of air, filling her lungs and saying, "Captain Noone was right . . . I shouldn't have come in. I . . . I'd best leave."

"Yes, ma'am. I think so," agreed the helpful man. "Have you got your legs?"

"Quite all right now, thank you."

He watched her leave before placing the cup she had used to his nostrils, smelling her. Outside, in the hallway, Noone took her by the arm and solicitously walked her to the elevator. "You look a little

103

pale and very tired, Robyn. I want you to go home now. Leave this to Thorpe's people."

"Leave Joe's murder to them?"

"Revenge and anger ate Joe's insides out, and you know that. He was half a man."

"Joe was more man than . . . than anyone I knew." She pulled from Noone and said, "This cab is mine." She rode down alone, in silence, glancing over the meaningless papers she had stolen from the crime scene. To her they made as much sense as the incidents of this night.

"Oh, Joe," she moaned and her heartbreak filled the elevator cab.

Melody Carter was a bright, young policewoman with long dark hair and dark features. She put her arms around Robyn and led her toward the car. "I'll get you home and put you to bed, honey," she said.

"No, I've got to get to Elena Hogarth."

"The FBI guys said Ovierto kidnapped her."

"That's the bull Thorpe is shoveling. I know better."

"Well, if she wasn't kidnapped . . ."

"They'll be all over her place by now."

"And every exit from the city, so how do you hope to locate her first?"

"Not sure, but I've got to try."

"Do you even know what she looks like?"

"I got a glimpse of her in a picture with her husband and kid while I was snooping around her office upstairs."

"Where to then?"

"O'Hare International."

"She'll be disguised—traveling under an assumed

name—if she's hiding."

"And Thorpe knows that, too."

"Are you sure you're up to this, Robyn?"

"Yes, now go!"

"Are you sure then that we ought to be grinding the same wheel as the FBI?"

"Are you going to drive or talk?"

"All right . . . all right . . ."

At the airport the vigil was long and fruitless until suddenly she saw Donna Thorpe in the middle of a circle of her agents. They'd come out of airport security and were now heading toward the terminals. They moved like one machine.

"Come on," she told Melody, chasing after.

"Robyn!" Melody rushed to keep up.

"Elena Hogarth," she shouted to Thorpe. "Have you gotten her into protective custody?"

The machine stopped when Thorpe did and all the eyes turned with hers. She stepped from out of the clutch of the black suits. "She had her own escape route planned for some time, it seems. As near as we can tell she is on one of several flights, but it's damned impossible to tell which. We're having the airports watched at each destination."

"She didn't have much faith in you, did she?"

"I hope it is not to her regret. Ovierto will not rest until he kills her."

"Why? What is driving Dr. Ovierto to make him so obsessive about Hogarth, Oliguerri, and the other scientists?"

"A man like Ovierto has only one reason to kill, he enjoys it, and he knows we value our scientists. In his warped brain that translates to a much higher score than if he were cutting up prostitutes or home-less people like Jack the Ripper."

"He places a higher premium on these kills be-cause you do?"

"We, the government. Now, I must go."

"Back home, to retrench? Where was that? Ne-braska?"

Thorpe took her aside. "Look here, Muro, I ad-mit that I thought of working with Swisher the mo-ment I knew Ovierto was heading for Chicago, but only because I knew Swisher was a tough, reliable cop. It was not my intention to see it end this way."

"You knew Swisher was reckless, and your trained boys are not. Most of you people have little families and backyard barbecues to look forward to in the evenings and on weekends. You used Joe like a wild card in a pat deck. And he got off a couple of shots, and with better luck, he might have ended your problem—but he didn't. Instead, he took two shots that should have gone into you."

"Are you through?" She had a stricken look on her face but she quickly replaced it. "I lost my closest friend and partner to this bastard Ovierto, too, in a much more cruel fashion than Joe's—ahhh, why am I trying to explain anything to you?"

"That's right. You don't owe anyone anything, least of all me, do you? You don't have to tell me why Ovierto is systematically killing off the top minds in the country, none of it. It's all classified, isn't it? Isn't it?"

Thorpe wheeled on her heels and returned to the center of her entourage, and they began to march away again. Behind them they heard Robyn Muro continue to shout, "You're all a bunch of killers, aren't you? Aren't you?"

Melody pulled her back as they watched the silent FBI machine move out onto the tarmac where Thorpe boarded her helicopter after a few perfunctory remarks to Jack Harris's replacement. She glanced up to meet Robyn's eyes, which were still on her, just before disappearing behind the black glare of the bubble.

One of the FBI men came back inside and straight up to Robyn. He extended a note. "From Inspector Thorpe," he said, leaving it with her.

"What is it?" asked Melody.

Robyn opened it as the helicopter began its ascent. The note read:

If you want to help Hogarth call me — Thorpe.

Book Two

Time is like a river made up of the events which happen, and a violent stream; for as soon as a thing has been seen, it is carried away, and another comes in its place, and this will be carried away too.

Marcus Aurelius, Meditations.

. . . in my age, as in my youth, night brings me many a deep remorse. I realize from the cradle up I have been like the rest of the race—never quite sane in the night.

Mark Twain

Chapter Twelve

He had not been idle the days following the attack on him at the Fermilab in Illinois, and now Maurice Ovierto was putting the finishing touches on his latest taunt at the FBI's premiere inspector, Thorpe. Chained to a bulkhead in the rusty old freighter that he had been using as his base of operations in the Portland-Seattle area was the third of his slaughter victims. He needed three body parts from three distinct individuals quickly to make his plan work. The parts would round out a little package he wished to forward to Thorpe, a little joke he had arranged both to alert her to the fact that he knew Hogarth was somewhere in Washington State, but also to continue his thoughtful, concerted effort to drive Thorpe out of her mind. With each cut, each death, each "gift" to her, he knew he was eroding away her strength and resolve, peeling back the layers of her all-too civilized veneer, scratching at the demon within her. He was molding her in his image, to one day be as unfeeling as he had become.

As for alerting the FBI to the fact he knew they

were holding Hogarth somewhere in the vicinity, his ego could do nothing else. He had once again made fools of them in Chicago. Now, if they dared oppose him again, he'd make fools of them in Seattle. Besides, he enjoyed the game. Alerting them to his whereabouts also had the effect of causing them to show their hand. They'd likely make some troop movements, roust the Hogarths out to remove them to yet another location. It could only serve his purposes.

His mind was filled with these thoughts even in the midst of the dirty little butcher's theater he had created of the old ship he had purchased, moored here at the forgotten end of a dying pier where a tuna cannery, unable to compete with the majors and the save-the-dolphins movement, had left the area bleak and useless save for the few ships plying the Pacific for oysters and shrimp and a unique little area where pearls were bartered.

He had purchased a few of the pearls himself, paying twice their value, knowing he was being hustled. But he didn't care, for the idea that the pearls gave him was exquisite. It was when he learned that this area was the only area left in all of Seattle that dealt in such trade that he knew his idea had come to full fruition.

The dark interior of the ship was perfect for the work. His victims had been chosen at random, off the street, for no other reason than that they were at hand. He glanced at his watch, a sterling silver Rolex that told him it was almost midnight, three days after Chicago. Not a bad average for a killer, he silently quipped.

He wore a blue surgeon's gown and mask and was nude beneath these. As he approached the woman chained to the corner braces of the bulkhead, he saw that the drug had now completely worn off. She was fully conscious, fully aware of her situation and of the fact that he was coming back for more. He had forced himself on her earlier, but it hadn't been good. She had been too out of it. The tension was not there.

Now things were different. The pupils of her deep brown eyes were so dilated as to appear to be those of a frightened horse. Even her sweat-drenched body added to the moment, as did the wild, flowing hair. He stood about three feet from her, taking her all in, smiling behind the mask, the blade as thin as spaghetti but large enough to reach from his hand at the base of his chin to the forehead.

"I'm here with you, my dear. Dr. Ovierto is on the job," he said with a little laugh, savoring the moment. "I just need a little something from you, my dear," he continued in his best bedside voice, as if he were about to take her pulse or a little blood. "The doctor won't hurt you."

The blade and the exaggeratedly pleasant voice made her tear at her bonds and scream against the gag, which was soaked with her spittle. "Here, let me make you more comfortable," he said, taking away the gag. "Isn't that better?"

"Why? Why're you doing this to me?"

"It's the only way for me."

She was a hooker who had responded to the wrong john.

Now the thin, stiletto blade that gleamed under the single bare light told her she was going to die here. She pleaded with him.

"Don't beg! Christ, I hate that."

"All right, all right . . . whatever you want, but—"

"I want your Adam's apple."

"What?"

"I need a box of them."

"What?"

113

"I've got two, and I need a third to round out the set."

"What?"

He stepped closer again, forcing a fresh gag down her throat. She began to thrash.

He stood back to watch the thrashing. A completely helpless victim, thrashing, eyes registering total fear: this was enough to make him bulge below the surgeon's gown with an erection. He knew he couldn't fight his *base* instincts, even though he wanted to finish the package for the early mail. But he knew how weak he was in the face of a thrashing woman, and so he put the knife aside for now, resting it comfortably on an old crate within reach. Atop the crate there were numerous mouse droppings. On another crate a plate of oysters, half-eaten, remained to fill the room with an odor other than that of the fear and perspiration coming off the woman. A third odor welled up from the keg of preservative and disinfectant he had days before prepared for this, the final night of his triple Seattle killing spree, which would keep the Seattle authorities quite busy.

His ultimate plan — given the time before he must move in on Elena Hogarth — was to take each of the bodies and place them at three distinct locations where they would be found, each with its throat missing, presumably cannibalized by some mad-dog killer. At the same time, he meant to leave enough of the evidence — perhaps even one of the bodies — here, aboard ship. And, time permitting of course, to also place with that third body his old colleague Dr. Rosenthaler who would stand in for the Seattle mad-dog.

The possibilities excited his imagination still further.

It would make for a great hullabaloo and he liked big hullabaloos, especially those that he had himself created from scratch.

Earlier, he and Charlene, the prostitute chained now to the wall, had enjoyed the oysters, although he had had to force-feed several of the last ones to her, explaining to her about their special properties as an aphrodisiac. She didn't even know what the word meant. But then, it wasn't her brain he was after. He had himself swallowed a number of the oysters but none of those he had laced with the thiopental sodium, an anesthetic. He had eaten two or three just in order to keep her calm at the outset of their "arrangement." He had joked with her and teased her with pearls, taunting her by spitting out several little gems, as if they'd been discovered in the oysters. This made him laugh and it made her say he'd have to pay her with cash. Once he pushed two one-hundred-dollar bills into her purse where she'd slung it over an old chair, asking her how much she was worth, they had begun their picnic in full earnest. . . .

Now he came again at her.

He lifted up the gown and became excited as she watched, and the fear in her seemed to subside somewhat. She probably thought he was just kinky, and that all the nonsense with the knife and the threats, the rape, and the chains was only for this.

She stopped thrashing to allow him easy access, and he immediately felt the shift and sensed that the tension had sapped from her; certainly, the level of fear had decreased. Deflated. He felt like a deflated balloon from his chest down, with this sudden change, and now, even as he rammed hard into her, his right hand reached over to the crate and lifted the thin blade to her throat.

He gauged her by the tension this created.

"Good," he said. "That's better . . . better."

She gurgled under the gag which he reached up to with his left hand and snatched away.

115

"Scream if you like," he told her. "I like screams."

She obliged, but it wasn't right. Her screams now were theatrical, he thought. She needed more motivation. He pressed down on the blade which instantly severed tissue at the throat, the blood trickling down between her breasts, toward his penis.

Her fear rose perceptibly and now radically as the knife drew more blood like a pipeline sunk for oil.

He felt himself coming.

He moaned and repeatedly shouted, "Good, yes, yes! Good! Goooooooooood!"

As he climaxed in her he rammed the knife deep in at the same instant. And began cutting. And she began screaming in earnest. But the screams turned to bubbling gurgles as he continued to surgically slash in controlled movements. He cut out a square of flesh at the center of her throat, a box around the Adam's apple. He worked at removing the vocal box. Only the severed chords made her screams stop.

Down in the hold of the old ship, no one could hear. In two other areas of the ship, he had taken the throats of two others, one a man. Now, with his bloody prize, naked and drenched in her blood, he opened an old keg that he had earlier filled with cleansing solutions and formaldehyde disinfectant. Two other such globs of flesh swam in the solution beside it.

He'd have to work most of the rest of the night to get the package out to Thorpe by morning. It would take some clean surgery to deposit his pearls inside the Washington State apples he intended to send her.

Behind him the prostitute was dead from a combination of trauma and blood loss. He'd clear her away later. For now, he had work to do. His mind worked at a feverish pace. His base sexual needs gratified, he now meant to satisfy something less degrading to him-

116

self. He meant to satisfy his gamesmanship with Thorpe.

He looked back over his shoulder at what was left of the woman and said to the carcass, "Was it good for you, Thorpe?" This made him laugh.

He went up to the captain's quarters above the hold, where, in a refrigerator, he kept a stainless steel dish on which all of his instruments were laid out in a row. He set these up on a table in the room. Taking a second steel dish, he returned to the death hold and lifted out the first victim's throat box. He carefully covered the other two and returned to the captain's cabin where he clicked on the TV and listened to the "Arsenio Hall Show" as he began carefully removing the layers of tissue encasing the hard ball of the Adam's apple.

The solution had done its work well, not only keeping the matter preserved and clean, but pliable. He made another cut just as the audience on the TV broke into laughter at something Arsenio said to his guest star, John Candy.

John Candy told Arsenio that he had an Uncle Timmy in Cleveland that wanted to sleep with Hall. More laughter but this time a little nervous.

Ovierto made a neat, near invisible incision in the Adam's apple before him. He worked with surgical gloves on, and beside him, in a clear dish, three shimmering pearls of dubious quality had come to rest at the center.

Candy's punch line came: "But he was talking about Fawn! Fawn!" he repeated. The audience laughed more naturally, if not raucously. But Arsenio had his arms in the air. He didn't get it.

"Fawn Hall, not *Arsenio!*" said Ovierto, thinking Candy's so-called joke was a stupid blunder and that Arsenio was getting sick of such flak and was slow on

117

the uptake, but that the audience was the worst for laughing at the inane remark. People were sheep, he had decided long ago. Everyone laughed and applauded when a light went on, like Pavlov's dog.

Hall was now trying to elicit some information about Candy's latest picture.

Ovierto pressed into the slit he had made in the apple one shiny pearl. The tweezer had made its deposit perfectly.

"Good," he said to himself, examining the work. Now he just needed to suture it with the finest material he had in his black bag. He went straight to this part of the job, knowing that as the tissue dried it would show more of the suture.

It was fine work, and in anticipation of this part he had secured a large magnifying glass to his head. Candy and Hall's voices continued at the back of his mind, but now he spoke to himself. "Just like the jeweler's work. There . . . there . . . yes . . . yes . . . yes."

He breathed deeply when he had finished the first one. A glance at his watch told him it was past two. Nerve-racking. He wondered if he could possibly manage all three tonight and get them out in the morning. Debating it was taking up valuable time.

He returned for the second apple in the barrel, continuing the painstaking work. The TV was flashing scenes from an old Bogart movie. He liked Bogart and wondered why he had never been cast in the role of a doctor. He had seen this particular movie when he was just a boy of eleven, he remembered. He hadn't had a bad upbringing, and he had had a great career spread before him when he had finished medical school and had gotten his position under Rosenthaler. But they— Thorpe and the others—they had changed all that . . . changed him, Rosenthaler among them.

But Rosenthaler had gotten his. . . .

Now serving out his life in a mental hospital not far from here.

But maybe Rosenthaler had suffered enough. Maybe the man ought to be put out of his misery. It had been almost five years, his suffering. Why not show a little mercy, he asked himself as he made his way back to the instruments to finish his night's work.

It now remained for him to wrap the package properly, address it, and put stamps on it.

Exciting . . . all very exciting . . .

Chapter Thirteen

Lincoln, Nebraska

For Donna Thorpe home was fast becoming as much of a problem as her work, since it appeared that Jim was suddenly — *at least it seemed sudden to her* — no longer supporting her. She'd told him all that had occurred in Chicago, sparing no detail in what felt like a confession, for she did feel remorse over the deaths of those that Ovierto had killed, particularly Joe Swisher. She could only tell this to Jim, along with the rest of it, along with her obsession with this case. But he shut her out, saying he did not want to hear another word about it — about the mistakes in Chicago, the mistakes in Houston — none of it. And for the first time in their marriage he grabbed her by the wrists, and, hurling her toward the mirror, shouted, "Take a good look at what you've become, Donna! Look, look!"

She fought against his hold, knowing that if she wished she could put him on his back in an instant.

He forced her eyes round to the mirror. "You and this monster you're chasing, girl, they're becoming one! One!"

"No!" she maneuvered his arm into a gyrating twist and suddenly had him in a choke hold, forcing his right hand against the small of his back. She'd shouted to him to stop it several times, and their shouts drew the children to the door.

When the children saw them fighting, it did something to Jim. She quickly released her hold. He pretended a smile and lied to the children, bundling them off to bed, but when he returned he was icy cold, seething. In the dark where they lay side by side, unspeaking, his voice sounded like a bell tolling when he finally spoke. "I'm divorcing you, Donna. It's over."

"What're you saying? That we can't work this out?"

"I don't believe there is any way to—"

"We can try counseling," she suggested.

"It's beyond that."

"What do you mean, beyond that? We haven't even tried."

"But we have, in a sense. I've listened and you haven't, all our married life. There's no getting through to you, and the idea some day I'm going to get a call from that grim reaper, Sam Boas, that you've been—"

"That's not ever going to happen," she insisted.

"—killed! I'm tired of sitting back, waiting for that call. Maybe that doesn't make me much of a man . . . maybe getting an arm broken by my wife doesn't make me—"

"Oh, Jim, please, you know how much I love you! How much I need you."

"No, no I don't know anything of the kind. I know you have one overriding desire, the same desire that's been the basis of your life for six years. I'm just not able to continue this way."

"Then I'll try to change."

"Inspector Donna Thorpe will never change."

She reached out to him, but he pulled from the bed, taking a pillow and a blanket with him to the guest room.

She cried alone in her bed, worrying about the children in all this, wondering what her life would be like without Jim, and wondering if he meant to fight for custody of their kids. Exhausted, tearful, filled with regrets brought back from Chicago, she felt as if her world were coming to an abrupt end. Depression painted everything darker and darker until the blackness without her became a blackness within. At the root of all her sadness and remorse was Dr. O. Now the bastard's ugly influence was destroying her marriage.

The following morning, early before the children awoke, she found Jim in the other bed, and she curled up beside him there, feeling like a little girl, her entire being shaking. Her uncontrollable shaking woke him and he put his arms around her, pulling her into him. She nestled in the crook of his arm and began to kiss him about the chest, interspersing her kisses and caresses with promises.

"I'll just stop," she said.

"Stop what?"

"Pursuing that bastard."

Jim was silent a long while but his body began to respond to her touch. "Is that possible with you?" he asked.

"Damnit, I'm not bound hand and foot to Ovierto!"

"You had the case stripped from you, and yet you pursued him to Chicago."

"On a tip," she half-lied. "There wasn't time, and no one in D.C. was buying it, and—"

"So, you took up the standard once more, and once more me and the kids have to wonder if you're coming back alive. Isn't there enough crime in Nebraska to fulfill you, Don?"

"Yes . . . you're right . . ." she sniffed back tears. "It was wrong to go."

"Things like that . . . you're the chief. You could have coordinated the whole thing from here. Why place yourself in such danger?"

"I won't do it again."

"You put me through hell, you know?"

"Yeah, yeah, I know."

"And while it was going on, this manhunt of yours . . . you never gave me a thought."

"Not true," she said, sitting up. "I called and—"

"You called to touch home, to recharge your batteries. Don't try to fool yourself. When you're working no one's on the planet other than you and the creep you're after."

She shook her head. "You're being . . . you're—"

"Concerned? Worried sick? You bet. And while we're at it, I'd like my children to have a mother."

"That's not fair!"

"We're going to wake them to this, if you don't hold your voice down."

She breathed deeply, nodding. "I didn't come in here to fight."

"No?"

"I came in to say I was sorry, and maybe find something under these covers." She lifted the sheet.

He smiled in spite of himself. "Do you mean it, about quitting this obsession with Ovierto?"

"If he'll quit—"

"No, if you'll quit!"

She hesitated a moment. "I'll . . . I'll . . . I can't promise anything other than I'll do my best to stay in Nebraska."

He reached down, brought her lips up to his and kissed her tenderly. " 'Bout all I should expect to hear from you," he said.

"It's a start."

"No, this is a start," he said, kissing her ferociously,

123

sending his tongue deeply into her mouth. His sexual maneuvers were rough and he ended their lovemaking with a pounding of himself deeper and harder and deeper into her, all as if to make up for the arm-lock she had placed him into the night before. Neither experience had given her any gratification, except that now, perhaps Jim would reconsider the rash words of the evening before.

Later, breakfast with the children was relaxed and pleasant. Just before she left, Jim made her promise once more to end her obsession with Ovierto.

She told him to consider it done.

She was met downtown with news that sent her reeling back to those moments in bed with Jim, the promise at the door. Her superiors at Quantico had faxed new orders for her. She was to go full-steam ahead on the Maurice Ovierto case. The information was sketchy, something to do with her being the only field agent who had had contact with Ovierto, and secondly that no one else had placed him in Chicago as she had. Apparently, her report had made an impression on someone high up. She'd been careful to give her report a proper framework, saying that her Nebraska office was in pursuit of information on a Nebraska homicide that could have been Ovierto's first abduction-murder, and that the trail had led them to Chicago. The rest of the report was fairly accurate, detailing how agents such as Jack Harris had died, and how a Chicago cop named Joe Swisher had also met his end. According to the report, Swisher had been involved in a mutilation case that might be the work of Ovierto. He had contacted her in Nebraska, offering the tip only if he could be in on the bust.

So far as she knew, no one questioned the particulars of the deal she and Swisher had arrived at, which had been exactly what she had counted on. With the possible exception of Robyn Muro, no one in the CPD was squawking either. And now this—a coup of sorts! Quantico admitting to a mistake, reinstating her, with obvious limitations. She would remain in Nebraska, but every shred of information on Ovierto would filter through her offices.

Obsession, or hard-won right to see a case closed? No matter what terms she might use, no matter how she put it to Jim, it was going to be a blow to him. She had no choice now in the matter. It was a direct order. She only wished that she hadn't promised. . . .

She was still responsible for the safety of Elena Hogarth and her family. She had worked tirelessly to see they were intercepted by agents at another corner of the continent, where they were being safely detained now. It was all her ballgame once more, and she didn't need to couch her terms in the muffled wrapper of an ancient case, nor employ the services of another Joe Swisher. It was too bad about what happened to Swisher, and she felt remorse for Muro, who loved the man, but at the time the CPD connection had been necessary to keep her hand in the game.

She hoped that no one would ever know how strongly she felt Swisher's death.

Jim was wrong about her resembling Ovierto, dead wrong. Ovierto felt no remorse for any of his actions, and for a time she had believed that she could work that way if need be . . . but she couldn't. *Not as tough as I thought I was,* she told herself now.

In the squad room the atmosphere was mixed. Some men were missing. Victims of the Chicago debacle. But now they had been given the full green light to seek out and reek revenge on this bastard, Ovierto. The orders to her were read aloud, and they ended with a chilling line:

The Company is now involved in the search for Ovierto, and if the CIA gets him before we do, we'll never live it down, so it's shoot to kill, Inspector Thorpe, shoot to kill.

Boxes upon boxes of records were shipped to Nebraska; all the paraphrenalia of a six-year-long manhunt. It almost seemed as if Quantico believed that by shipping everything to Nebraska along with Thorpe their problems with Ovierto were over; that it was now a Nebraska field office problem, like a simple tax evasion rap, or a whiskey runner, or an ordinary kidnapping. It seemed as if Washington wanted to wash its hands of the ugly matter. And it also seemed as if she now had been cast in the same role as she had cast Joe Swisher.

She'd heard nothing from Robyn Muro, and in talking with Brian Noone she learned only that Muro had been promoted and was still working on the Stavros case.

Ted Lowenstein, a young new member of the team, who had been summoned out of the squad room when a package had arrived that looked suspicious, returned now to tell her that the package was addressed specifically to Donna Thorpe.

Donna went down the long corridor to the steel-reinforced, concrete bomb room where the package had first been taken. Ted's expertise equipped him to pry open tricky packages, and now he was decked out in the pads and the oversized catcher's mask and mitts, but he said there was no bomb inside.

"How can you tell?" she asked needlessly, knowing it had been X-rayed.

"Just doesn't have the feel of a bomb. Too light for one thing, and we peeled away the outer layers, and the dog doesn't smell anything he's trained on, so—"

"So what's that odor?" she asked, feeling her brain go

into a spiral of memories. The odor was familiar. It was human decay, a stench like raw chicken left in the heat for two days.

Ted said, "I think you know."

She'd acquired some kind of reputation, after all. These young men in the department had been aware for years now of how Dr. Ovierto had singled her out to receive his grisly "gifts."

"What markings were there on the outer paper?"

"Addressed straight here."

"He knows I'm here. What else? What about postmark?"

"Hard to tell?"

"What do you mean, hard to tell?"

"Smudged over badly, but I think it was Portland, Oregon."

"Oregon?"

"Yes, but—"

"But what?"

"Had a little stamp on it, rubber and ink pad stamp with a little message."

"What message?" She lifted the outer paper with tweezers to read it for herself. It seemed a logo of sorts from a grocer. It read: *Washington State Apples Are Great Apples.*"

"Jesus, how can he know about Washington! Christ!"

They had relocated the Hogarths to Seattle.

"You want me to open it? The box?" he asked.

"I've got to get some air first," she declared, fearful of what she might find inside, and rushed to a special phone that had been set up specifically to contact the agents watching over the Hogarths. She had to hear for herself that nothing untoward had happened to anyone in the family.

Nothing had happened in Seattle. She felt a sudden relief. She alerted the field agent to the fact that Ovierto might now know their location, and that there might be a change in the works, but that the family was not to be told as yet.

Then she went back to where Ted had remained with the frightening package, which was little more than a three-by-four-inch box once the outer, larger boxes had been removed from around it. It sat on the table, the contents fully exposed when she entered. Ted stood in a corner where he had backed away, and vomited repeatedly.

Thorpe stared rigidly and fixed her emotions like steel against the sight of the pulpy tissues and lumpy balls in the interior of the box. They looked something like turkey parts, but were instantly recognizable as human.

But she wouldn't give Ovierto the satisfaction of getting to her again. She just wouldn't. She vowed she wouldn't.

Chapter Fourteen

November turned into December, and still Robyn couldn't get past Joe Swisher's death. The funeral had been hell for her, but Joe would have loved it. Over half the cops in the city had turned out. He did have more friends than he had realized. All day at the wake cops came up to her with stories about Joe, often how Joe had saved their necks in a tight spot, tales he had never told her. The age difference between them, ten years, had never been so evident as at the wake, with this procession of policemen from Joe's past moving by his coffin. Several times she had been moved to tears, but her overwhelming emotion that day was one of pride to have been Joe's woman.

Her bitterness toward Donna Thorpe not only lingered but grew. She'd been careful with the files that Peggy Olson had lifted from Joe's place only an hour before the Feds burst through the doors. She had placed them in a safety deposit box. Noticing the amount of time she spent locked away with the contents of that box, the people at the bank were beginning to think her strange. She read and reread every file, every scrap of paper, for a clue to Ovierto. She began to hate the man beyond any hatred she had ever known. She read of the deaths in England, in Atlanta, and of the FBI agent, Sykes — Thorpe's partner. Ovierto was a one-man firestarter, keen, even brilliant,

129

and given totally to the darkest side of mankind, the side that made it entirely possible to believe in Satan and a Hell.

But there was something missing from all of the information provided Joe Swisher, something vital. There was no file on Ovierto himself, no background information, nothing that might hint that he was bound to become an assassin. He was just referred to as a mad M.D., a maniac with a scalpel.

Where had he gained his medical knowledge? What schools had he attended? Where did he practice? At what stage of his career did he go mad? Who was his first victim—and why? Why?

According to Donna Thorpe there was no why. She knew that Joe wouldn't push for such an answer, that Joe acted on what was at hand, that he always did. She knew Joe well from his own file, from information supplied by Joe's shrink. She knew that if Joe took the assignment he wouldn't ask a lot of questions, that he'd just see a challenge, plunge in, and either kill or be killed. . . .

Now Thorpe was swinging a lure in front of her eyes, but the lure wouldn't work, not without full disclosure, a thing of which Thorpe seemed incapable. So, she had put the idea of working with Thorpe out of her mind. It had worked for a day, two days, three . . . and then it came back, creeping in, taking over her waking hours, interfering with her daily work, of the work being done on Stavros with Peggy and Melody, of which Captain Noone had approved. Until now the notion of going after Ovierto on any terms offered her, had seemed like an irresistable gleaming diamond, but the Stavros case continued to keep her busy.

The Stavros case was coming along well. Peggy and Melody had proved her right. With dogged determination, the three of them had retraced Stavros's day before the killing. It had taken a great deal of overtime, knocking on doors, interviews, and even a full-blown stakeout. The case was shaping up to be a "family-related" crime of sorts, since the victim was sleeping with another man's wife. The chief suspect was a man named Dominic Gotopolis, a big, proud Greek who worked in a construction pit and wore a hard hat home each night. His wife had apparently "disappeared" since the Stavros killing, and neighbors feared that she, too, was dead.

It took weeks of dredging up circumstantial evidence enough to interest the D.A., who finally ordered a search warrant on the basis of the information the policewomen had obtained. Now they were ready to go in, and the warrant specified they could enter while Gotopolis was away. They did so quietly, with the eager help of the maintenance man's wife, one of their key sources of information.

The big second floor apartment was completely dark inside, and everything was a mess. The man was obviously living alone. There were clothes everywhere in need of washing. Peggy went down one corridor that led to the bath and a back bedroom. Melody rummaged about the living room area and kitchen. Robyn heard a mewing like a cat from the master bedroom, and she pursued the sound.

There was no need for guns, and yet she felt strange not having hers raised. Usually when they made a warrant search, they had to first subdue the people inside the house with threats of violence. All of the shades here were pulled and the curtains drawn, leaving the bedroom as dark as night. There was someone on the bed.

She went instinctively for her gun at the same time that she flicked on the light. What she saw made her gasp. "Oh, my God."

The lady who had gotten them through the door screamed and crossed herself. "Please, keep back," said Robyn as Melody gently moved the lady back and Peggy rushed in.

Peggy said, "Oh, Jesus . . . oh, Jesus."

It was Mrs. Gotopolis, and she was alive, but she was beaten beyond recognition. She was tied to the bed, a starved woman below the bruises—shapeless, in her late forties, and nude. There were welts all over her body where she had been beaten, and her eyes were pulpy, cut like a boxer's so that she could hardly focus on her rescuers.

Peggy saw the misshapen, desiccated piece of human flesh that hung, like a broken light socket, from tape at the ceiling over the woman's head. "What the hell is that?"

"It's something I'm sure Mrs. Gotopolis is glad she can't see any longer," Robyn whispered in Peggy's ear. "Stavros's penis."

Beside the bed she saw the homemade whip of rope and a broom handle that Gotopolis had created for the occasion. Some metal instruments lay alongside the bed as well.

"Call 911," said Robyn. "Get a medic team down here now!"

Peggy gladly rushed for the phone so she would not have to see anymore. Melody hung at the door while Robyn put a soft hand to Mrs. Gotopolis's temple. The woman flinched like a frightened animal. "It's over," said Robyn, "We're here to help you."

"HowwwpppP meeeeeeE," the woman rumbled, her lips a bloody pulp.

Robyn started to untie the ropes but suddenly stopped. She looked up at Melody, who stood frozen in the doorway. "Get down to the unit, Mel, and bring up that Polaroid."

"Polaroid?"

"Do it!"

Melody's mouth fell open, but she nodded and disappeared. Robyn continued to talk soothingly to the victim, and she found a blanket to lay across her, but she didn't want to disturb another thing in the room until she got pictures. Peggy returned saying, "Medics are on the way."

"Where's Mel?"

"Don't know."

"Get her, will you, quickly."

Just then Melody returned with the camera. "Take some shots from every angle," said Robyn as she removed the blanket over the woman. "Mel, do it."

"I . . . I can't." She pushed the camera into Peggy Olson's hands.

Robyn tore it from Peggy, who merely stared at it. "We've got to document this just as it is if we want to nail this bastard." She began snapping shots, moving about the room.

The landlady was upset at this, shouting and gesturing. Peggy tried to calm her. Melody opened a window for air and sucked at it. When the landlady disappeared and they were listening to the photos being snapped, Melody said to Peggy, "Is that something she learned from Joe Swisher?"

"Just doing her job."

"Sure . . . getting good at it, too."

"Mel, she wants one thing and that's—"

Suddenly Gotopolis was in the room, upturning furniture and shouting, "What are you doing in my house! My house! With my wife! My property!"

He charged at them like a bear, picking Peggy up and throwing her into a wall. Melody brought up her gun but the bull had hold of her wrist. She dropped the weapon, her hand white from the lack of blood, and he sent her hurtling through the window she'd opened, careening down the two flights to the pavement below.

At the bedroom door Robyn had him in her sights. "Hold it, Gotopolis! You're under arrest for murder."

"Murder! Is it murder to protect your wife from filth?" He came at her.

"Stop where you are or I'll—"

His stride was so great he was atop her when the gun went off, blowing a hole in his chest. His shirt was afire with the powder for half a second as he exploded backwards and over the sofa that quickly soaked up his blood. He was dead.

Peggy had had the wind knocked from her, but she had stood against the wall with her own gun trained on Gotopolis when Robyn had warned him to stop. She would have fired if Robyn hadn't. She still held her gun on the dead man when she said, "My God, Melody! The window."

Robyn was already perched there, staring down. A crowd had gathered around Melody. The ambulance's lights and siren spread the crowd. Even before they got to Melody, Robyn was crying, "Is she all right? Is she going to be all right?"

"She'll live. Taken a bad hit, but she'll be all right."

"Get someone up here. We've got another victim," she shouted down. She then turned on Peggy and asked, "Why didn't you fire?"

"I was going to but—"

"Going to but? Buts and ifs can get you killed in this job, Peggy, remember that."

Peggy swallowed and realized she was still holding onto her gun. She holstered it, watching Robyn Muro go back into Mrs. Gotopolis's bedroom. From inside she heard Robyn talking calmly to the woman about how everything was going to be fine now. She looked in to see Robyn undoing the woman's bonds. The penis had already been ripped from the ceiling thread and Robyn had put it out of sight.

She telephoned Thorpe for the sixth time, but this time she determined to let it ring and to actually speak with the

FBI woman. Jack Harris, the Chicago FBI agent who'd died along with Swisher, had been a friend of Robyn's as well. It had been through Harris that she had learned so much about the iron lady, Thorpe. She wondered how Thorpe would react to her calling.

"Muro, it really is you," she said when she came on.

"Have you had any further leads in the Ovierto matter?"

"Not much. Why are you asking?"

"Curious."

"I see."

"What about Elena Hogarth?"

"Safe for the time being."

"You have her then?"

"That's right."

"I read about a body found in a mine shaft in Denver. One of yours?"

"The rest of Bateman. A policewoman led us to him after some convalescence. She met with Ovierto out there on a routine call."

"And she came out alive?"

"Blind for life, scarred for life . . . but alive, yeah."

"Son of a bitch."

"My sentiments exactly. Oh, by the way, I understand congratulations are in order in the Stavros case."

"I called —"

"Yeah?"

"I want in. I want Ovierto."

"Good . . . good."

"Good?"

"Great. We can use your help."

"It doesn't change how I feel about you."

There was a moment's silence before Thorpe said, "I understand that. I don't have too many people I can call friend, unlike you."

Robyn swallowed hard. Lately, she didn't have too many friends either. "I'll need help squaring it with

135

Noone."

"Leave your captain to me."

"All right, manipulation seems to be your specialty."

"Can you be ready to leave at a moment's notice?"

"Where to?"

"Seattle. Ovierto is on the scent again and this time we're not going to lose."

"You want me to babysit Hogarth?"

"She's got a sitter. I want a shooter. You're the best, so I've heard."

"I'll be ready."

Chapter Fifteen

The call came in the middle of her restless sleep. It was a male voice, very dry and to the point. "Be at O'Hare Airport, ready to proceed to Seattle, Washington via private jet. Look for hangar nine at the Flying Tigers terminal. You'll have to get a car to take you across the tarmac."

"Will Thorpe be there?"

"She will see you in Seattle."

"Who is this?"

"Dr. Samuel Boas."

"Boas?"

"On my way to Seattle from Washington."

"I'll be there in an hour."

Robyn rushed to dress, and in a little over an hour she was finding a seat on the empty jet. Behind her came a tough-looking man of perhaps fifty-eight or fifty-nine. He held a black briefcase, and when she said hello he merely groaned and took a seat, fastening his belt. He paid her no further mind.

The jet taxied out and took off like a kite. Below her Chicago looked like a field of jewels. She tried to go back to sleep and was almost dozing off when the elderly, thin man shook her. "No time for that now," he said. "Here are the photos and information you require, Officer Muro."

"Who are you?"

"FBI coroner out of Quantico . . . Boas, Sam Boas, remember? I thought you were briefed on this?"

"No . . . I mean, not about you. What are we looking at here?"

"Apples," he said enigmatically.

She squinted. "Apples?"

"These are three Adam's apples that that butcher sent into HQ in Nebraska, to Thorpe. He killed three people in the Seattle area just in order to send Inspector Thorpe some Washington State *apples*. Sick bastard."

"He's telling her he knows where Hogarth is being held."

"Exactly. Telling her he intends to get her at any cost, and there's nothing anyone can do to prevent it."

She stared anew at the photo of the large jar of formaldehyde in which bobbed the Adam's apples. She felt a sudden rush of nausea at the sight, failing the test, she supposed. She tried to cover it with talk. "When did . . ."

"Three-ten yesterday, UPS from Seattle." He mercifully put them away.

"Where is Hogarth being kept?"

"She and her family are to be relocated. That's your job, isn't it?"

"Yeah, I suppose it is. How large a family is it?"

"Here." He spread out a display of pictures of the Hogarths in various homey scenes. Mr. Hogarth was a tall, dark man with angular features, while the child was pudgy and round-faced, looking more like her mother about the eyes. Robyn guessed her age at seven or eight.

"Cute as a button, isn't she?" asked Boas. "You know what Ovierto would do with that button?"

"Unimaginable."

"Think the unthinkable if you want to understand this maniac," he said.

"There is nothing he is incapable of, is there?"

"Absolutely nothing."

"How long has he menaced Thorpe?"

"Six years . . . or it will be soon. The first two was taken up by her and Sykes tracking him down, and she was almost killed when he turned on her. He escaped from those idiots in Houston while she was still healing in a hospital there. It's a wonder he didn't kill her in her hospital bed, because he left a momento beside her bed, a pair of eyes he had ripped from a guard. Ever since then, he has taunted her. It's like having an evil personal demon who torments you. It's driving her crazy."

"I can imagine." But she really couldn't imagine.

He gave her some additional files to study. Most of it she had already seen, duplicate information she'd had from Swisher's cache of files. Dr. Boas went back to his seat and slept the rest of the way to Seattle. She, too, caught up on her sleep, but it was fitful.

When the plane landed, they were met with an entourage of Seattle FBI agents. She was told that Thorpe wanted to see her and Boas. They were taken to the Hilton in downtown Seattle. Boas was quiet the entire way, except to say, "I am getting old for this . . . too old."

"Why are you here all the way from D.C.?" she asked.

"Because I am the best, and Thorpe needs me."

"You have some loyalty to her?"

"I know of no agent who has worked so hard to bring in a man. Yes, yes . . . you might say I have some loyalty to her . . . yes."

They arrived amid the bustling, busy downtown traffic at midmorning, going for the suite where Thorpe was staying. They'd been instructed to use a rental car, no limos, which had upset Boas to no end. And here they were meeting Thorpe not at the Seattle FBI Bureau but at the shining, gleaming, sleek, steel-and-glass Hilton, where an enormous fountain greeted them.

Upstairs in Thorpe's suite they found a fully working, functional setup, with officers and computers hard at work. Thorpe had obviously gotten someone in Washington on her side, Robyn thought, impressed with the hardware assembled here. Thorpe cautiously offered her hand, and Robyn took it with equal caution.

"After our last meeting, I wasn't sure you'd come."

"What's going on here?" asked Robyn, ignoring Thorpe's remark.

"We're linked with every system in the city and every breaking event and arrest down to a simple bust on the street. We're electronically watching for any sign of Maurice Ovierto. We also have on file here every known loony in the city and we're cross-referencing with people Ovierto has known in the past."

"That's something I wanted to talk to you about, Ovierto's past. Just where did he come from? What created this kind of a maniac?"

"Very little is known of his childhood and upbringing, but what we have is here, and it is open for your perusal, along with anything else we have."

"You can find no direct connection between him and these scientists he is bent on killing?"

"Only a guess at best."

"What guess?"

"All of the people he has killed have been valuable to their governments and to a joint venture between these governments."

"And what venture is that?"

"It has to do with space technology."

"Space technology?" She thought of Fermilab. "Physics?"

"Astro physics, yes. I know very little of the details of the . . . the venture myself. It matters little. What matters is that this maniac has determined that no peaceful, joint efforts on the part of our various governments will take place, so long as he is alive. I think he just has set himself up as the destroyer of peace on this planet."

"But he was once in medicine—"

"A surgeon."

"He was never involved in this venture with NASA?"

"Only in his mind."

"Meaning?"

"He learned of it from one of his early victims. He believes that if he can frighten us enough we'll turn over all the data on the project to him. He believes it will give him the power to rule the Earth."

"Would it?"

Thorpe laughed. "It is a project aimed at the peaceful application of astromedicine, that is all."

"What's the name of this project?"

"I'm not at liberty to discuss any such details with you."

"Ohhhhh, partners to the end."

"I'm not your partner in this. I'm your superior, and if you can't accept the fact that there is some information too sensitive to pass along to you, then you'd best get back on a plane for Chicago."

Robyn considered doing exactly that for a moment before saying, "No . . . no, I'm in for the long haul."

"Are you sure he hasn't left Seattle?" asked Boas, who'd only just returned from a bit of catching up with some old friends and colleagues in the Seattle area. "He's done it before, creating big red herrings, sending us all to Cleveland or to Upstate New York only to find it was for nothing."

"He's here," said Thorpe.

"How can you be sure? Those apples? He could still be—"

"I know," she said firmly.

"You've concentrated on former associates in the city?"

"Asylum types he has known."

"How do you know who they are?" asked Robyn, curious.

141

Thorpe took her to a computer terminal and pressed a few buttons asking for a cross-reference on anyone known to have ever associated with Dr. Maurice Ovierto living in Seattle. There were six names on the list.

"Remember the poor slob he roped into his net in Chicago, the guy that was riddled with bullets who was happy to stand in for the great and powerful Dr. Ovierto?"

"So, you're having these people watched?"

One of the names appeared to be a woman, Lynn Janklow.

"We have watched them day and night."

"You seem to know more about this creep than anyone."

"It's like keeping tabs on Satan."

"Where's Hogarth and her family being kept?"

"Before we move on that, are you sure? Sure you want in?"

"Yes."

"Ovierto would like nothing better than to have you tied on a slab somewhere, under his scalpel, do you understand?"

"Yes."

"He's more than cruel—"

"I know what he is."

"—and a woman as . . . as beautiful as you . . . well."

Robyn blushed a bit before saying, "Dr. Boas has already tried dissuading me. You don't have to go on."

"It's just that with you," her hand came up almost imperceptibly, "Ovierto would see to it that your death was long and torturous. He . . . he has a fetish about stretching pain and torture to the limits of human endurance, especially with pretty women."

"He's apparently done exactly that with you . . . for what? Six years?"

Thorpe's lower lip trembled and their eyes met.

"Somewhere, I'm sure I'm in his computer."

"His computer?"

"He keeps a computer record of various effects that his different techniques bring about . . . various forms of torture on anyone he has . . . mutilated."

Robyn sensed for the first time the depth of the mutilation to her psyche that Thorpe had endured.

She clasped Robyn's hand, depositing something into her fist. She thought it was a key, but looked down at a vinyl packet with two pills inside. "Cyanide," said Thorpe. "You may need them."

Robyn was shown a place where she could freshen up, make any calls she wished, and catch up on the jet lag, while Thorpe and the others made preparations to move the Hogarths from danger. Whatever those plans were, Robyn had not as yet been told, and she was getting increasingly nervous about the part she was expected to play. Was she here to be another drone for Thorpe? That was not the way she intended to operate.

She went for the door to find a phone. She didn't trust that the one offered her by Thorpe was bug-free. Downstairs, in the lobby, she found several pay phones and called Precinct thirty-one in Chicago. She got through to Peggy Olson.

"Robyn, it's you. What's going on around here?"

"What do you mean, Peg? Peg?"

"Captain Noone's put out an All Points for any calls coming in from you. Wants to speak to you. It's like all hell's broke loose here."

"Noone? *What?* Suddenly he can't do without me?"

"I think it's a little more than that, Rob."

"Jesus, what could he want?"

"I don't know. Only he knows. Want to bite the bullet?"

"May as well, things here are kinda slow for the moment."

"Patching you through, and kid, be careful around those FBI creeps."

"Gotcha—" but Peggy was off.

Noone came on all bluster. "All right, Sergeant, I hope you're pleased with yourself."

"Sir?"

"The files, Muro . . . the stolen ones, the ones Joe Swisher was supposed to have hidden in some hole somewhere, were found in your safety deposit box."

"What? How, who gave authorization to go into my—"

"You're dealing with the fucking G-men, Sergeant. What'd you expect?"

She thanked God that she had brought the papers from Oliguerri's desk with her. They hadn't left her bra. Anyone wanting them would have to kill her for them. "They found what they wanted then."

"Real swift, that Thorpe. She invites you out West and moves in on you here. You're swimming with sharks, kid."

"So I'm learning."

"But taking those records, that was stupid, Muro. They could charge you with theft, obstruction of—"

"I think Thorpe has bigger plans for me than that."

Noone was silent for a moment. "Robyn, why don't you come back home. You're needed here. Let them take care of that whacko, Ovierto."

"No, Cap, I'm in it for now."

"Watch your backside, girl."

"Thanks, Captain, for the concern."

"They think you've got something else belongs to them."

She played dumb. "Oh?"

"Something out of Oliguerri's lab . . . some papers."

"I wasn't in there long enough to—"

"To have a drink of water?"

144

He knew . . . they knew. The papers she had taken from the lab must be important and were likely the reason Thorpe had invited her in. What was so important about them? The figures, the equations, the words themselves, which were in his Nigerian tongue? "I took the files because they were in Joe's place. That's all I took, Captain."

"You wouldn't lie to me, would you, kid?"

"No more than you would lie to me, sir."

This silenced him again. She took the opportunity to say, "Look, I've got to go. I'll check in when I can."

"Do that . . . do that."

When she hung up the phone, she wasn't sure who she could trust any longer. And she wasn't sure how long she could hold onto the notes from Oliguerri.

"There you are," said Thorpe, who was suddenly beside her. "It's time to go. I've had Walter take your things to the car at the rear of the hotel. It's time to move out."

Who was Walter, she wondered—her best trained sniffer? Had he gone through her bags before taking them to the car? "Thank you . . . very thoughtful of you," she said, accompanying Thorpe. "Listen, Inspector Thorpe, don't you think it would be best if we could try to trust one another, since we are going to be working together?"

"But I do trust you, Sergeant."

"Not quite enough. I understand your people looted my safety deposit box in Chicago."

"I wasn't aware that the Chicago Bureau had taken such steps." She stopped, staring at her, giving Robyn the benefit of an "ah, ha!" glance. "So, it was you who made off with the files I'd left in Swisher's care."

"Don't give me that. You knew all along. You knew it when you invited me in that night at the airport."

She half smiled at Robyn. "You're very smart, Robyn—as smart as you are beautiful. So, you know what we're really looking for. Why don't you tell me

145

where it is?"

"All I took were the files."

Thorpe dropped her gaze, considering this. "All right . . . all right, then that would mean that our fiend, Dr. Ovierto, has what we want. That information could make him even more dangerous than he already is."

"What information is it, and how does it make him more dangerous?"

"Sorry—"

"Oh, shit! You're sorry . . . you can't tell me . . . top fuckin' secret, is it? Having to do with this God Project you were talking about upstairs?"

"Pythagoras is not my concern! Ovierto is!"

"That's the name of the project?"

"Forget it. Concentrate on Ovierto, damnit."

"Be a good soldier, huh . . . just do my duty, like you do yours, and let other people make the moral choices?"

"Don't talk to me about morals. Morals . . . what good are they when you're hunting a demon?"

"If you don't hold onto your morals then you become the demon."

"Nice speech, Sergeant, but give it a rest! Please! After you see the results of this Devil's work, and then you imagine a potent weapon capable of destroying whole populations falling into his hands . . . then you tell me about morals."

Walter honked the horn just outside the rear door as the two strong-willed women bared their teeth at one another. Finally, Thorpe said, "I wasn't always an Inspector . . . wasn't always an FBI agent, but I have always been a woman, Robyn, and I'm telling you woman-to-woman that there is only one objective here, and that is to see Ovierto to his grave any way we can. Now with this document which you most certainly have tucked away somewhere . . . possibly on your person . . . we might lure the bastard to us, and when he gets close enough to two such women as we are, he will not live to move away from us. Is that clear?"

"I don't have it," she put out her arms in supplication. "Do you understand?"

"Then we must assume he has it, since Hogarth's testimony is that the notes were in the lab when she went out to Swisher."

The mention of Joe's name used like a pawn in her game, coming from her cold lips, made Robyn walk away from her and get into the waiting, unmarked police car behind Walter.

"You don't get it, do you, Muro?" Thorpe said when she got into the automobile. "We are all of us expendable in this, all of us."

Robyn said nothing, feeling the scratchy papers against her breast. She realized that all that stood between her and Thorpe, with her goonish Walter, all that kept them from strapping her to a chair and ripping her clothing away, was her gun and something she hadn't expected from Thorpe, forbearance.

Chapter Sixteen

The Hogarths were being held at a heavily guarded, fortified location, a building which was a failed winery, largely empty, with a connecting house, all in Spanish architecture surrounded by gently sloping hills, overlooking a lake which could be viewed from the elaborate, wraparound veranda. Windows studded this veranda on two levels, and it gave some cover from the sun and the rain which was plentiful here in Washington. It had rained now, off and on, since Robyn's arrival. But for now the sun was out, covering the dry December lawn with a glistening sheen.

There was a long approach to the "safe" house where the Hogarths were virtual prisoners to the situation. Robyn imagined it was most difficult on the child, but then, having the child in such danger must be equally difficult on the parents.

Robyn was escorted into a very beautiful, spacious house, whose rear windows overlooked the lake. She was introduced to Mr. Hogarth, who apparently had had enough introductions to officers to last him a lifetime. He went back to his book and his martini without a word.

"He's a college professor," said Thorpe, as if this explained his rudeness. "Philosophy."

"Where's Mrs. Hogarth?" Thorpe asked an armed man at the window.

He pointed, "At the lake."

"What the hell're they doing down there?"

"Easy, Malloy's with them."

"They shouldn't be outside! Those were my orders."

"The place is guarded on all sides, including the lake."

"Come on, Muro," said Thorpe, rushing out the back.

Robyn caught up to her and they made their way down stone steps for the water, where the child was puttering about the chilly shallows, playing chase with minnows below the surface, while her mother watched, doing some upright sunbathing in a low-cut print dress, her bare arms goosebumped with the cool air. From her stance and the nervous activity of her hands, it looked as if she'd just come away from a fight with her husband.

From across the lake a small boat was chugging closer, the sound of the motor meshing with the sound of birds in the trees. The sun-dappled water made the boat and the man a black silhouette against the water, but Robyn saw the man at the tiller raise something — an object like a gun — and point it toward them. Was it one of Thorpe's people? Just then there rose an explosion from the house that rocked the ground, sending Robyn and Donna Thorpe toppling. Thorpe came up firing at the man in the boat as other agents rushed in toward the flaming house and winery. The boat swung around. Robyn aimed for the motor and put a slug into it before it was out of range.

Mrs. Hogarth and the child were screaming in one another's arms in the shallows where Elena Hogarth had grabbed up her baby. Thorpe rushed into the water, continuing a fire which was useless since Dr. Ovierto was out of range.

Using a hand-held radio she snatched from her pocket, Thorpe called for her men to circle the lake. She shouted for men on boats about the large, winding lake to pursue Ovierto. She pleaded for one of these boats to pick her up. All this time the child was screaming and Elena Hogarth tried to get her up, falling again into the water with her. Robyn rushed in to help with the child, throwing a coat she wore over the girl, who was screaming, "My daddy! My daddy! My daddy!"

Elena Hogarth hugged the child and the coat into her. Thorpe suddenly pushed them to the ground, a ping like a bee sting passing Robyn's ear. "He's got a scope on that thing! Get to cover, now!"

But Ovierto was toying with them all, sending bullets just close enough to frighten them before he suddenly stopped, seeing another boat racing toward him with agents firing at him.

"Get him! Get him!" Thorpe shouted into her radio when the silhouette in the distance lifted a piece of heavy artillery and Robyn saw that it was a bazooka.

"Thorpe! He's got a bazooka! Call your men back!"

But it was too late. Ovierto fired and the boat carrying the agents exploded, the pieces raining down over the water.

"Christ, he turns that thing on us and —" Robyn tugged at Hogarth and the child to run for the other side of the burning house, beyond the smoke, for protection. Thorpe stood her ground, calling up a second boat of agents, who picked her up. They barreled toward Ovierto, who readied to fire, but something was wrong with his artillery piece; he turned, revved the motor to full speed, and raced off.

Robyn got Mrs. Hogarth and the child into the car which had brought her and Thorpe to the winery. Walter was nowhere in sight, most likely inside the house when it had blown with such an impact she guessed plastique explosives had been used. But how had the demon gotten in to place the charge, and when?"

"Get us out of here!" Hogarth pleaded with her.

Robyn hesitated. Thorpe and the others would continue their pursuit of the madman for as long as they

150

could. She had a distraught child and a frightened woman on her hands and must act now to get them to safety.

"We're getting the hell out of here!" Robyn declared.

Robyn wheeled the car around and tore from the grounds, leaving rising flames and a black cloud of smoke behind them.

"Where to? Where can we go?" asked Robyn.

"Anywhere! South . . . South here on 192. That will take you to the Interstate."

It sounded as good as any other direction to her at the moment, so Robyn punched the big sedan and rocketed south on 192, finding the Interstate and merging with the traffic there.

The girl continued to cry. Her mother damned Robyn and all her kind with a few cutting words. "You people can't protect us . . . no one can."

Robyn's nerves were frayed and she wanted to tell Hogarth to silence the kid, but she said nothing, her knuckles white against the steering wheel. They drove for an hour before the radio came to life and amid the static they heard a chilling voice say, "Daddy's dead, and mommy's .next . . daddy's dead and mommy's next."

Robyn shut it off, saying, "Christ!"

"He's a devil . . . he's everywhere," Elena Hogarth said, shaken. "How does he know we can hear him? How did he come on the radio?"

"Anyone with a police band can play electronic detective, Dr. Hogarth, and he doesn't know that we got his message. He's just firing in the dark."

"Like he destroyed the house? In the dark? Killed my husband in front of you people."

"I'm not FBI, and I'd appreciate it if you wouldn't lump me in with Thorpe's kind."

"You're all the same . . . Seattle police, FBI . . . what's the difference?"

"I'm a Chicago cop, that's the difference."

151

"The Chicago cops couldn't stop this fiend either."

"Joe Swisher was my partner."

This silenced her a moment. "I'm . . . I'm so sorry. He was a very nice man."

"We . . . we planned to marry some day."

"Now we have both lost our men to this madness . . . and poor Oliguerri . . ."

Robyn looked in her rearview and saw the anguish in the face of the woman, whose skin was slick with tears and an absence of makeup. Dr. Hogarth gasped several times, trying to regain her composure and strength for the child.

Robyn had switched off the radio to shut Ovierto up, but now she wondered if it had been wise. Good police work meant listening to the killer when he gave you the opportunity, but with the child in the car, she hadn't a choice. She wondered if such a consideration would have occurred to Thorpe. She wondered if Thorpe were not trying now to get through to them, worried silly about the whereabouts of her protected lady of science.

Quietly, she reached for the radio to switch it back on when she thought better of it. If Ovierto heard what was said between her and Thorpe, he'd find them. She thought better of making any attempt to contact Thorpe. Thorpe had become a kind of magnet for Ovierto wherever Thorpe was, Ovierto was sure to go.

She realized that Thorpe had found Hogarth in Seattle first, but now it dawned on her that Thorpe had made no effort to relocate the Hogarths from here before now; she had baited Ovierto, *using* these people. It was Inspector Thorpe's style, all right.

Robyn drove on to the border, crossing into Oregon in the pitch dark, finding a small, unremarkable motel where they would stay the night. The neon-lit sign read *North Star*.

"We'll get a room here, move on when its light," she told Hogarth.

Elena Hogarth, tending to the child asleep in her lap, said nothing. Robyn saw to the details, taking one room for the three of them and obtaining a folding bed for the girl. Once inside, Robyn claimed the bed nearest the door, not at all sure that Hogarth wouldn't run if she had the chance, as she had in Chicago. Robyn had ordered a pizza be delivered to them, and they ate enough to fill their stomachs.

The little girl could hardly eat, however, and she returned to the safety of sleep. Robyn observed the tenderness between the mother and child. When she was sure the girl was asleep, Hogarth came back to where Robyn sat watching the news. "She's devastated," she told Robyn. "She'll never recover from seeing her father die like that."

"If she's anything like you, she'll fight back."

"How do we fight a maniac like this man?"

"Any way you can."

They sat in a deep, blue-lit shadow, staring at one another. Elena's eyes misted over. "She's my baby."

"I know you're scared. So am I."

"That doesn't quite reassure me, knowing that."

"But I'm good at my job. You're safe."

"For the time being . . . but for how long?"

"Dr. Hogarth, tell me about Pythagoras."

She looked stricken. "What?"

"The project you and Oliguerri and the others were working on, the thing that's making this crazy man chase you across the country to destroy you and your family."

"It's got nothing to do with the project. I've been assured of that by—"

"By Thorpe?"

"Yes."

"Thorpe is almost as warped as this creep, Ovierto. Now tell me about Pythagoras. Tell me. You've got to trust someone."

"I never even told Randall."

"Dr. Hogarth, please."

"No, I . . . I couldn't."

"Not even if it helps save you and your child?"

She looked from Robyn to the child and back again. "How can it help?"

"Anything that helps me understand this creep better will only help our chances."

"Pythagoras . . ." she said it as if it were a curse. "Wish I'd never heard of it."

Robyn gently nudged her on. "You've got to trust someone."

Her sniffles subsided as she began to talk. "It's a major undertaking for space, astrophysics and medicine . . . that is it began that way, as a benevolent proposal for a humane program that would rid the world of any number of diseases—"

"From space?"

"Without space it would be impossible."

"Is it possible?"

"We were close . . . very close. Dr. Oliguerri held the key."

Robyn thought of the papers Oliguerri had left behind, the ones she carried now, the ones Thorpe wanted. "How close?"

"Everyone else had perfected their part. Oliguerri's was the most difficult, and I was assisting him the night . . . when he was killed. This monster, this Ovierto, he does want the research, doesn't he? Doesn't he?"

"It certainly appears so. He wants to make some sort of a trade, the lives of future victims—scientists—for the information."

"I suspected as much, but Thorpe—"

"Thorpe has her own view of matters."

"And you?"

"My concern is with protecting you, and, to be honest, getting Joe Swisher's killer."

"At least you seem . . . honest."

"I'll show you just how honest."

"What?"

Robyn reached into her bra and brought out the folded pages of Oliguerri's work. "I don't know if this means anything, but you're the first one I've shown it to."

Elena Hogarth gasped. "It's Oliguerri's work . . . his final conclusion on the project."

"Can you read it?"

"Somewhat. He enjoyed the secrecy of his unusual language. It was as good as a computer code, but he taught me some. The figures of course . . . yes . . . yes . . ." She went into the reverie of those engulfed in the fascination of their work.

After giving her ample time to look over the paperwork, Robyn asked, "What does this all . . . mean? That your Pythagoras project is workable?"

"Possibly . . . possibly . . ."

"And what would this be worth to a foreign government?"

"Hmmmmmph, billions."

"A cure for diseases of—"

"It is a double-edged sword."

Robyn stared into the dark eyes of the scientist. "There is a potential then for destruction?"

"Yes."

"So, Thorpe wasn't bullshitting about that much. Just how destructive could this thing be?"

"It could wipe out whole populations. What's worse it could turn whole populations into mutants."

"If that's true, why did you continue to work on it?"

"Why did men build the first cannon, the atom bomb? To see if it could be done. Not that Oliguerri and I didn't have our reservations. We spent many restless nights with ourselves. It all started out harmlessly enough . . . the application of concentrated sun rays to destroy toxins and

155

waste sites, in fact. Benevolent enough for you?"

"But it got twisted?"

"It was taken a step further, to help in diseases, to actually pinpoint and alter genetically impaired T cells—"

"T-cells?"

"—in the human immunological system."

"A concentrated laser from outer space sifts the sunlight into a beam that can destroy cancer cells in a man on Earth?"

"Yes . . . our beneficent repast from space exploration and laser technology with the help of Fermilab. Don't you see what it could mean? The long-term results, possibly wiping from the planet all genetically impaired cells of any kind. Oliguerri imagined an Africa free of disease."

"Pretty heavy stuff," Robyn said.

"But we both immediately recognized the dangers, as did others. The first fear was that some one person gaining control of this would, well, control all medicine, since medical practice as we know it would be . . . well—"

"A thing of the past. No more surgery, for instance."

"Yes."

"Ovierto was a surgeon, you know."

"There are more lethal problems with the technology," she replied.

She stood and paced before Robyn, gathering her words. "It took Ibi and me months to determine just how lethal after our initial discovery. You see, what one can do in solar laser technology, one can undo just as quickly."

"Depends on whose wielding the laser scalpel, you mean?"

"Precisely. Whoever controls this thing has the power to nuke whole populations, and there'd be no place to hide. It would make what we're doing now, hiding from this maniac, playpen time by comparison."

It was like letting the genie out of the bottle and taking your three nasty wishes only to lose your soul to the genie.

156

"Genetic altering from space?"

"Or genetic dismantling . . . one step beyond gene splicing, call it gene dicing," she said. "God, why didn't we shut down like Cartier wanted."

"Cartier, the English scientist killed by Ovierto?"

"Yes. She called it the power of Hitler to the tenth power. Imagine, Sergeant Muro, implanting a genetic malady or an immune deficiency in an entire race, and you have the dark side of Pythagoras."

Robyn considered what she was hearing carefully, trying desperately to place Ovierto in, but he seemed a square peg here. "Space," she muttered, "final frontier of what, man's ignorance, fears, hatred. Why *Pythagoras?*"

"Greek philosopher . . . took it from one of my husband's books. He was first to suggest that the Earth revolved around the sun, and that was in 500 BC. He also believed that the sun revolved around a fire at the center of the universe, a kind of cauldron of the universe . . ." She stopped to gather her strength and her thoughts. "He was quite ahead of his time, spoke of the harmony of the spheres, and proposed the theory that all phenomena may be reduced to numerical relations—"

"So, you named it for a dead man."

Dr. Hogarth frowned at this. "Most things are . . . named for the dead. Pythagoras also believed in the concept of the soul, and I liked that. He believed in a life of moderation, and he took a keen interest in medicine."

Now Robyn stood to stretch, shaking her head. "To your knowledge, Ovierto knew nothing of this technology?"

"Nothing, but information in the scientific community of this size . . . well, it's like any other community . . . news travels. We'd tested the laser with several dump sites before I ever heard of Ovierto. Mirrors were already in place at the orbiting stations before all this . . . this madness coming at us. The physicists worked out the necessary concentrations of sunlight required, along with the engineers who'd actually designed the laser itself. Hundreds of people worked on some portion of the whole."

"But few people knew of the whole, right?"

"Yes, correct."

"Like you and Oliguerri."

"Yes."

"And you never spoke of it to your husband, ever?"

"Only in the most general terms, and the most glowing. I didn't burden him with the razored side."

"You told him you named it Pythagoras?"

"Yes, tried to involve him a bit. We were having difficulties communicating lately, and—"

"I see."

Dr. Hogarth returned to the laser itself. "People like me, bacteriologists, microbiologist, we became most important to the project. Without us, it wouldn't come off, and we knew this. We understood the diseases we were going after. We understood cell biology, reproduction, disease. Most people connected with the project were kept in the dark about its ultimate goals, for good reason. Oliguerri and I, along with Cartier, were among the few to make waves about the direction the research was suddenly being forced to take, one of a military nature, one of biological warfare."

"This was work done with NASA?"

"They were taking the payloads up. The Defense Department got into it afterwards. We tried telling them that countless experiments on disease cures in space are yet to be done, but they took a different view, an industrial application view at first, to do away with waste and toxins we earlier had no idea of what to do with—a true boon, really."

Robyn put her head in her hands. "But it's all gone sour somehow, don't you see?"

"Yes . . . yes, sour, after the tests."

"The tests?"

"Los Alamos, seemed the proper setting . . . history, all that."

"How long ago were these tests done?"

"Oh, six years, I'd say."

"Six years?"

"Yes."

"About the time Ovierto became a problem for the FBI."

"I'm not sure about that."

"But I am." Robyn paced, trying to make the connection. "When you were at Los Alamos, were you secretly brought in, housed, all of you?"

"Well, yes . . . all very hush-hush. Didn't see my daughter for almost a year. My husband was ready to divorce me at that point."

"Ovierto was there."

"What?"

"At Los Alamos. He was there, on hand. Either legitimately or illegitimately, he was part of it. He had to be, don't you see?"

"Well, now you mention it, there was a surgery, a medical team."

"Were there any accidents? Anyone hurt?"

"We . . . I was never aware of anything of that nature, no. But then . . ."

"But what?"

"We were pretty well confined to one work area. There seemed to be a great deal going on elsewhere, however, but at that time there was no thought of human experimentation."

Robyn was skeptical. "How sure of that are you now?"

"I . . . I don't know."

"Ovierto may have been more involved than we know."

"No, I never . . ."

"He gained access to the safe house, wired the place . . .

159

how? He either had a contact among the FBI men or someone in the house."

"No . . . you can't think—"

"I'm just thinking out loud. I didn't know your husband, but I've seen husbands do worse to their wives than blow them up."

"He loved Rachel . . . perhaps not me, but he would not have harmed Rachel."

"I'm sorry, but I have to think of every possibility."

"It had to be one of the agents."

"As well it may have been." Robyn dropped it.

"Although he was acting rather . . . *strangely.*"

Robyn said, "We'd best get some rest." She took the notes stolen from Oliguerri's lab, folded them up once more, and readied for bed. She waited until Elena Hogarth went into the shower before she hid the papers. No sense taking any chances. She found a drawer, placing the notes beneath it in the rear. When Dr. Hogarth finished showering, Robyn went in, taking her gun with her, ever cautious. When she looked back, she found that mother and daughter were asleep in the big bed, the child having stirred in the interim. For a brief moment, Robyn stared at the scene of mother and daughter wrapped around one another.

She'd found her bag in the trunk of the FBI car, but Hogarth and the child had no clothing whatever with them. She had invited Elena Hogarth to fish through for anything she thought might be comfortable for the child to sleep in, and anything she, herself, might use, either tonight or in the morning. Dr. Hogarth had graciously thanked her.

Robyn grabbed some sleepwear herself and returned to the bathroom. Leaving the door ajar, she quickly showered. Under the soothing stream of the hot shower, she wondered where Ovierto was at this moment and where Thorpe might be. Other than the fact that Ovierto was still at large, they knew nothing, and it wasn't an enviable position to be in. On the other hand, calling in to Thorpe could tip Ovierto off to their whereabouts. The man was a cunning demon, after all.

She wondered how much Thorpe knew about Pythagoras. She had played dumb, acting the good soldier who just follows the dictates of her superiors, not caring to know the particulars of Pythagoras. If she chose to be in the dark about what the governmental scientists were working on and what seemed to be driving Ovierto to murder upon murder, then she'd have to be rudely awakened. However unlikely it seemed, Thorpe had genuinely detached Ovierto from Pythagoras. Why? Didn't she see the connection? Or was she too close to the trees?

And what about the government's plans for Pythagoras? Could they be every bit as sinister as those of Dr. Ovierto in the end? Robyn had been disappointed by her government before, but this . . . this could go far beyond disappointment.

In any event, according to Hogarth, Oliguerri's final written words were worth a great deal to the authorities, far more than a human life or two.

Robyn returned from her shower refreshed but agitated by her thoughts. She lay down on the bed and felt every muscle weighted down with fatigue and draining tension. Sleep, if it came at all, would be a mixed bag of anxiety and wonder.

"What've I gotten myself into?" she asked the silent room.

Chapter Seventeen

The following morning they were out before dawn, continuing on the Interstate only briefly before Robyn decided to veer off for the old Pacific Coast Highway. She'd always wanted to see it, and besides, Thorpe would be looking for them everywhere, making the Interstate dangerous for them. She still wasn't certain that she wanted to be found, not just yet, anyway.

Ovierto's communication had told her one thing, that the evil genius had escaped capture once again. Had he been calling from his hideaway, or a car, or his plane? He obviously had a fortune to squander in his quest for Pythagoras. To some degree, she felt comforted knowing there was a reason, after all, for the man's madness, his obsession, that it was not just a deranged fixation on driving Donna Thorpe as mad as he was.

She switched on the radio in order to learn what she could from the calls. Every law enforcement agency in the West was alerted to the car, down to the license plates, and so too, then, was Dr. Ovierto.

"We have to ditch this car, get something else," Robyn told her charges.

"Why are we hiding from Thorpe?"

"Thorpe is not your . . . Thorpe draws Ovierto."

She had almost said that Thorpe had used them all to bait Ovierto in Seattle.

"If we could get to an airport, fly out," suggested Hogarth.

"All the airports will have men looking for us, two women traveling with a child, but if we did it separately . . . maybe. Where would you like to go?"

"Vermont."

"What's in Vermont? Relatives? Relatives are not good. Ovierto, Thorpe . . . both will know about any relatives."

"Friends I haven't seen in years."

"You don't mind endangering—"

"Well, what else can I do?"

"We can go back to Seattle, make a deal with Thorpe."

"What kind of deal?"

"We've got to get Ovierto off your trail. We've got to set up a decoy operation. I'm a decoy cop. With the right makeup, I could look like you. We can leave a crumb-trail to me for Ovierto to follow while you and Mindy can be properly relocated. No more playing tag with this monster."

"What makes you think Donna Thorpe will be willing to do it your way?"

"It's the only way she's going to find you."

She pulled over beside the road to take in the view of the Pacific. She'd never seen it up close like this before, so much peaceful water at the surface, teeming with unrest and frenzied feeding below. She had stepped from the car, taking the keys with her, to view the panoramic sight before her. The child got out to stretch, followed by Elena Hogarth with a resigned look on her face.

"All right, but Thorpe will want the papers, too. You know that."

"Yes, I know. I also know that they're not safe on me or you. At least she can place several concrete walls between that information and Ovierto."

"And you . . . it places you in great danger to impersonate me."

"That's my job . . . besides, just standing here beside you places me in as much danger. I think for your sake . . . for the child's sake, we have no other choice but to follow the FBI program. But there won't be any deal unless we get real assurances from Thorpe that it'll be done speedily and properly, so that you will remain safe. I'm beginning to think that means without computers." She thought of what Thorpe had said about Ovierto's computer. She wondered now if she was in his files.

Elena Hogarth stared now at the sea. She then said, "I believe I can trust you. All right, we do it your way."

"Frankly, it'll look a lot better on my record, bringing you in, than if we were hauled back, me in cuffs."

Robyn began to notice the low hum of the airplane in the distance, but her eyes fell on Mindy, who was rummaging about the woods here overlooking the beach and asking if she couldn't go down onto the sand.

"No . . . be careful there, Mindy . . . Mindy," Dr. Hogarth was saying when Robyn realized that the plane was flying straight in at them. She didn't know a great deal about private planes, but it looked like a Beechcraft, a sleek, bright dart coming at them.

"Get down! Get down!" she shouted and leaped to the earth at once, seeing Hogarth cover the child with her body. Gunfire rained down, barely missing them as the plane pulled up.

Mindy was screaming from beneath her mother. Elena was hit. Robyn stood and fired every round in her gun at the disappearing plane, placing two bullets in the wing section before it was out of range. She then rushed to Hogarth and the kid, seeing the blood. Hogarth was alive but nearly unconscious.

The plane was banking in the near distance, preparing to come around again.

"In the car! Get in the car, Mindy!" said Robyn, trying to cope with Elena.

"No, no!" shouted the girl.

"Get in!"

The girl instead helped her get her mother to the car. Robyn said, "We've got to get out of here!"

She then rushed around to the wheel and realized that the keys were missing. She saw them lying in the dirt in front of the car where she had dove earlier. Overhead the plane was coming in low again.

She punched the radio, calling for assistance, telling anyone listening who they were and that they were under fire from Ovierto's plane. She then ran around to the other side and grabbed Elena up in her arms, shouting for Mindy to run as far from the automobile as possible. "Hurry, hurry!"

A line of fire began at the ridge and cut through the car as they leaped into the brush amid trees, an explosion from the vehicle rocking them, sending flames into the pine needles where they lay. The car exploded a second time, sending up a choking gas cloud.

"The papers," moaned Elena.

"I have them."

The plane moved off again. With no place to land, with trees all around, Ovierto must be stymied, unable to see them where they hid but pleased with his pyrotechnical display. Robyn said over and over to herself, "Come on back, you bastard, come on back" as she reloaded her .38, her heart pounding. Ovierto gave it up and did not return.

* * *

Seattle's seaport was a bustling place in the city, where merchants and customers met below the watchful bows and sterns of enormous freighters. Tug boats sounded and moved about the harbors like terriers while clouds of seagulls and pelicans followed the fishing boats as if guiding their direction. The place was busy with people as well, from the tourists to the dock officials and seamen coming and going. It was a little corner of the city where privacy could be had amid the noise. Drugs were sold straight off the ships, and raids had netted whole bundles of hashish coming in under various ingenious disguises, along with cocaine and other illegal narcotics. Amid the scars of the older section of the docks an old freighter stood twenty-nine feet high beside the pier. Moored from stem to stern with four lines, the *Zimbabwe Jewel*, though rusted red with age, appeared to be winning the tug of war with the dock trying to hold her. She'd one day take the moorings away with her through sheer and constant friction between the two, as the water gently rocked the lumbering monster. From all that anyone could see, the old freighter was a long way from her home port of Rhodesia. But recently, there'd been some scuttlebut about the pier that she'd gotten new owners, and that she was now registered with the Port of Seattle by a man named Bateman.

Inside the rusting tub, all was still and silent, save for her ropes and creaking bulkheads and the hummed tune of the insane man who had bought her and would come and go from her on occasion without ever having been seen. No one knew what the future held for the unlucky *Zimbabwe Jewel*.

Dr. Maurice Ovierto had made a substantial cash down payment on the ship, using it as his dumping ground. Three Seattle citizens were taking up space in

166

it now, their bodies beginning to annoy him with the stench. They'd all had their throats surgically removed for the apples he had wanted so to send to Thorpe. Thorpe was such a fool, he thought; she didn't know how deep was his reason for driving her mad. After all these years, she still hadn't put it together with her father. What did he have to do, spell it out for the bitch?

Senator William P. Thorpe, who had secretly spearheaded Pythagoras and who had contacted his old school chum, Dr. Louis Rosenthaler, who in turn had called on Dr. Maurice Ovierto to set up a surgery and medical facility at Los Alamos for the government, a very special, high-priority event to test the results of certain lasers on human disease organisms. Ovierto had always had a touch of madness in him. He believed it was genetically transmitted, along with his other condition, a metabolic disease due to disordered hemoglobin synthesis called porphyria. It ran in families, and it caused him episodic abdominal cramps and pain, as well as changes in the skin, neuritis, and mental changes. He knew of the various drugs and foods that could trigger an attack of the disease, the same which had caused the madness of George the III of England. With the laser, he had taken a calculated risk. The result was *the man he was today*. He owed it all to Thorpe's father, in a way. . . .

He had set up several radios in the old ship, a police band, as well as a ham radio and a simple AM/FM for local news. He also had a small TV in his captain's quarters here. He'd brought in a bucket of chicken and on his return had found rats feeding on the remains of his last meal — as if they hadn't enough to feed on in the ship.

Since Pythagoras's early stages of development, six years before, he had had more attacks than ever, and their duration was longer. But he knew that in the six years since the failed experiments and mistakes at Los Alamos the scientists responsible for Pythagoras had continued to work on the problems and resolve them. He knew that his own disorder, as well as countless others, could be cured, and he knew that a world riddled with genetic disorders would pay dearly for Pythagoras, perhaps even *his* price.

His disease made him sensitive to light. His skin would bubble from it at times, when the porphyrin hormones were running high in his liver. The hormones had caused coma in him, hallucinations, nerve damage, seizures, and difficulty breathing. Before the experiment he had been able to live with the toxic levels, but he'd believed in the project and so subjected himself to the effects of the laser. Rather than reduce the power of the crippling disorder, it had doubled it. What other effects the laser had on him, on his brain, he could only guess at, but he believed it had made of him a cold, sociopathic creature capable of feeling nothing for his own victims. Or was it all an excuse he cared to feed himself so that he might do whatever he wished to whomever he wished and not feel a thing?

Either way, Thorpe was at fault, along with all the scientists behind the creation of Pythagoras. Now they must either deal with him or die. He'd gone to great lengths to bring Thorpe to her knees, and perhaps she was ready to bargain.

He looked out a porthole to see a tug passing by. All looked peaceful from where he sat. He was unsure if he had been successful in killing Hogarth and the others, but he was fairly sure that he had. It would send a clear message to Thorpe, finding the child's charred bones amid the wreckage.

He thought of sitting across a table from Thorpe, answering her questions, answering all the questions that troubled her sleep, all the whys that she seemed incapable of seeing on her own. And he knew she was no dummy, despite his rage toward her and his desire to hurt her as her father had hurt him.

As for her father, there'd been no way to get at him. He'd died of a sudden heart attack long before. But Rosenthal, now there was a man on whom he had been able to wreak his revenge in full. He'd left Rosenthal a crippled madman.

Rosenthal was here in Seattle, in an asylum. Thorpe knew this much, and she had had the asylum watched, but now, with Hogarth gone, she'd pull back her forces and he'd go find Rosenthal and tell him how he could get his mind back.

As for Randall Hogarth, he'd gotten what he deserved. Ovierto had met him soon after the Hogarths had arrived in the city, convincing him that with Pythagoras in their hands they could rule the medical world together, that he, Ovierto, would need a spokesman and a front runner so that he might remain a silent partner in the multi-billion dollar scheme that could lead to universal domination. Hogarth's morals and his "philosophy" had never been so tested before. He did exactly as he was told, but he never knew what hit him. He'd thought he and the girl would escape death. They would step out of the house at nightfall to gaze at the stars, at a safe distance from his doomed wife. But Ovierto had seen a different scenario unfolding; his mind spurring him on to do what his hand itched to do, he had seen it played out and surprised everyone, including Randall. He had obliterated Thorpe's oh-so-careful hideaway.

He was much pleased with himself. He went back to the chart room, where he had installed a computer. He turned it on and pulled up the file he wanted. He'd gotten the information required to access Thorpe's computer from Bateman, who had become a sniveling creature in the end. He had used Bateman's code at first; this was soon cut off to him, yet it had been long enough for his computer to take over on a modem and begin a random selection to search for Thorpe's code. For some time now he'd known her every move before she did.

He decided to call her electronically. By the time they traced it he'd be gone.

He typed out his message and it was conveyed to her terminal in Nebraska. From there it would flash to any other she might be using.

Donna Thorpe hadn't slept since Hogarth and her child had disappeared with Robyn Muro. She paced before her people at the Hilton suite, where all information statewide and along the coast was being monitored. The car was found, charred to the tires, at an overlook point along the Pacific Coast highway. The news burned like ice through her veins. The information was helpful in giving them a lead and units had been dispatched. She wanted to rush there herself, but she was suddenly stopped by one of the computer clerks, who said there was a Priority One message coming through for her on her terminal.

She went to the terminal, pressing her code. It was either news from Quantico or Nebraska, she wasn't sure yet.

Then it came up.

Hogarth is executed. Give me Pythagoras and the killings will end.

"Bastard . . . bastard's on line. Corey, Corey, trace this. Get on it and work on it until you drop. This damned job is Priority One for your people. Got that?"

"Yes, Inspector, right away."

She grit her teeth. "So, he wants Pythagoras. Don't we all," she said to herself. Then she ordered a man to bring her car around. "We're going to Oregon."

"That won't be necessary, Inspector," said one of her agents who handed her a radio receiver headphone. "It's Muro."

"Muro, you damned fool! Where are you?"

"Never mind where I am. I'm alive, and lucky—"

"I know, Hogarth and the child are dead. Ovierto has just told me so along with the men who found the car."

"Ovierto?"

"The bastard just contacted me."

"He wants Pythagoras, the whole thing, doesn't he?"

"Yes, yes, he does."

"Are you going to deal with him?"

"Yes, we are."

"Washington approves?"

"To hell with Washington. This is my call."

Both of them knew that their conversation was being monitored by Ovierto, and they fed him what he wanted to hear. Thorpe played off her beautifully, Robyn thought, if only because she really did believe Hogarth and the child dead. Robyn decided to keep it that way until she could speak to Donna Thorpe face to face.

"With the information Hogarth had," Thorpe continued, "we have a complete package on Pythagoras. I say we give it to him before more lives are lost."

"But if he uses it for . . . for evil . . ."

"It will take years before he can mount anything useful. To get the kind of technical assistance he needs—"

Robyn disagreed, knowing that Pythagoras could bribe anyone, but she said, "You're right. It may be our only chance to end this senseless killing spree."

"We can't risk another child . . . other people any longer."

"No . . . I don't suppose *we* can."

"We've got to deal with Ovierto . . . do what he wishes, whatever is necessary. I'll see you back here shortly."

"It would be shortly, if you'd send a car for me."

"Hold on. Let's secure this line."

Thorpe did so, scrambling the signal before taking any further information from Robyn.

Chapter Eighteen

Dr. Samuel Boas was one of many associate clinical medical examiners and pathologists who worked at FBI headquarters in Quantico. At least, that is how he viewed himself. He was in fact the director of the enormous and multifaceted FBI labs, in charge of their smooth operation, the budgeting decisions and allocating time and resources among departments, persuading them to cooperate and sometimes "share," like good boys and girls there in the big sandbox when samples came to them from law enforcement agencies across the nation. The FBI crime lab at Quantico had become the ultimate in forensic medicine, forensic psychiatry, toxicology, ballistics, and questioned documents.

Before becoming the chief of such a prestigious operation, he had been the director of the SFPD Crime Lab in San Francisco. He'd served as a consultant to universities and hospitals from D.C. to Hong Kong. His training had recently taken him into hypnosis, domination, terrorism, and victim behavior. He had been on a panel formed to understand what had occurred at Jonestown, what kinds of controls Charles Manson managed over his murderous "children," how

Patty Hearst became a bona fide SLA member, and how others, held captive for years, were turned into true slaves to their masters, as in the California case of the woman called K who had for seven years endured captivity and brutality until she became the perfect slave.

Boas belonged to a host of associations, and he wrote and published papers each year on these and related topics, as well as his well-known textbooks on forensic medicine. He had worked with the U.S. Department of Justice, Scotland Yard, Hong Kong, the CIA, the LAPD, the NYPD, and many others throughout his long career.

And he knew the toll Ovierto was taking on the one victim he had once physically scarred. He had tried to warn Donna Thorpe about this before. It was one of the reasons he had flown to Seattle to see her face to face, along with the information he harbored about those disgusting Adam's apples, three hardened lumps of flesh now. But hidden within the curled folds of these three masses of the largest laryngeal cartilage in the throat he and his staff had discovered an amazing thing.

Boas had held Thorpe's attention long enough for him to go over his concerns for her personal health and her mental state. She blew up at this, they had argued, and she immediately saw him as the enemy, as if he had been sent here by her superiors to watch over her like some aged vulture, to which charge there was some truth. He had so upset her that she had shut him out suddenly. Her interest in this cop from Chicago was her new obsession, and she had rushed out of the room and down to the lobby in search of Sergeant Muro.

He hadn't been given a chance to tell her about the

pearls! And then all hell broke loose at the so-called "safe house."

In the meantime, he had consulted with several old friends, posing them a hypothetical about a police person and a fiend she had been chasing for six years now. He told them every detail that seemed relevant for them to reach a conclusion about the long-term effects of such a relationship as that between the sado-mashochistic Ovierto and the steady officer Thorpe. They in turn had asked a thousand questions which helped to bolster the hypothetical, such as those concerning her personal supports. He told them of the rocky home life and the fact that the murderer had killed her lover.

To a man, they agreed with almost all of his own assessments of what Thorpe was going through, and yet there seemed to be no way to communicate these concerns to her. She closed him out. She needed someone she could wholly confide in, but he seemed not to be that person.

And yet his superiors believed that he had some magical quality or trick up his sleeve to garner that very prize from Inspector Thorpe — her complete trust and confidence. He didn't like the role they had cast him in, didn't like going behind Donna's back, trying to convince Washington that she was all right, and that they hadn't misplaced their trust.

Boas had been in forensics for the better part of a half a century, but he had never seen anything like the cat-and-mouse game being played out between Donna Thorpe and this madman, Ovierto. Somehow Ovierto knew her every move, and he even played the forensics people for fools on occasion, as he had with the Adam's apples sent to Nebraska. The men there hadn't seen the careful, almost invisible work done by the mad doctor, whose hands must surely be skillful indeed. He'd hidden a clue in the folds of skin in the laryngeal tissue.

Boas had come to Seattle for good reason. If Ovierto were here, perhaps what he had found embedded in the flesh of the apples could help Thorpe. He had kept his find to himself, telling no one, not even his assistants. He had not told Thorpe, either, why he must see her in Seattle.

She had told him to come ahead but said that on his stopover in Chicago he was to pick up a passenger, a policewoman named Muro. The doctor agreed to do so, and he agreed to share his lurid files with Robyn Muro if that would make everyone happy.

When he had finally gotten Thorpe alone to tell her of the bizarre find, she'd bolted from him, discovering that Sergeant Muro had disappeared, locating her in the lobby of the hotel. It wasn't until a day later, after he learned of news of the attack at the winery, that Dr. Boas had again been able to get Thorpe alone, insisting on ten minutes.

Thorpe looked as if she'd gone without sleep all night, and Boas guessed this was the case. "I've got to get back to D.C. in a few hours. Now, you're going to listen to me."

"Of course, Dr. Boas, what is it?" she said, ransacking the room for the water, ice, and booze. Boas had noticed the drinking before.

"It's about Dr. Ovierto's most recent gift to you, the gift of the apples."

"Yes, what about them?"

"Embedded in each was a *pearl*."

"A pearl?"

"Not your most exquisite pearls, but yes, pearls. Here they are."

He placed them in a clean ashtray he found on the table between them. He stared at the glistening, white-and-ivory beads as they collided with each another. "What do you think it means?"

"Who the hell knows with this son of a bitch? Casting his pearls before . . . swine? We being the swine?"

"Yeah, like him to illustrate his point in such a fashion. Showing's definitely better than telling so far as Ovierto is concerned."

"Any rate, I've done some checking around the piers and—"

"Why Boas, *you?*"

"Just an itch I had to scratch. Any rate, the pearls come in at only one location."

"Pearls? Imported to here?"

"Yes, from the Hawaiian Islands, New Zealand, Australia and China, but they all go through customs and customs is located at Pier Thirty-four. Now, I figure, these being obviously untouched—"

"Boas, you old hound. This could be important."

"Why the hell do you think I came all the way from D.C.?"

"Who else knows about the pearls?"

"Not a soul."

"No one?"

"You and me." He could see her pulse pounding in her temple. "This could be it. Could be it . . . could be . . ."

"I wish I could stay to see it through, but—"

"Get clearance. We may need you. Tell them I want you here, Doctor, please."

He frowned. "I've been away too long as it is."

"Try."

"All right, but it will be useless."

"Thanks, Dr. Boas . . . thanks."

177

"Thank me *if* and when it pans out."

Donna Thorpe didn't waste a moment more, leading the convergence on Pier Thirty-four at the Seattle Port Authority. The Port Authority officers were waiting outside a hulking old ship that looked as if it were bleeding rust, the name barely discernable where it had worn away: *Zembabwe Jewel*. Thorpe could feel her pulse racing. She sensed he was here, puttering around inside, doing something trivial like putting on his socks or going to the john. Seattle police had still been unable to locate the three John Does whose throats had been cut for their voice boxes. Perhaps, she thought, the bodies were in a refrigeration hold on board the ship. Boas had told her that two victims had been women, the third a man.

She indicated with an angry gesture that everyone was to keep down and keep still. They moved out quietly from the custom's building. "We go in with extreme caution," she told the others, four of her Nebraska men, two Seattle agents, and another five Port Authority policemen. They started up the ramp.

The ship was large, lumbering atop the water like a city dump on a barge. Odors welling up through the unused holds reminded her of dumps also.

"She's an old steamer, original registration Rhodesia," said the head of the PA men. "Now it's registered to a Mr. Bateman—"

"Bateman?" She knew he saw her shiver. She had already begun to feel certain that this was one of Ovierto's dumping sites. Like the Colorado mine shaft, it would appeal to him. Now the mention of a registration to a man named Bateman—it had to be more than coincidence, and knowing the dark sense of hu-

178

mor Ovierto possessed, it certainly seemed the work of the monster.

She signaled for some of the agents to go forward, others aft, as the PA officers guarded the decks. Boas was on Thorpe's arm, and now he brought out his own revolver as they descended the metal stairs into the semidarkness of a hold. The stench was unmistakable and overpowering in the dark, the odor of decaying human flesh accompanied by the sound of feeding flies and gnawing rats.

"I think you can safely say we've found his leavings," said Boas with the tone of a man resigned to the worst.

She turned on the heavy-duty lantern given her by one of the PA guys, and at the end of its flash she saw the raw, skinned body of a long-legged woman being devoured by rats.

"*Jeeeeezusssss,* oh, God!" she said. "You picked it, Boas."

"I'm going to need some assistance from an SPD team."

"Foster, go up and make the request."

"There's only one body here," said Boas, going closer, chasing off the vermin with gunny sacks filled with rotten vegetables.

"The other two are here, somewhere," she said.

A shot was fired in another part of the ship, far to the bow. "Come on," she said to Boas who ambled behind her, as she pushed through a door and found herself in a narrow passageway, rushing forward. "I want that bastard! He's mine!"

The pair clanged along the metal walkways, up ladders and through hatches. "Do you know where you're going?" shouted Boas when suddenly she shouted, "Duck!"

Shots rang out and Thorpe fired once, twice, three,

179

four, five, six times, drilling the man who had fired at her until his body was rammed against a bulkhead, blood oozing out of his chest where each of her bullets had hit him. Boas got to his feet, watching from below on the ladder, his eyes even with the floor above, at eye-level with the newly killed man. He'd watched the body slide to the floor in a dark shadowed corner of the room she'd burst into. It was the galley and the man had pulled down pots and pans over himself as he'd fallen backward.

"I got him! I got the son of a bitch!" Thorpe was elated. "It's over! Christ, it's over."

She was so overcome with excitement, she felt faint. Boas made his calm way past her, going to the dead man. Other agents were converging on them, someone saying, "All right! All-bloody-right! It was the rats . . . I fired on impulse."

"We've got a body at the stern hold," said a third agent to Donna Thorpe. "What've you got here?"

Thorpe turned when they entered the blackened galley and she said triumphantly, "While you *Wild Bills* were shooting rats, I got him! I got the bastard, Ovierto. I got Dr. O. Tell 'em Boas. Tell 'em!"

"It's not him," said Boas dryly.

"What?"

"It's *not* Ovierto."

"Pull off the makeup!" She rushed to the bloody corpse and tore at the gray-to-white hair, the scalp, the neck. There was no makeup.

She was shaken. "Who is he? Who the hell is he?"

"He fired on you," Boas reminded her.

"But who the hell is he? He's not one of ours, not PA."

Boas fished for some identification. He found the light and read, "William Rosenthaler, M.D."

180

"Rosenthaler! Damn, damn! Search the rest of the ship for Ovierto! *Now, now!* And take extreme care!" she shouted at her agents, knowing that Ovierto was not here; that he had set up Rosenthaler to stand in for him at this location as he had Deter Fomichs in Chicago.

"Rosenthaler was a friend of your father's," Boas said.

"I know that."

"I had thought he was . . . dead."

"He was institutionalized some years back when Ovierto got to him. Literally drove him mad. Up until yesterday, I had an agent guarding the asylum, but after the loses we sustained at the winery . . . he was pulled."

"Don't blame yourself, Donna."

"Who else do I blame, Doc? I'm in charge, and Washington's turned it back over to me since I pegged Chicago as his next target. Now this."

One of her agents popped his head back in. "We've found another body, stuffed in a bin."

"That's number three," said Boas. "*All* will have had their throats surgically removed."

"And Rosenthaler makes four," she said, staring at the man at her feet.

"Come on, Donna. I'll take charge here now," said Boas. "You get back to HQ. Come on."

Boas led her out and only the open air of the sea above decks brought her around. She straightened, pulled free of his guiding hand, and said, "I'll see you off when you finish here. Don't have to tell you — anything you find that might help, let us know. We were *close* this time, thanks to you, Doc."

"Yes . . . yes, we were."

"Too bad it's not horseshoes, huh?"

"Now there's a game I can keep up with," he said with a little laugh. He snatched out a filter-tipped cigarette.

"Thought you gave that up?"

"Did . . . but times . . . like this . . . call for a smoke."

"It was nice having you with us, Dr. Boas. Wish you could stay."

He laughed. "You *have* been away from Jim too long!"

"Hey, Boas, if I weren't married . . ."

Now the older man blushed. "And if I weren't old enough to be your father."

She kissed him on the cheek and for a time they stared out at the harbor and the open sea in the distance, sharing the moment. It was short-lived; a few seconds later one of her agents told her that Muro had been located and returned to the Hilton.

"She'll be waiting for you," said Boas. "Go easy on her. She did what she thought was right."

"What she thought was right. That's the problem. She's a loose cannon."

"Perhaps what you need . . . a loose cannon."

"I've tried that route before with her boyfriend."

"Ahhh, Swisher . . . yes . . . too bad."

"She's only here to avenge him."

"And she blames you?"

"Lot of that going around."

"You can't take so much on yourself, Donna."

She looked back out at the ocean, seeing whitecaps and swells in the distance beyond. Life was getting too large and overpowering, like the ocean, she thought. But she said, "You know anyone else who's going to take it on? Even Washington has learned there's no one else, that I know more about Ovierto than anyone."

182

"You knew about Rosenthaler."

"Yes, a friend of my father's, and a man who knew Ovierto before Ovierto went mad."

"Are you saying he is getting closer to you?"

"If my father were alive, I'd guess him to be Ovierto's next victim."

"But since he is dead? What is the O's next move?"

"I don't know. He'll find another way to humiliate me. Although I can't think of much that is more humiliating than drilling Rosenthaler six times."

"He fired first. It was pitch in there. You did what anyone would do."

"Exactly . . . exactly on schedule, as we dance on Ovierto's bloody puppet strings. The evil bastard. What's his next move? Since he believes Hogarth dead . . . who will it now take to sate his appetite?"

Chapter Nineteen

When Robyn Muro returned to the Hilton head-quarters of the FBI, she made out a report and saw that it was filed via the computers, stating that Dr. Hogarth and her child had died in the fiery car and that she had barely escaped with her own life. In the meantime, Dr. Hogarth and the girl were on their way to friends in Vermont. The computer cover story, Robyn guessed, would work, because like Thorpe, Ovierto had begun to trust computers more than he did people. Of course an FBI forensics team was out at the site of the charred car by now, and so Robyn had to convince Thorpe of the strength of her plan.

To judge by the field reports coming in, somehow Ovierto was gleaning information. He had somehow tapped into the system; add hacking to his list of crimes. He could not ever be underestimated.

Everyone at HQ was as frightened as cats, waiting for Donna Thorpe to return. She had come to a similar conclusion about Ovierto's infiltration of the computer system they were using since she'd ordered no reports in or out until her return from wherever it was she had gone.

Now Thorpe and Boas burst in, Thorpe coming

184

straight for Robyn, her anger unguarded. "You had no right to endanger Hogarth in the manner you did! What do you think we're running here, a summer camp? So you can showcase your skill with a car and a gun? This is a team effort, Muro, and you'd better learn that from this moment on!"

"Just hold on a goddamned minute!"

"No, you hold on! Inside, in the private room, now!"

Boas made an apologetic frown behind Thorpe. Robyn followed her into her private chambers.

"All right, where's Hogarth?"

"She and the child are safe."

"Don't hold out on me, Muro. Where are they?"

"En route to Vermont."

"How?"

"Greyhound bus to L.A. They'll fly from there."

Thorpe seemed to soften. "You did well pulling her out of harm's way at the winery."

"What the hell happened out there?"

"Place was set to blow. Don't know how . . ."

"Think I do."

"Oh?"

"Seems there was some friction between the husband and wife. Anyway, if Ovierto got to him—"

"But he saw Hogarth outside when he detonated the house."

"He likes his fun and games strung out. You know that better than anyone."

"So he does. He left us with a few more presents out at the docks."

"Huh?"

She explained to Robyn what had occurred at the old ship, and how she had mistaken Rosenthaler for Ovierto. "Human calling card," she said, finishing. "Now, speaking of calling cards, where's Oliguerri's notes?"

"Only if we work together, Thorpe."

"What the hell do you call what we're doing?"

"As equals."

"Equals?"

"I don't come under your FBI dictates."

"Shhhhhit, you Chicago cops . . . all alike, male or female . . ."

"That's right."

"All right . . . we work together on an even footing until we catch this creep."

"I have your word on that?"

"Done."

"See, I know your father was behind Pythagoras from the beginning, and that it's just possible that Dr. Maurice Ovierto knows that, too, and—"

"How did you come by that ridiculous—"

"Senator Thorpe had great ambitions . . . like his daughter."

"You don't know what you're talking about. My father's career involved improving the National Debt, housing for every American, feeding the poverty-stricken. He had nothing to do with Pythagoras."

"Hogarth confided in me. The truth now."

Thorpe's mouth fell open. "Hogarth told you this . . . this nonsense?"

Robyn saw that she was in a mild state of shock, that she hadn't known that her father was involved from the beginning.

"Rosenthaler . . ."

"What about Rosenthaler?" asked Robyn, probing.

"He's the man I killed on the ship. Ovierto set him up to be gunned down by me."

"Donna, it's been personal with Ovierto from the beginning."

"Why . . . how did I miss it?"

"Too close to the trees? What difference does it

186

make. Now we know, now perhaps we can do something differently."

"As a child, I recall having met Dr. Rosenthaler. I was . . . had to be seventeen. He and my father had long, serious talks."

"Rosenthaler was kidnapped by Ovierto, I understand, and driven into his own madness?"

"Yes . . . some years ago. Ovierto thought he could get what he wanted from Rosenthaler. He got other names . . . names of people now all dead."

"We've got to take control of the situation now."

"We begin by taking control of Oliguerri's notes."

"Exactly."

"Give him what he wants . . . except we doctor them."

"Can you get us an expert on the Ibo language? It will have to look authentic."

"Yes, I can arrange it."

"Then let's get to work on it. Here's the document taken from Oliguerri's office."

She watched as Robyn pulled it from her bra and flattened it out on the table between them. "Dr. Hogarth looked it over closely. She says it is the formula, and that with it, Pythagoras can go into effect. Without it, no."

She picked it up, stared at it and seemed to take in even the aroma of the document, breathing deeply. "If this had fallen into Ovierto's hands, I shudder to think—"

"He never got near it. Bastard almost charbroiled it along with me. By the way, I put two bullets in his plane. You may want to have your people go to work on any planes getting their tails patched. A little old-fashioned police work might turn up his plane, and if we could ground the creep—"

"Good idea . . . and good work, Robyn. Maybe we

187

ought to look into inducting you into the agency."

"Not a chance."

"We'll see."

Robyn changed the subject. "What do you think his next move will be?"

"He's already made it."

"The ship?"

"Prior to that, he contacted us."

"Contacted you how? Don't tell me, via computer?"

"Yes, as a matter-of-fact."

"Demanding Pythagoras or what?"

"Or there'll be more deaths."

"So, we create a package for him and then what?"

"We wait for his next communication, make the drop, and hope we can somehow track him."

"Put a honing device in the package? It'd never work with him. He'd find it in a second and stick it on a dog."

"Something new we've developed. It's so thin that it's stitched into the bag and looks and feels like the cloth. We'll put a standard bug in, but the frequency will be different."

"Sounds good . . . good."

"Only hope he contacts us before he does anymore devastation."

"Have you any idea who he'd go after next?"

"Several possibilities. Boas and I had thought he was getting personal with Rosenthaler. I had known the man."

"I see."

"My family's in Nebraska," she said weakly, obviously worried.

"Maybe it's best to move them. But if you do so, use Western Union. It's safer."

"I'll do that."

"What about your mother?"

"Buried alongside father."

"In-laws?"

"Both gone."

"Then I'd just see to your immediate family . . . get them to high ground."

"Yes, thank you. My Jim, and the kids, about all I have aside from this . . ."

"Understood . . . really. What other targets?"

She had a list of some four high-powered Pythagoras project scientists who remained alive other than Hogarth.

"Are they all at safe locations?"

"They've all got guards around the clock; they've all been uprooted and are relocated."

"Dates, names, addresses are in the computer?"

"Yes, we'll have to scramble them again."

"I would if I were in your shoes."

"It'll be done."

"Anything else? Anything?"

"Any way he can hurt me? Sure, a thousand ways . . ."

Robyn saw a near-beaten, tired woman before her, a woman who needed a stalwart friend. Joe, despite his rancor, had a certain respect for her, and now Robyn was beginning to see why. But Ovierto had worn her down like erosion against a bald hillside. The roots of her anguish were exposed. Robyn found herself unaccountably drawn to the other woman's misery and sadness and she moved to hold her without reservation. Thorpe responded with unabashed sobbing. Robyn held her tighter, telling her she understood.

In a moment, Thorpe raised her hands to Robyn's face, holding her softly between her hands and kissing her on the mouth, her tongue probing deeply. Robyn held her back and looked deeply into her imploring eyes for some time, trying to determine what was happening. Robyn had enjoyed the moment's respite of warmth between them after all the enmity of the weeks since their first meeting, but she'd formerly felt this woman was the chief cause of Joe's death; could they now be sharing a moment's passion? She wasn't certain she wanted it, but now Donna Thorpe was disrobing, dropping the veneer of the business suit she wore, exposing her firm, high-peaked, full bosom to Robyn, who hadn't made love to another girl since junior high days. Robyn felt a little giddy, a little confused, and a lot dizzy as Donna said, "Robyn, I just want to lie down with you . . . just for a short while . . . please."

Robyn started to say something and catch her breath at the same time, but Donna took her in her arms and forced her tongue even further down her throat. Robyn had been without a man for a long time now, since Joe's death, and she was feeling an incredible need welling up, a need she hadn't felt for Donna Thorpe before now, and yet here it was, pressing in, impaling her on Donna's tongue, the woman's warm breasts like large hands feeling her.

"Take your clothes off, Robyn . . . please . . . please."

"Is it safe . . . are we . . . will anyone walk in?"

"No one comes in without my say-so."

Robyn tried to catch her breath as she undid the buttons of her jumpsuit. Donna began to help, tearing at the buttons with her teeth and with a laugh. It was obvious Donna needed a complete distraction, that she needed to black out the events of the past weeks, to totally forget Ovierto and his wickedness, to cover herself with something that was not wicked but loving, and Robyn was that something.

Robyn returned her kisses now feverishly, her hands delicately playing over Donna's breasts, rising to her long hair. Donna half knelt, taking Robyn's breast in

190

her mouth, flicking the nipple wildly with her tongue, driving Robyn into a mindless blue to red to white color behind her closed lids, making her moan.

"Come to the bed," said Donna, urging her there. They fell across the spread, laughing as Robyn tried to get out of the remainder of her clothing. Donna had somehow magically become completely naked, and now she moved over Robyn like an energetic lizard, flicking her tongue everywhere, working her way down and down on Robyn, when suddenly Robyn saw Dr. Boas at the doorway. Robyn flinched at the smiling old man who just stood there watching and admiring.

"Dr. Boas!" she gasped.

Thorpe raised up on her hands and looked between her breasts at the interruption. "Damnit, doc . . . don't you know how to knock?"

"I did. You didn't hear? Anyway, I was worried you'd kill her. I see . . . I see, I was mistaken. Carry on. I'm gone."

Boas disappeared. Thorpe brought her face back around to Robyn, her long hair playing over Robyn's ticklish belly. Their eyes met and Thorpe began to laugh at the intrusion, and this made Robyn laugh and pull Donna down to her, smothering her head in her own breasts and feeling the volcanic tension of the last few days exploding out of her, the magma of her insides boiling up and away.

They waited to hear from Ovierto, but as they waited, they tracked, attempting to pinpoint his movements. One trail that was being followed up was Robyn's suggestion regarding places in this vicinity where the plane might be patched. Thus far, however, it had turned up nothing. Nor had searches of local air fields. Ovierto was invisible once more, blending in like a chameleon.

Robyn and Donna Thorpe didn't talk about the sex they had shared. It seemed that if they spoke about it, it would be spoiled. It was not like Robyn's relationships with men, which she always felt it necessary to talk about afterwards, usually responding to the male's need to be reassured of his performance. Such reassurance was unnecessary here, and the sex had not gotten in the way of their working together.

Boas had returned to D.C., and no one else knew. It added a new dimension to her relationship with Donna Thorpe, like a new facet on a diamond or a many-sided die.

In the last few days they had put together a bogus Pythagoras package for Dr. Maurice Ovierto. It consisted of the information needed to put together a geodesic-shaped contraption, out of which the only laser that might come was a laser of the color spectrum.

Robyn had worried that Ovierto would see through it too quickly, but Donna assured her otherwise. In the meantime, Donna's family was relocated from Nebraska to places unknown even to her. She wanted it that way, saying, "The least I know, the least he knows . . . all the better."

"You're sure there's no one else close to you he might target?"

"You," she said with a light smile. "Or the men I work with."

Robyn looked closely into her eyes, feeling strongly for her, realizing their differences still remained. Yet she had changed, as had Thorpe. The other agents hadn't been blind to the change, either. "You're sure? No one?"

"It's so frustrating. I know . . . *we* know . . . that Ovierto is preparing some catastrophe, some punishment against me—"

"Because you are your father's child."

"—and we can't stop him."

"Let's get lunch," Robyn offered.

She smiled. "Good idea. I know just the place."

As they left, Donna left strict orders as to where to contact her if anything came up.

Over lunch Robyn got her talking about her father, Senator Bill Thorpe. She described a kind, caring man whose only interest in Pythagoras was in reducing suffering and disease in the world. Rosenthaler, too, was interested for the same reasons. Rosenthaler had been Chief Medical Advisor to two presidents and the two men knew each other intimately.

"To fully understand what happened with Ovierto, we have to gain access to your father's project files," Robyn told her.

"Don't you think I've already tried that?"

"You mean even you have been denied access?"

"Exactly. It's top level only."

"But now you hold a bargaining chip."

"Oliguerri's final work?"

"Hogarth said it was right . . . that it was the key to the entire project."

She shook her head. "I don't know . . ."

"Why not?"

"Because, damnit, I'm good at what I do, and I've never—never withheld anything from my superiors."

"Maybe it's time you did."

They sat in silence for a while, before Robyn said, "I believe that Ovierto was a member of the medical team at Los Alamos during the initial testings of Pythagoras, and I believe something happened out there . . . something that turned Ovierto into what he is today."

"Speculation."

"He was there, Donna."

Thorpe stared into her drink for a time. "All right. I'll see what I can get from Washington."

"You'll do it?"

"This could end it for me . . . blackmailing my own government . . . me."

"Tell them it's the only way if you're to ever understand Ovierto, to find his weaknesses."

"Do you really think he has any weaknesses?"

"Everybody's got weaknesses."

"Even demons?"

"Even Ovierto."

She nodded. "Let's get back . . . put in the . . . the *request.*"

"You'll never get it as a request. You've got to use your trump card."

"I don't need you to tell me how to massage my own superiors, Muro."

"Hey, I'm only trying to help, all right?"

"All right. I mean, I know . . . I know."

She looked weary, and the edginess in her voice combined with an electric energy which was deceiving, for while her body and mind seemed charged with power, it was a power that seemed to be using up her reserves, as if she were on an alternate generator. Robyn guessed that she had spent the night thinking of her children, her husband, the home that she had let slip away from her. Robyn knew that it had been the groundswell of her emotions, and that it had turned to quicksand, and Robyn wondered if she had added to the quicksand.

As if reading her thoughts, Donna gathered herself in and reached out to Robyn, taking her hand in hers. "I never thanked you."

This confused Robyn. "For what?"

"For . . . for forgiving me, for Joe."

194

"I never said I did."

"No, you never put it in words."

Robyn considered this and what she felt. She still felt Swisher had died needlessly, and that this woman had contributed greatly to that needless death, but she also had had time to realize that Joe loved danger, and that it was Joe who wanted to be in the thick of it. He could have turned Thorpe down, and no one would have blamed him. Her trickery, working on him through the Stavros case, had had little to do with Joe's ultimate decision.

"He make a pass at you?" Robyn asked her point-blank.

"No," she lied. "He loved you very much, and I . . . I couldn't be sorrier for your loss."

It was uncharacteristic of Inspector Thorpe to say as much, but Robyn had watched her closely these last few days, and it appeared that she was a ball of twine, slowly unraveling one moment, tightly in control the next. She was on what Ovierto might call his satanic roller coaster ride.

Perhaps the best place for her now was back in Nebraska, close to Jim and the kids, to return and fight for that part of her life before it was completely lost to her. Robyn suggested this.

Donna looked away. Anywhere but in Robyn's eyes. "I'm afraid that it's already too late for that. No . . . best move I can make is D.C. Get at those records. I'll make arrangements."

Robyn put out a hand to her and she took it as if it were a life preserver, pulling Robyn into her. They held onto one another for a long time.

Book Three

What need is there of suspicious fear . . . if thou seest clear, go by this way content and without turning back: but if thou dost not see clear, stop and take the best advisers . . . keeping to that which appears to be just. For it is best to reach this object, and if thou dost fail, let thy failure be in attempting this.

Marcus Aurelius, Meditations.

I have always felt friendly toward Satan. Of course that is ancestral; it must be in the blood, for I could not have originated it.

Mark Twain

Chapter Twenty

St. Francis of Assisi Cemetery, Washington D.C.

Dr. Maurice Ovierto had unlimited funds to draw upon in two Swiss bank accounts. He had obtained most of his money from victims like Rosenthaler, who signed over all of their money to him in an attempt to save themselves from Ovierto's wrath. Ovierto had taken the money, but it had only worked to a certain degree, postponing the execution of the death sentence.

Ovierto had learned that with enough money a man could buy anything—*anything*. Satisfy any lust, cause any amount of mayhem. He could even buy murder, but this he preferred to do himself. Currently he was buying ghouls, graveyard ghouls; for enough money could buy enough men and enough tools for the job he had in mind tonight on a chill December eve in Washington, D.C. amid the gravestones of the long dead. He needed a pair of bodies, and to the men who were being paid well beyond their day labor job fees he must have seemed both a godsend and an extraordinarily selective body snatcher, for they had had at first to forage through the cemetery for half an hour before he pointed to the graves he wished unearthed.

They were at bottom now, the mud and mire streaming from their clothes while Ovierto stood by untouched by the soil. They had reached the concrete encasing the coffins that lay side by side, the two that he wanted. The men set the small charges that would crumble the concrete vaults, turning them into rocks which they could remove by hand.

They timed the small explosives to go off just as another jet swooped in low for nearby Washington National Airport. Ovierto wondered if Thorpe were on the plane. It was unlikely, he decided, since she probably thought he was still in the vicinity of Seattle, a continent away.

At any rate, she was in for a grand surprise when she did return to D.C.

The men were over top of the caskets now. Ovierto ordered the body bags be sent down. He didn't particularly wish to see the couple's desiccated bodies. The woman had been in the ground for over six years, the man three. There wouldn't be much left of them, and he had to watch closely lest the fools he had hired tried some shenanigans with whatever jewelry they might find down there. For this reason, Dr. Ovierto climbed down with the bags personally as the lids were being pried open and smashed.

One of them popped open like the trunk of a car when a hasp was broken; foul gases sent the men back. Maurice Ovierto went closer. It was the man. Not so high and mighty anymore.

But the hands were bare of jewelry and nothing on his wrists marked him. Ovierto silently cursed this fact.

"Open the other one—hurry!"

This was done within minutes. On the hand of the

female skeleton grinning up at Ovierto there was a lovely diamond with a gold band, and this brought a smile to Ovierto's lips. "Good, good night's work," he said as if to himself and the desiccated remains of the woman and her mate. For a time the men he had paid so handsomely watched uneasily as he pulled forth a pair of needle-nosed pliers and began to tug on the dead woman's skeletal hand, wrenching it back and forth, holding firm to the wrist bones that began to rattle, until he plucked the left hand completely off. This he placed in a small bag he had pulled from his coat pocket.

"Get her in the body bag and to the van," he ordered the men as he proceeded to the male skeleton and worked for much longer at removing the right hand, mostly bones to which a few tatters of sinew doggedly adhered. In a short while, Ovierto had removed a hand from each of the corpses. Then he climbed the ladder back out of the six-foot trench, ordering that the second body be taken to his van.

Ovierto looked back at the gravestones and the gaping holes. "This'll kill her," he said to himself and then laughed the laugh of the mad. "Kill her . . . kill her . . ."

Another day and night went by in which Donna Thorpe flew back to D.C. to make her "request" in person and to view the documents on Pythagoras, should she be allowed to see them. A day later she contacted Robyn by phone and told her to catch the next flight out for D.C.; she wanted her at the Defense Department the following day at exactly 9 A.M. With still no ripples from Ovierto and things in Washington State pretty slow, Robyn was glad for the change.

She'd been getting pressure from Chicago to return home to her job there. In D.C. her captain wouldn't so easily find her, and, she admitted to herself, she'd begun to want Ovierto as much as Thorpe did.

In D.C. it was cold and raining at the Pentagon where she was met by Donna Thorpe wearing a blue serge suit, the one she'd been wearing the day they had made love. They exchanged an awkward moment of pleasantries when suddenly Donna kissed her on the cheek and said, "You were right. It took time, but it worked. We're going in to see Pythagoras."

"Great, Donna."

"They're not happy about it, but they fear Ovierto a lot more than they do us."

"Us?"

"I told them it was the two of us or no deal. I want you in. In fact, I want you in the agency."

"But I've got a job back in Chicago that—"

"Forget that. The agency is for you. You're a natural. We need talented women in the FBI. Oh, we'll talk about it later. Let's get in out of this muck."

The Pentagon was enormous, living up to the expectations and cinematic recreations of the place created in Robyn's mind. It did not let her down in the red tape department, the number of doors and levels of lieutenants they were filtered through before arriving at a room that appeared to be hermetically sealed. There were no windows or decorations, only an enormous antique pair of tables and chairs that reminded Robyn of the Chicago Public Library's golden oldy furniture. The lamps hanging low over the tables enhanced the dusty-library image.

They were left here alone in the empty room, and here they waited for ten minutes before a door at the rear of the room, opposite the one they had entered, opened. A man with two stars on each shoulder, a general, approached with an armful of documents and files. He did not introduce himself. He seemed angry, put out, his big jowls set hard when they were normally like Jell-O, Robyn guessed. He simply placed it all at the end of the table and disappeared the way he had come.

The two women went to the files and Donna divided them down the middle. "We've got two hours."

"Two hours?"

"All they'd give us."

"But what about the laser itself?"

"I've seen it. It's fully operational. It just hasn't performed accurately. Oliguerri held the key."

"Now they have it, do you trust them to use it wisely?"

"Yes, yes, I do."

"Responsibly?"

"Absolutely."

"Ovierto finds out, he's going to go on a rampage . . ."

"That was one reason they were anxious to cooperate. They're afraid."

Robyn nodded, understanding. "Of course . . . enough publicity brought about by Ovierto and this could go public, and maybe it ought—"

Donna grasped her hard by the wrist and Robyn saw that she had placed a finger to her lips, indicating the place was bugged.

Robyn nodded. "I mean, it would be unfortunate, I mean."

"Best get to work here."

For the next two hours they scoured the files, Donna taking particular interest in anything having to do with her father and Rosenthaler.

"Here," said Robyn suddenly, "it's Ovierto."

There was a photo of a much younger Dr. Ovierto in white lab coat standing side by side with Rosenthaler. Ovierto had done his residency under Rosenthaler as some kind of boy genius, rising rapidly in the hospital in Houston. There was some indication the two men were very close and that some of Rosenthaler's advice to Senator Thorpe concerning Pythagoras might have actually come from Maurice Ovierto.

They read further, Donna looking over the discovery of Ovierto's definite tie with Pythagoras with a mix of fear and fascination. "Then he *was* there, during the testing."

"And there was some human experimentation going on."

"Ovierto's history," she said, "here it is."

There were several biographical pages on Ovierto, information that had been concealed and sent to the deep for years, kept even from the very government agency mandated with locating and destroying Maurice Ovierto.

Just then the general returned. Two hours had gone by in a flash. He said he'd come for the files and he began to silently scoop them up. Donna Thorpe pursued him through the door, however, shouting, "General Wright, General Wright!"

He turned, gave her a demure look and said, "I believe we have no further dealings, Inspector."

"The hell we don't!"

Robyn stood by, staring a hole in the general.

"Agent Thorpe, we have been true to the spirit of our arrangement, and we have followed your instructions to the letter. Now, the deal is over."

He turned the documents over to an aide and they began to move off.

"Ovierto was part of a human experiment with Pythagoras, wasn't he? Wasn't he, damn you!"

The general turned, his face livid, rushing back at her like a rhino. "This meeting is terminated! Do you understand?"

"And my father? How was he terminated?"

"That's madness, to suggest that—"

"Pythagoras became too big for the senator when your side learned of its military applications, isn't that right?"

The general said angrily and lowly in a growl, "Just do your job and get Ovierto, and quit making wild accusations that have no foundation. Your father died of a heart condition, I am told."

"He didn't have a heart condition. He never had a heart condition."

"Heart attack then."

"Yes, while in his office, working late . . . alone."

"I have nothing more to say to you, Inspector."

"I'm sure you don't."

Robyn put an arm around her and led her away from the retreating figure of the big man with the stars on his shoulders winking back at them. "You work your whole life for what you believe in, and some fat fart like that kicks it all right out from under you," she said to Robyn as they searched for their way out of the gigantic labyrinth.

They didn't notice the handyman who was at work in a corner area where electrical conduit and pipes created a maze in a box. The man's hands worked deftly among the jumbled wires. He wore a jumpsuit and a ball cap and sucked on an unlit cigar, observing the no-smoking rules of the government facility. He watched Thorpe and Muro go by with a twinkle in his eye, for now Maurice Ovierto was sure he had come to

205

the right place to continue his struggle against *them*, against all of them.

Ovierto moved from the electrical box here to the phone lines in the basement, the tag on his chest indicating he had gotten clearance to do work in the building. He had followed Elbert Mackey from here the day before, taking his truck, his tools, his clothing, and his life. Tapping General Sampson Wright's phone line would be a simple matter.

"We have it, Mr. President," he mimicked the officious General Wright. "We have Pythagoras."

"Not quite," he replied to himself in his own voice, "because the price is going up." Inside his tool chest he had the makings for a bomb. Infiltrating the Pentagon with an unassembled bomb was a great deal easier than trying it with an assembled one. . . .

When Donna and Robyn got back to Quantico there was a small package waiting for Thorpe, and as it was rank with a sickening odor, and the handwriting was his, it was obviously from Ovierto. It had taken some time to determine that it was safe to open the package, that it contained no bomb, but the emotional explosion it caused in Donna Thorpe was enough. The contents spilled out with black earth, a pair of desiccated, bony hands, one with a ring on it. The sight made Donna gasp, back away, almost fall, and grab for some anchor around her as she weaved. Robyn rushed to her, supporting her, but she pulled away and ran from the room, vomiting and crying.

Robyn lifted the message rubber-banded to the skeletal left hand as she stared at the beautifully set diamond on a lacey ribbon of green gold on one finger. One of the hands was larger than the other, a male's hand, while the left, with the ring, was a female hand. Donna used tweezers to pry open the message. It was a sick rhyme that read:

Sykes was fun
   and Bateman more,
but nothing compares
   with a mothering whore
and a bastard's corpse . . .

They helped vent my spleen
   in a rollicking cemetery scene
Here in old D.C.
   at beautiful St. Francis of Assisi . . .

It came clear to Robyn. She hit an innercom button and called for assistance. Several agents responded quickly to her call for any information on a graveyard disturbance in the area.

"Something went out over the wire about ten this morning," said one of them.

"Where at?"

"Assisi, about an hour away."

"Are Thorpe's parents buried there?"

"Yes, as a matter of fact. What's this all about?"

"Christ . . . Christ . . . the bastard's turned into a ghoul, a body-snatching ghoul. Can you get me out to the cemetery?"

"Right, no problem. Come along."

She told another agent to tell Thorpe that she would check out the cemetery, assess the damage done, and get back to her.

On the way, Robyn realized that not only was Ovierto in D.C., but that he had been in the city for some time. She prayed he had not done any more harm to Donna than he had already inflicted. She detested the maniac for his methods, for Joe's sake, and now for Donna's.

At the large cemetery the roads swelled and rolled about the graves like a park path. The groundskeeper who had called the police earlier was excited to learn that the FBI had been called in and said it was no ordinary case of cemetery tampering, that it was an out-and-out body-snatching. In fact two bodies were missing, a couple by the name of Thorpe. Robyn wanted to see the empty graves and the ground around them. She called for the local police, asking them questions of the crime scene as it had originally been found, and when the police questioned her interest she grew angry.

"The man was a goddamned senator, and that interests the FBI." The other agents, rather enjoying her performance, didn't reveal the fact she was not FBI.

Soon she heard from Donna, who was on her way out.

Robyn told her she could take care of matters there, but Thorpe was stubborn and she was coming on.

At the graves' bottoms, far below the headstones with her parent's names engraved on them were two gaping holes where the coffins had rested, their fronts smashed open. Donna didn't need to see this. It was obvious he was trying to break her as he had Rosenthaler, to send her over the edge.

Robyn tried to stop Donna at the gate, pleading with her, telling her that she was playing right into the maniac's hands. "He wants you to go in there and stand over those empty graves and keel over, kid. Don't you see that? Don't you see it?"

208

"Out of my way." Donna made the car lurch forward, tearing away from Robyn, but Robyn held onto the side, walking swiftly, continuing to plead.

"They were never here anyway, your parents! Their bodies, yes, their husks, empty shells, but not them, Donna! Donna!"

Thorpe stopped the car she was driving and rested her head on the wheel, crying. Robyn reached in and held her head in her hands, saying, "Go on, cry it out."

"I don't want to cry," she said. "I want to kill him."

"You and me both."

She dried her eyes. "Then let's get back to work."

"Now you're talking."

"How did he do it? Two graves in one night, one man?"

"He had help . . . lots of help, according to the local cops. Probably hired help."

"I got the paper sent to documents. They're trying to learn what they can from it. Strange stationery, almost like rag paper."

"Yeah, I noticed that."

Robyn came around, got into the car and saw that the other woman was staring out at the silent cemetery, her parent's grave sites out of the line of their vision, over a gently sloping hill. Noise rose from that direction, where the other agents and the locals were talking over the horror of it all. "Come on," said Robyn, "let's get out of here."

"Yeah . . . you're right . . . you're right. And thanks, Robyn."

"What do you suppose he's done with their remains?" Donna Thorpe asked Robyn hours later at headquarters, out of the blue.

"I wouldn't even hazard a guess . . . not with this

209

guy."

"Profile guys can't even get a fix on Ovierto."

"It'd be a lot easier if they had those Pentagon files," replied Robyn. "Like the business of his having bouts with some disorder?"

"What's that?"

"Something I saw as I was rushing through the information General Wright so graciously provided us."

"What kind of disorder? What was the name?"

"Iiiiiy . . . can't recall, Poppy something or other."

"Damnit, think."

"It looked like paprika or poppy-riaya. Noticed it just as Wright returned."

She called for Boas to come over to her temporary office here. Boas did so, and on entering he greeted them both warmly. The pleasantries over, Thorpe told Robyn to tell Boas what she had seen on the reports on Ovierto.

Boas nodded several times and grunted.

"What does that sound like to you, doc?" asked Thorpe.

"Porphyria?" he asked.

She said, "Spell it . . . no, no, write it out for me."

He did so on a chalk board behind him.

"That's it," said Robyn.

Donna asked, "Are you certain?"

"Absolutely."

"All right, Boas, tell us what you can about the disorder; is it rare, for instance, and is there medication for it, and if so would it have to be prescribed?"

"All of the above."

"Now we may have his Achilles heel! We've got to contact every M.D., every pharmacy — put it on their damned computers that we want to know about any dispensing of the drugs someone in his condition

210

would require until we can check them out. If we move fast, before he has a chance to replenish his supply—"

"However you want to handle it, Inspector," said Robyn.

"We alert every agent, get the entire agency on this."

"Good thinking," said Boas, writing out a list of the kinds of medication a man of Ovierto's age would require to combat the disorder. "Primarily this new miracle drug called tertracychterane, for advanced cases."

"Now, we turn the tables on him," Thorpe said firmly, the image of her parent's bones in an evidence box clearly before her. She had obviously returned for the ring, however, and had recovered this, for it flashed at Robyn from her finger.

Chapter Twenty-one

Time passed. And then came more time. A long day and night stretched into two.

And they waited to hear from the villainous Dr. O, who had chosen to let time pass in order to drag out Thorpe's anguish over her parents' remains.

Robyn Muro had watched helplessly as Donna had taken first to drink and then to self-recriminations. She spoke often of having missed her chance to kill Ovierto the first time around. Any reassurances Robyn gave her that she'd get another chance fell as flat as clichés in a hospital waiting room. Robyn stayed close by her side, but there was nothing she could do to ease the pain, and the waiting was taking its toll on her as well now. She imagined it was like waiting for a strike force in a war, a strike force you knew was coming at you, but there was no escape—only the waiting.

"Let's get out of here," she suggested, "go to dinner," she pleaded, "see a movie, maybe . . . anything."

"You go ahead. I'm not very good company lately."

They were at the apartment they'd shared since arriving in D.C. Robyn was no longer on the payroll of the CPD, and a threat hung over her head that if she did not soon return to active duty there she'd be terminated. All of this news seemed not to phase Donna in the least, and for this reason Robyn was beginning to get annoyed with her. Finally, she said, "Look, we've got to talk. I'm going back to Chicago in the morning, pick up my duties there. I've been offered a lieutenant's position—"

"Joe's old post?"

"Yes."

"And lieutenant's pay?"

"Equal pay, yes."

"Maybe we'd better talk at that. Let's find a bite."

They took a cab to a restaurant a few miles from the apartment and were soon seated opposite one another and looking into one another's eyes over a bottle of Zinfandel. "I haven't been very pleasant to be around lately, I know," said Donna. "My husband is . . . he called last night . . . filing for a divorce . . . wants custody of the children . . ."

"Oh, jeez, Donna, I had no idea. I'm . . . what can I say that won't sound hollow?"

"It's just that now I need you more than I ever did," she replied. "And I wish you'd reconsider . . . stay on."

Robyn looked away. "I don't know."

"I've got papers in the works for you to become an agent, Robyn. We . . . the department . . . need you. I'm not just being selfish here. I mean it."

Robyn reached across and placed her hand on Donna's, saying, "I'm sure you do."

The restaurant was large and busy and bustling with people and waiters and the noise of dishes, but Robyn felt for a moment as if they were completely alone, the only two people on Earth who understood the enormity of the problem they referred to as Dr. O. Donna said, "You've been a great comfort to me, you know?"

"How? I haven't done anything. I haven't known what to do."

"Just being near, Robyn."

They'd ordered earlier and now their meals arrived. Robyn dug into her pasta salad while Donna cut into a Quiche Lorraine. After a few bites, Donna tensed, her fork jabbing at something in her food. It was a finger bone with a message wrapped about it. Donna lurched away from it, shaken and cringing. Robyn grabbed it up whole in her napkin and said, "Stay calm, kid . . . stay calm. See if you can place our waiter! It could be *him!*"

Robyn tore open the message as Donna tried to pull herself together, to find the professionalism that Ovierto had so carefully eroded, and to fight back.

Robyn kept saying, "He's here! Somewhere here! We've got a shot at him."

"What . . . what does it say?"

Robyn read from the note:

Your parents' parts are on ice for now, perfectly preserved, save for the parts I've had to use to convince you that I am serious. Now, Donna dear, you'll hold hands with me or their bones will be cleaned and sold for what they'll bring. A simple ransom is all I require: your parents for Pythagoras. And you're to come alone. No girlfriends or boyfriends in the department.

"Where? Where is the drop?"

"Upstate New York at the Massena, New York dam on the St. Lawrence Seaway where the locks are. He says you'll know what to do when you get there. He says if he smells backup agents, you'll never see the bones."

"Let me see that," she said, a tinge of the old toughness returning to her voice. "The bastard's holding two dead people hostage."

"And he brought the message right to us and we never saw him."

"Don't take another bite of your food. No telling what's in it."

"Where's the guy that waited on us?"

"Come on!" she said, stuffing the note and the finger bone into her coat pocket, rushing for the kitchen, where a confused maitre d' tried to stop them. Robyn flashed her badge at the man and he relented. Donna pushed through the kitchen, staring at the people there, forcing her way to the rear door and out into the night. Robyn caught up as she prepared to fire at a figure in the distance who was walking away.

"You're not sure it's him, don't do it!"

A dog came bounding up to the man she was about to shoot. The man tore a stick from the dog, threw it and the dog gave chase.

"There!" said Robyn, pointing to a figure in an overcoat running deeper into the park.

"Come on!" They ran after the fleeing man, going deep into the park, below a viaduct and along the water's edge. In the distance stood the Washington Monument, lit against the sky. The fleeing man was running in the direction of the Lincoln Monument. If he got across the grounds he could hail a cab and disappear into the city.

He had a good lead on them and he appeared only as a shadow on the horizon. He could be a jogger, another mistake. Thorpe couldn't afford any further mistakes and she slowed in her pursuit, saying to Robyn, "We've got to split up! You that way. Circle around. I'll meet you on the other side. He gets a cab, and we've lost him. And remember, he a master at disguise and sleight-of-hand."

"Got it. Go!"

They didn't see one another for ten minutes, each

continuing in a dead heat after the fleeing shadow they prayed was Ovierto.

Robyn came up from the south end, and in the distance she saw Donna coming on fast. Between them, climbing a restraining chain link fence, was the man in the overcoat, lumbering over into traffic, trying to hail a cab on Constitution Avenue, where the cars whizzed by like electronic flashes.

"Stop! Police!" shouted Donna.

Robyn cried out, "Hold it, or I shoot!"

The big man didn't seem to fit, Robyn thought; his size was much bigger than Ovierto's profile indicated. But then, he could be wearing lifts and padding.

"Geeeeeet awayyyyyy from meeeeeee!" he cried, turning and lifting a large knife that flashed, reflecting the orange street lamp.

"Put it down!" shouted Robyn at the same moment the man turned and ran out into the traffic, dodging cars. Donna and Robyn climbed the fence. Together again, they parted traffic as best they could, trying to keep track of the weaving figure of the suspect as he disappeared into the enormous, sprawling Lincoln mall that was lit like a temple before them.

"Damnit, he'll disappear in there!" shouted Donna.

People in cars cursed them and Robyn lifted a finger to more than one of the drivers as they weaved across Constitution Avenue. Someone threw a smoking pipe from a car window at them; another man threw catcalls instead.

Inside the mall, there were several directions the big man might have gone. If he wore a disguise, the men's room for a quick change, Robyn suggested. There were several levels to the mall which crisscrossed and tangled about themselves in a kind of concrete taffy pull, and it was fairly crowded with people.

Robyn located a map, but Donna knew the place

well, and so she pushed on. Soon they were outside the men's room and nodding at one another. Donna kicked through the door, and they rushed in, bringing up their weapons. Men inside at the urinals responded with curses and confusion.

"Police!" shouted Robyn out of habit.

"FBI business," said Donna. "You, you, you! Out!" she told the men who were obviously not what she wanted.

"Out of the stalls, now!" shouted Robyn.

A flush and a young teen stepped from the only occupied toilet. He was shaken and unnerved by the women holding guns on him.

"Come on!" shouted Donna. "We've wasted enough time here."

"Maybe this guy knows the back areas here," suggested Robyn.

"So do I. Come on! Ovierto isn't getting away from me this time."

Robyn could hardly keep pace with Donna as she rushed from the men's room down the long corridor to a door marked Mall Personnel Only. They pushed through and ahead of them they heard the movement of a caged animal knocking over items in his way.

"It's him! We're back on!" said Donna, cocking her weapon, holding it to her cheek in the semidarkness of the mall's back corridors. It seemed like a human maze, filled with the debris of a merchant's nightmare — discarded, disused, abused, and broken items, stacked boxes, trash, mannequins staring from vacant eyes, dollies, and half-filled racks. Ahead of them they heard whimpering and heavy breathing.

"We've cornered the bastard," said Donna.

"Are you sure it's him?"

"Of course it's him! You saw the knife."

"He's too . . . too large."

217

"Disguise."

"I'd have noticed our waiter if he was that god-damned large!"

They faced a dead end but there was no one in sight. There was a door at the back. Along the sides were naked, statuesque plastic women and men leaning in rows upon one another. The opposite wall was covered with a pair of gurneys filled with cardboard.

Robyn crossed to a door, but found it electronically bolted. "No one's gone through here."

Donna indicated the gurneys with a flick of her gun. They approached cautiously. "He's a brutal bastard," Donna said. "Doesn't deserve to breathe another breath." She reminded Robyn of Joe's death, of Sykes, Bateman, and what Ovierto had done to her.

"I'm going to pull it over," said Robyn, taking firm hold of the gurney and bringing it down with her weight, spilling the useless contents all about them. There was no one inside. They approached the second of the gurneys. There was no doubt now.

"Wait," said Donna, taking out a book of matches and lighting them.

"Donna!"

But she cast them into the cardboard collection which ignited like old rags. "Let the devil take him!" she said, laughing.

As the flames whooshed upward, Robyn said, "No!" and pulled this gurney over as she had the other, singeing her hair as she did so. The flaming cargo spewed across the floor, and, at the same time, the mannequins behind them exploded outward, hitting both of them as the hiding figure of the big man came at them with the knife.

Donna's gun had cascaded from her. Robyn brought up her weapon and fired as the knife came at Donna's eyes.

The gunshot was like an explosion in the confined area, and it sent the lumbering man in the overcoat sprawling against the wall, his blood smearing in an uneven line behind him as he slid to the floor. He was so stunned he could not move, and the huge, ebony-handled kitchen knife lay on the floor beside Donna Thorpe, who picked it up and stared at the helpless figure before her. Donna's arm arched upward, the knife flashing death as it came down, but Robyn grabbed her arm to put an end to the thrust. Their eyes met; both women were breathing heavily and shaking.

"Let me go! Let me kill him!"

The big man before them looked up with pleading eyes, blubbering something unintelligible, crying.

"Look at him now!" shouted Thorpe. "Go ahead, plead with me, Ovierto! Beg! Beg for mercy!" She pulled free of Robyn, the knife still clearly in her control.

"Donna! It's not him! It's not Ovierto!" Robyn shouted.

Thorpe froze, looked from the dying man to Robyn and back again. "It's . . . it's just another of his disguises. That's all. He came at us with the knife! It's him."

"It's not Ovierto," Robyn said firmly, taking the knife from her. "Look closely at him. He's a dupe, another stand-in for Ovierto."

"Oh, Christ . . . Christ . . ."

"Get the lights turned up in here, and get an ambulance," Robyn told her.

Thorpe did so but not before Leonard Groiler was dead. A check of his work permit made it clear that he was a former mental patient with some retardation who had been working at the restaurant about the kitchen. Robyn was certain that an FBI check of

219

Ovierto's acquaintances among the mad of the world would show that Groiler was one of them. He had done exactly as Ovierto had instructed, playing his part to the end, made to fear these two women who were bound to come after him with guns.

Chapter Twenty-two

At the Lincoln Mall the scene was chaotic until Dr. Samuel Boas arrived to take charge of the body, his familiar calm and dignified comportment lending comfort even to Thorpe, whom he took aside and spoke to. Thorpe was visibly crumbling, and Robyn feared she'd come apart completely. Boas gave her some sedatives and sent her home in a car.

Ovierto had them laboring under the delusion they were the hunters, when in fact he was the hunter, Robyn realized too late. Still, Groiler had come at them wielding the knife, and the shoot was a clean self-defense maneuver. Anyone looking at the evidence would have to grant that much.

Thorpe had shown Boas the note from Ovierto, and Boas had taken it from her and placed it in an evidence bag. But before she left, Donna pleaded with him to return it to her, saying, "It's come down to him or me, Sam . . . him or me."

Boas had argued, but she was adamant, refusing to leave until he returned the note to her.

"But it's evidence."

"I don't want anyone else knowing about it, Sam."

He relented, walking her to the car, putting her in the care of two other agents.

Meanwhile, Robyn, too, was shaken. The result of

her firing a weapon had been the death of a retarded man, knife in hand or not. No one walked away from a shooting feeling good about it, except in the movies. Taking Gotopolis's life was more of a reflex response to danger than anything else, and, given what she had seen Gotopolis capable of, she hadn't been overly remorseful. But the lumbering retard was very likely acting out of fear, threatened by a scenario placed in his brain by the sick predator, who had convinced him that he, Ovierto, was the only one he could trust. For this reason, she felt a great remorse for the man she had killed.

Ovierto had twisted them around his little finger again.

Why hadn't she seen it coming?

At what point could she have slowed the events?

Had it been necessary to fire as she had?

Could she have wounded the man enough to stop his assault?

Had she time for two shots instead of the single deadly one to the chest?

If she hadn't fired, wouldn't Thorpe have been killed?

A thousand questions about the seconds it took to kill Groiler.

Donna was blaming herself, saying that she should have known what was going on, angry at herself for not seeing it for what it was. Robyn had spent the last half hour trying to convince her otherwise, but to little avail.

Now Robyn was being questioned by another FBI agent, a guy named Riley. Riley was good-looking in a quiet, reserved way; something about his manner calmed her, even though his job, obviously, was to get a clear picture of what happened. He, like Boas, wanted to see the note that had come, presumably, from Ovierto. She promised him he'd get it tomorrow, if she had to pry it from Donna's grip. She was tired, weary, and weak.

"Let's get out of here, then," he told her. "They've got more than enough help. Let me take you home. Where are you staying?"

Boas watched them leave, and Riley exchanged a wave with Boas as he got into his side of the car.

Riley was perhaps thirty, thirty-two, about Robyn's own age. He asked her if she had any intention of taking the FBI exams to become an agent.

"No, just working this one case with Donna . . . Inspector Thorpe."

"You two've become quite close. Staying with her here in D.C. What's the address?"

"You seem to know a lot about it. My guess is you know the address."

"Refresh my memory."

She rattled off the street number, and a silence settled over the car until he said, "Everybody in the *club* is concerned about her, that's all, Muro. It's got to be tough being the sounding board for a brutal, sadistic man like Ovierto."

"Yeah, you could say that."

"She's not . . . coming unglued, is she?"

"Thorpe? You kidding? She's like nails."

He laughed lightly. "I've heard that. But even nails get rusty."

"What the hell are you fishing for, Riley? What's your job, anyway, some kind of Internal Affairs officer? Checking on Thorpe, chasing buzz-bull and rumors?"

"I've worked similar cases, and I'm just worried about her, all right! Everybody's worried about her. Everybody."

"Who is *everybody?*"

"The entire Bureau."

"Her superiors, you mean."

"You're pretty shrewd at getting answers yourself," he conceded. "Look, if you are her friend, you'll sit her down and tell her she's looking at a lot of flak on this and what happened in Seattle, not to mention her pushing some goddamned four-star general at the Pentagon against the wall."

"She didn't push anyone—"

"Pushed, pressed, probed, whatever term you want to apply."

"Just tell me something, Riley, whose side are you on?"

They'd arrived at the apartment, and the car came to a screeching halt. Riley had opened his door to come around when she said, "Don't bother. I know my way up!" She slammed her own door and rushed from him.

Riley pounded the top of the car, obviously unhappy with the way things had gone. He chased after her and caught her at the elevators inside where the light was muted.

"I thought I made it clear that—"

He cut her off. "I've got a team of agents working under me, good men, and we'd like to help any way we can. Soon as Boas told me about the note . . . well, I figured, we have a clue, a way to track Ovierto this time."

She was interested instantly. "What are you saying?"

"I've already got my guys canvassing every cold storage facility in D.C."

"Cold storage?"

"For the bodies. If he's going to attempt an exchange, he's got to put the bodies on ice, right, for a while?"

She considered this, a small half-smile coming

224

over her. "Riley, you may have something there."

"I worked a few years in morgues to pay my bills. I know a little something about bodies."

"So, how do we go about this?"

"Bills of lading have to be worked out, if he ships the bodies to Canada."

"But he could just fly them himself. He's got a jet."

"A Lear or something, isn't it?"

"Beechcraft."

"Hot little numbers, but the bodies would be easily detected, as old as they are. The odor alone—"

"So he has to send them commercially? In refrigeration?"

"Unless he's lying to her . . . unless he has no intention of making an exchange."

"He'd do it, one way or another . . . to humiliate her further, to hurt her. So, he'll want the bodies in place."

"So, you trust he'll take the bodies to the Canadian border, to the St. Lawrence Seaway?"

She bit her lip and nodded, and then said, "He's sadistic where she is concerned. He very likely has a plan to . . . to . . . I don't know, set their remains on fire or send them into the seaway, God or Satan knows . . ."

"So, we canvas every possible route out of the city Ovierto's grisly cold storage container might take, check all bills of lading and zero in on any heading to the seaway area either in the States or Canada. My guess is it'd have to be within a hundred-mile radius of the dam and the locks there."

"You've thought a lot about this."

"As I said, I've already got men working on it."

"Orders from above?"

His hesitation told her it was so, but she didn't push it when he said, "My unit's a troubleshooting unit."

"Right now, Thorpe can use all the help she can get. I think I speak for her."

"I'd say you were a good friend, Robyn Muro."

"I try to be. Right now, Donna doesn't feel she has many left in the department."

"Perhaps we'll have time to become friends as well."

"You and Donna?"

"You and I." Then he qualified it, saying, "All for one . . ."

"Maybe . . . maybe. I'd better go up now, see how she's doing."

"Right . . . right. I'll be in touch tomorrow."

"Good. If we can locate and hold that shipment, we may have the key to destroying Ovierto."

"Possibly," he replied without the faintest notion of what was swimming about in her mind. "We'll work on it all night, until we're satisfied we have something. Get back to you if we've got anything," he promised with a boyish flick of his wrist in her direction.

"Thanks Riley, thanks." She turned and went into the elevator, a glimmer of sudden hope filling her mind. She had an idea, a way to get close to Ovierto, close enough to blow him into his own eternal grave, but it all hinged on Riley's success in finding that container and getting to it in time, and on a little assistance from Boas. She imagined it was time that the sting was reversed and that she and Donna now sting Ovierto. It would be risky, very risky. But it was a way.

Her mind raced with the mad notion, but she knew she'd have to keep a cap on it until every detail was worked out. She believed she'd need Boas's help along with what Riley could supply. She didn't want to raise any false hopes, so when she entered the apartment, finding it darkened, she decided not to wake Donna. But then she realized there was someone sitting alone on the sofa chair.

All about her, strewn on the floor, were photographs, and Donna Thorpe sat among the images of her parents and her children in the dark, a drink in one hand, her gun in the other. She looked suicidal.

Robyn went to her, going to her knees, asking for the gun. Donna gave it up without a fight, saying, "I won't make it that easy for the bastard."

"Good . . . good girl. Now, come on. I'm putting you to bed."

Donna kissed her lightly on the cheek and said, "You're so good to me, Robyn." She was in her robe, her voice slurred by the drink. "I thought maybe you'd left me, too."

"No, no Donna . . . I'm here . . . I'm here."

There was a sudden noise just outside the windows that opened on a small veranda. The sound made her grab the gun back from Robyn, turning for the window, her robe flying open, revealing her body beneath.

"Donna, away from the window!" Robyn shouted, but Donna tore at it wildly, sending it flying back on its castors, and leaping out with the gun fully extended, shouting, "Come and get me, you son of a bitch! Come and get someone who can fight back! A live target!"

Robyn rushed out to pull her down, her own gun pointing at the young teens who had snuck out onto the veranda opposite, knocking over a metal table while in the throes of passion.

The terrified young people rushed inside under a chorus of apologies from what must appear a pair of crazed females. Robyn now confiscated Donna's gun and ushered her back inside. "Jesus, now will you take those sedatives Sam gave you and get to bed!" Robyn was more upset and frightened than she was angry. Donna latched onto her and cried into her midnight blue blouse.

* * *

After that the night had passed quietly. Donna awoke before her and was on the telephone when Robyn stirred. "Coffee's on," she told her, pointing to the kitchen. Robyn heard snatches of her conversation. "Syracuse? That's as close as you can get me? Shit . . . What about Canada? Ottawa looks closest."

Robyn saw that she had an atlas in her lap. "You're not going up there alone, Donna."

"I'll do what I have to do. I've always done what I had to do. Why quit now?"

Robyn went to her knees before her, pleading, "You can't play by his rules. With him there are no rules, only that he gets his prey, and right now—"

"Don't try to cheer me up," she said. "The die is cast, kid. It's either him or me."

"This isn't some goddamned wild West show. The man has to be stopped, and you're going up there at his request, alone! It's suicide!"

"Suicide if I don't do anything."

"There may be another way."

"No, there's no other way."

"Look, we've got people working on running down the . . . your parents' remains. We figure he's shipped them via a cold storage container of some sort, and Riley—"

"Riley?"

"Yes, he spoke with me last night."

"Paul Riley?"

"Yes."

"He's no good . . . no help! His coming in like this, it means one thing. I'm seen as a liability by my own people. Bastards . . . they're all bastards . . . afraid of their own shadows, afraid of what we know about Pythagoras, afraid we'll go public."

"Aren't you getting a little paranoid about—"

"Paranoid? Paranoid? Christ, you're naive for a cop."

"Donna!"

"Sometimes paranoia is the only thing keeps you on top in this business."

"But if we can find the crate, we could use it against Ovierto. I have a plan."

"There's only one way to get Ovierto now. And it's a one-woman show, Robyn."

"You're talking foolishness, recklessness. I won't let you face him alone, Donna. Never in a thousand years!"

"I have no other choice, damnit!" She pulled the phone from Robyn, who had grasped it. "Don't try to get in my way, and don't follow. You follow and I lose . . . I lose my parents . . . I'll never forgive you, Muro . . . never."

"Donna, I could go in your place. You're in no—"

"No! Not a chance."

"He's got you rattled. You aren't thinking straight. You aren't thinking like an FBI agent any longer. And that's just what he wants so that he has the edge."

"I'm taking the dummy package to him."

Robyn could see there was no dissuading her. Donna went back to the telephone conversation. "Ottawa, fine . . . fine. Do it." She gave the flight salesman her Visa card number. She obviously wanted to leave a clear trail for Ovierto to follow. She was already dressed and she got to her feet. "I'm taking an early flight. Ovierto will be watching, one way or another. He'll see me clearly enough and follow. He'll contact me about when and where, when he wants to. I'm sure I can count on his being thorough."

Robyn had every intention of following also, but she said nothing, going for the coffee instead, saying, "Damn you, damn you! Go on then! It's obvious nothing else matters to you any longer! Go!"

Robyn had hoped she'd hit a chord that might hold

her, but she had played her wrong, and now the only sound in the room was the echo of the door as it slammed behind Donna. Robyn rushed to the door and pulled it open. At the end of the hall Donna looked back, holding her bag.

"The guys call me the Iron Bra! Don't worry, Robyn. I can do this. I can take him."

"Don't go. Not alone . . . not like this, playing his way."

"It's the only game in town."

The elevator door opened and she stepped in and disappeared. Robyn rushed back into the apartment and quickly dressed, letting her makeup go. She was about to bolt for the airport when the phone rang. She hesitated but then picked it up.

"Riley here," said the voice. "Agent Paul Riley."

"Yeah, any luck? Anything at—"

"As a matter of fact, yes."

"You're kidding!"

"Not a bit."

"I want all the details but—" she stopped, considering Donna Thorpe, picturing her boarding the plane for Ottawa, the capital city of Canada. Robyn had vacationed there once and had marveled at the changing of the guard at the government houses, the lumbering double-decker buses, and other British sights that made the tourist believe she was in London.

"Where's Thorpe? This ought to go to her," said Riley.

"Listen, Riley, you and I are going to have to play a little game of hide-and-seek, if you indeed know where Thorpe's parents are."

"Right now they're in a storage house called Wellington's—"

"In Ottawa, Canada?"

"Yeah, how'd you know?"

230

"Guesswork."

"Some guesswork."

"Listen, Thorpe's on her way up there now. Can you get clearance for a jet to get us up there immediately? It may mean the difference in getting Ovierto or not."

"You're damned straight I can. But where's Thorpe?"

"Thorpe's taking a commercial flight, to give Ovierto a false sense of security."

"Good . . . good."

"I'm on my way," she said. "Don't leave without me."

"You've got some kind of plan cooking?"

"Cooling . . . cooling, you might say."

As soon as Riley hung up, she dialed Boas and told him as quickly as possible what the situation was and that she needed some very special medical help. "Will you trust me? Will you come to Ottawa with me?"

"Yes, of course, but I don't understand what it is you need. You'll have to be a damned sight more specific."

"When I see you, I'll explain."

Chapter Twenty-three

Ottawa, Canada

"Benz-PW6, not even the Ruskies know about this shit. Highly experimental, Muro, so you'd better be damned sure . . . because I don't like bitching vegetables." Dr. Boas said, holding up the substance in a tube to his eyes as the plane taxied to a stop at Ottawa Regional Airport—a secondary airport where they might avoid detection by both Dr. Maurice Ovierto *and* Inspector Donna Thorpe. From here time was of the essence, and the drug that Boas had confidence in would soon play a vital role.

"How does it work?" she asked, a little apprehensive now that they were so near their objective.

Agents of the Canadian Secret Police had been placed close to Thorpe, watching her every move. These men were in contact with the Mounted Police who were in turn watching Wellington's Cold Storage Plant on the periphery of an industrial park in an area dominated by a stone quarry.

Boas took her hand in his. "You will be conscious throughout, but your blood pressure, your heart rate, everything will be slowed to a near standstill, a cryogenic live state."

"Duration?"

"Time varies with different people, but yes, on average, you should come out within the allotted time, so long as Ovierto doesn't deviate from the course you have designated for him, which is in all likelihood a possibility. In which case, you must go to a second injection, or you will most certainly freeze to death in that damnable box. Are you certain that—"

"Yes, I'm certain. We'll never have another opportunity like this one. Now, let's move."

The plane came to a standstill and they were quickly disembarking to the waiting pickup trucks below. They had made it clear to the Canadians that what they required was not limo service but a pair of beat up pick-up trucks. These Riley and another agent took charge of and drove Robyn and Boas in separate trucks to Wellington's, where the waiting frozen container, holding what she suspected were Thorpe's parents, would be found, if their information was good. In the meantime, the crate at Wellington's was being watched closely by Mounties in decoy dress, acting as workmen at the cold storage facility. So far as anyone knew, Dr. Maurice Ovierto had not come for his cold storage container.

"We've got to rush," Robyn told Paul Riley.

"Doing the best I can with these road signs, Sergeant."

They were both on edge, as jumpy as a pair of cats. He said in the quiet of the cab, "Maybe . . . maybe I ought to go with you, inside the crate, I mean."

"No need for that."

"But the weight differential alone will tip off the doctor."

"We've got sand bags for that."

"Suppose the bastard decides he wants to take off

another piece of them? Opens it up, and finds you . . . locked in under the influence of that drug, unable to defend yourself . . . Christ, I'm not sure I can just stand by and watch them fetch your parts out of there."

"Where you from, Riley?"

"What?" The question caught the tall, handsome man off guard.

"Where the hell are you from?"

"Missouri, originally. Grew up in D.C."

"The 'show me' state, huh? Then you get a good dose of the capital and you really get cynical."

"My cynicism has nothing to do with it. There's any number of things could go wrong with this harebrained scheme of yours."

"Harebrained? Now's a fine time to voice objections."

"Now . . . now, I know who you are. Look, it just makes sense that both of us go together."

"Thorpe doesn't know about this."

"What?"

"She has no idea we're here."

Riley considered this.

"It's the way she wanted it. No one but Ovierto and her."

Riley looked at her as if she were mad. "And you let her come ahead anyway?"

"Have you ever tried to stop her when she's made up her mind?"

"Yes . . . without success . . . sorry. Look, this just adds to my reasoning. I should be there with you."

"Why? Because you're a man?"

"Because, damnit, I'm another gun."

Robyn dropped her gaze, bit her lip and pouted a

moment before saying, "Well, I can't say that I'm not a little scared."

"You'd be dangerous if you weren't."

"All right, we both double as the cargo."

"Let's get to work then."

At the storage facility they carefully pried open the box that contained Mr. and Mrs. Thorpe's remains, placing them into a second container which was earmarked for shipment back to Washington, D.C. There was little doubt that Ovierto had no intention of coming near Wellington on his own and that he would send flunkies to do the actual carting; little doubt also that Maurice Ovierto would easily recognize any tampering, that he would recognize the box he had shipped here. They must be careful with the work, every staple and clamp straightened and driven clean.

Boas was overseeing the removal of the grisly remains of Donna's parents, taking great care with them, showing the deceased every dignity when an agent with cold hands dropped Mrs. Thorpe, the sound like a clattering of piano ivory against the icy bottom of the new crate. Boas shouted at the men to be respectful. He cursed under his breath and returned to face Robyn and Paul Riley.

"Muro, we could make contact with Thorpe now. Let her know we've located the bodies."

"No," she replied sharply.

"What?"

Riley nodded, agreeing with Robyn and saying, "Sergeant Muro's right, doctor."

"But she has a right to know."

"If we make any contact whatever, it'll tip Ovierto off to our whereabouts. It can only add ammunition to his camp."

"Besides," added Riley firmly, "it'd just take the edge off Thorpe; ultimately make her more vulnerable than she already is, and knowing her she'd want to go through with it."

"She wants Ovierto at any cost," said Robyn.

"You're sure, are you?" asked Boas.

"Yes, very sure."

"And you're sure about this?" Boas asked, pointing to the bottom of the cold container. "Why not fill it with sand? We monitor its movement from here, and that way—"

"All of that has been tried before with this guy," she said. "Tell him, Riley!"

"I'm going in with Muro," he replied. "And we do the sting as planned. No shadows, no electronic devices."

"Ovierto's known for detecting electronics and he'll spot a decoy operative a mile away. I don't want anyone out at the locks," said Riley sternly. "Do you men hear that? Everyone sits it out."

Boas looked from Riley to Robyn Muro, frowning and saying, "This is it then."

"The moment the crate is called for."

"You know that he has some nasty aim in mind, you realize, to destroy Donna Thorpe completely," said Boas. "You realize, don't you, that he has sure plans for this crate."

"That's why we plan to take precautions," said Riley, lifting a crowbar.

"That will be difficult to wield from inside."

"We've calculated the risks, doctor," said Robyn.

"Have you? Have you, really? Using an experimental drug, fighting back temperatures below freezing in order to surprise a madman . . . The whole idea is mad. Even if you survive the hour and a half to the border, we don't know if you will be in any condition to hold a gun, let alone pull a trigger. At least allow us to cut the freon lines early enough to—"

"No, no! If the box is dripping water, he'll know something is wrong!" she shouted. "We go as planned."

"Well, Riley, I see there's no hope of your talking sense into her."

Paul Riley looked at his new partner and said with a smirk, "No . . . no, there isn't."

"We're going to put this bastard away, Doc."

"Make a great retirement gift for me," he replied. "It's just that the alternative . . . well, I don't wish to think of it."

"Then don't. Just be ready with that juice of yours."

"The Benz-PW6, yes. Fortunately—or unfortunately—I brought enough."

Dr. Samuel Boas' gaunt, tall frame stood over Muro and Riley, staring down at them, wondering if they could see him with their four opened eyes staring back like the eyes of a pair of mannequins. Yes, Sam Boas thought now, they'd gone into the preliminary stages of unconsciousness; hopefully the injection had done its work. The pair were in wet suits at the bottom of the cold container, like a pair of frozen children. He wondered which was more dangerous, Ovierto or the tricky experimental drug. In laboratory tests it had worked, but that was under controlled conditions, and it had not always been without failures in the bargain. There could be long-term side effects, and if the biochemistry of the individual was such that he or she had a slow metabolic rate, death could ensue.

He had only moments to finish his part in the charade. The crate had been called for by a pair of dark figures brandishing the paperwork, large men with Eskimo-like features, whom he was told were Mohawk Indians.

Leave it to Ovierto, he thought. "Get the lid on properly," he ordered a pair of assistants who quickly closed out the picture of the helpless pair in the icy box.

"Out of sight, out of mind," he said quietly.

"We're not going to let them out of our sight," said one of Riley's friends, a man named Johnson.

"Orders, Johnson. We got orders to stand down."

"Wait a minute. I don't care what Riley or that cop from Chicago said to you, we're—"

"Not Riley, not Muro," he said flatly.

"What?"

He pulled out a envelope. "Read it."

Johnson did so. He saw that it was from the head of the FBI. It ordered not only Boas and the others to back off the rendezvous with Ovierto, but also Muro and Riley.

"We go ahead with this plan," said Boas, "and we say they left before we got the message."

"Will that wash?"

"They'll retire me a few months earlier, so? Let's help the Indians now."

Boas thought of his last few encounters with Donna Thorpe, his visit to Washington State in particular. He had had a secret reason for going to Washington beyond his personal reasons. His superiors had sent him. He was asked to give a full psychological profile not on the killer, Ovierto—as he

238

had long before done—but a profile on Inspector Thorpe. He had been sent to spy on her.

And now a command decision had been made, based on his report on Thorpe, he was absolutely certain, a decision which read: leave her in the cold where she has chosen to go. Ironically, Muro and Riley, also had chosen to go into the cold in an even more dramatic fashion. At any rate the three agents would be cut off, on their own, a policy which supposedly went against every notion the FBI stood for. But Ovierto had had his effect on more than just Thorpe. Ovierto had eroded confidences and trusts throughout the network. He had everyone running scared.

Holding Riley's pals and those agents who had worked with Thorpe back was going to be no easy task. It would mark him as a first class asshole, one of the ones who had turned his back on Thorpe. Only he had gone ahead with the mad, daring plan concocted by Muro and which, so far, had gone unreported to Washington.

He watched the others move the container onto a conveyor belt which ground its gears and whined and carried Riley and Muro out through a door where a Dodge pickup truck that had seen better days awaited it. The muscular pair of Mohawks hefted the crate with grunts but without any other signs of effort. Boas watched from the dark interior of the cold storage house, chilled to the bone, wondering if he had not sealed Muro's fate as well as Thorpe's.

The girls were on their own, except for Riley. Brave young fellow, Boas thought, before he rushed for the warmer outer offices of the warehouse where the other agents had to be told. His legs and back ached from age, tension, and frustration.

But he brought himself up to his full height and cleared his throat, drawing on his inner strength and his German heritage. He'd hold the others in check here until it was reasonable to assume they could move in. Thorpe wanted a showdown. Well, now she had gotten her wish.

Boas said a silent prayer for the rash Thorpe, the brave Muro, and the foolish Riley.

He confided in no one the strange message that had been relayed to him regarding an explosion at the Pentagon, a bomb that devastated an entire office, killing General Sampson Wright and his aide and destroying much property and information on Pythagoras. Boas silently cursed the horrid governmental project and all the calamity that it had fathered.

Wassssss re . . . mem . . . ber . . . ing.

Flashing back? Or was this real time?

Robyn couldn't distinguish past from present, sound from silence, light from dark. Her senses seemed embalmed, but not her mind and memory.

They waited for hours before anyone showed up with the paperwork for the crate. In the meantime, Riley had cleared the place of operatives. Only Boas, he, and Robyn remained to wait. And here they were, donning wet suits to retain some of the body heat until the drug should take hold. Riley nestled in beside her. Each carried a sidearm and an additional hypodermic filled with the fluid that would keep them from freezing to death. Getting inside, lying flat, making room for the crow bar and Riley, was a task in itself, and bits of debris from the previous occupants had clung to the bottom ice. It was like climbing into a cold, dirty refrigerator for a sleep. Boas quickly made the necessary injections and began tamping down the lid which, like the rest of the crate, had a wood exterior and hard plastic on the inside. On either side of them were several pairs of pipes that held freon. It was cramped and dark and freezing, but the amount of air would not be a problem for the short trip, especially since small, near-invisible wedges had been worked into the edges of the top. It was the only tampering they'd done, and so long as the box remained in cool areas, not much in the way of condensation or smoke would rise up and out.

Robyn felt the drug starting to take hold. She felt her tense body begin to float, almost as if it were above the floor of the crate. The place had become as black as a coffin, and she prayed it would not become hers and Riley's. She could no longer feel Riley, except for the mass that he represented pushing at her side. As for touch, she'd lost that altogether. Now she was at the mercy of the drug.

She could not hear herself. Could not hear her own heart beat or the whir of blood in her ears, nothing. She could not hear herself breathing, and the silence was fearfully deep and seemingly endless, like an unexpected pit that she had fallen into. She wondered what emotions Riley was experiencing. She wondered if the silence was driving him as mad as it seemed to be driving her. She felt no lifting and shoving of the crate as it was moved and she began to wonder if, indeed, it had been moved, or if the Dr. O had taken sudden control of the situation, come into the storage facility, and cleverly figured it all out, leaving her and Riley to die enclosed in the case of icy freon.

The darkness began to work on her mind also. She could see and think, yes, but all that she could see was blackness. All she could think was blackness. She and Riley had taken the place of the dead, and now they were returned to the grave site where the two Thorpes were interred, only it was them who were interred, and she now had awakened from the drug and found herself not in the storage box but in the earth!

How much time had gone by? How much? A few minutes? Ten, fifteen? An hour? Two? She'd brought a flashlight with her and she wore her watch, but she could move neither her hands nor her arms nor anything else. She was a prisoner of her own body. She began to imagine that she was sweating and that the beads of sweat were freezing over her skin, turning to crystals that itched and itched, but she was unable to scratch.

"Riley! Riley!" her mind screamed, but her mouth could not form the words; her every muscle had gone flaccid and numb. She tried to hear *his* inner turmoil, to hear his silent screams, but there was nothing to hear. She tried desperately to hear noises outside the box, but her sense of hearing, along with all others, seemed dead. She wondered if she were not dead.

Calm down, calm down! she told herself. She didn't have to fight to do so, however. *Any more calm and she would be dead,* she reminded herself now. If anything, she must fight to be less calm, to force herself to think of the reason she was here, surrounded in all this blackness, to remember Ovierto's ugly face and his uglier heart. She thought about Donna Thorpe and what Ovierto had put her through. She reminded herself that Donna was standing alone

242

against him somewhere outside this darkness. She held firm to that terrible thought.

Beside her, like so many potatoes in a bag, Riley felt like dead weight. He was likely struggling just as she was with the effects of the deprivation drug. Boas had said not to fight it, but she was damned if she could do anything but fight it. Still, only her mind seemed able to function. All of the other sense organs had shut down completely. Her fingertips felt like so many Paper-Mate pens attached to the club of her hand, none of it flesh and blood.

But while she felt cold, she was not shivering. The drug was doing its job. Now she had to place her trust in providence. But her breath seemed gone along with her feelings, and if she had stopped breathing . . .

Chapter Twenty-four

Cornwall, Canada

"I have many misgivings, believe me," Donna Thorpe wrote on the motel letterhead where she was staying in Cornwall, Canada, awaiting word from Dr. O. It was her final line in a letter she had post-marked for Robyn Muro in care of the Department at Quantico. In the letter she spoke of her regrets about Bateman, Sykes, Joe Swisher, and everyone else this evil had touched. She also explained that she intended to die if she must, but that she would take Ovierto with her. "Just be certain to bury me with the remains of my parents," she had finished.

She called the desk and asked if there had been any messages for her. Nothing.

"Can you get me a taxi?"

"Where is it madame wishes to go?" asked the French Canadian at the other end.

"The dam?"

"Do you mean the Saunders Dam?"

"Yes, I suppose."

"*Ahhhh,* that is no problem."

Thorpe considered this a moment. "Is there another dam?"

"There are many along the seaway. Iroquois, Ingleside, Long Sault . . ."

"Which is the largest."

"Oh, Saunders, madame."

"Where is the Robert Moses dam?"

"*Ahhh,* but the Saunders dam is the Moses dam! One half Canada, one half America." His manner seemed to say she was a fool.

"That's the one."

"*Ahhhh,* that is not difficult, madame."

"Thank you, I will be ready in fifteen minutes."

"I will have a cab for you then."

"Thank you."

"You are welcome."

"Oh, and the Eisenhower Locks? Are they at the dam?"

He laughed and quickly apologized. "No, no, madame, they are on the American side. You will have to go through customs over the bridge that you may see from your window."

She glanced out at the arching, towering bridge that spanned a section of the great seaway, crossing to what was called Cornwall Island on the map she had spread before her, a Mohawk Indian Reservation that straddled Canada and the United States. The Indians went freely across the border and through customs, being residents of both countries. That was how Ovierto would get the bodies where he wanted them to go, she supposed, if he indeed actually had them. He would use well-paid Mohawks who would ask no questions.

She only wished she knew the destination. Would he bring them to the dam on the Canadian side? The American side? Or would he take them to the locks? She did not know.

She quickly freshened up her face before going out to the waiting cab. Beneath her cream-colored jacket her .38 bulged. She had loaded it with ammunition that would explode outward on impact. Her purse bulged, too, with the bogus Pythagoras papers, which were stuffed with plastique explosives.

After a brief, pleasant drive, she was soon standing on the enormous wall of the dam, staring out over the superstructure from an observation tower that wrapped completely around it. A guide pointed out that halfway across began the American side, staring back at them through observation glasses, were the Americans visiting the Robert Moses dam.

She placed a quarter into one of the machines and viewed the panoramic plain along the mammoth seaway, a restful place overlooking the calm waters below, where fishermen in boats came dangerously close to the dam's intake valves. She asked a guide to point out the locks, and she found them in the near distance, east of the dam. From here it looked like any ordinary factory, though without the accompanying waste products being thrown up by the Reynolds Aluminum plant and the GM plant over on the American side. Still, the Canadians joined in the smog-making here in Cornwall, where a complete cumulus cloud with soft white edges, made of a stifling, malodorous sulfur from the wood pulp mill, billowed thick enough to throw a large portion of the old district into shade.

She had hoped she would be contacted somewhere along her tour of the dam, and she wasn't disappointed. She turned her attention to the American side, the dirty commercial field glasses shutting down just as she saw the man on the American side staring back at her. *It was Ovierto.*

She fought to find another quarter in her purse, the papers there in her way. She finally got the machine working again and stared at the empty window opposite some two hundred or so feet in the observation tower at the Moses side of the dam. The bastard knew exactly where she was. It was up to him now.

A man near her bent over to pick up some piece of paper that seemed to materialize from his palm. He then cleared his throat and said in a thick Indian accent, "You dropped this, missy."

The man hurried off as soon as he pushed the crushed paper into her hand.

She opened it and read the message that was clearly in Ovierto's hand:

Welcome to Canada. Now, proceed to the locks, alone. Wait there until further instructions reach you.

For the first time she was truly afraid. She checked for the cyanide capsule which she need only burst with her teeth to end everything. She didn't intend to be taken alive by Ovierto, if that was his intention.

Out of the corner of her eye she thought she saw the guard on duty here staring at her, but maybe she was just getting paranoid now.

She rushed back down, taking the stairs. Too impatient to wait for a crowded elevator to arrive, she searched the expansive parking area for the taxi she'd asked to wait, but it was gone.

"Damn, damn," she muttered before rushing back inside and asking the guard on the ground floor to call a cab for her. In a rather haughty manner that made him look more like a butler than a guard1 he indicated the pay phones. She went to the book, which was less than half the size of the D.C. phone book, and she located a cab company and called.

While she waited, she found a tourist map which showed the way clearly from here to the locks. When the cab arrived, she became instantly suspicious of the driver, who was rather clean-shaven, with closely cropped hair, broad shoulders, and a white shirt stuffed into black pants. She smelled Mounted Police all over him, and she guessed it was Robyn Muro's doing, siccing these guys on her for "protection." Damn her anyway, she said to herself.

As the cab pulled out she asked to be taken to see the Indian Crafts Museum on Cornwall Island. This was halfway across the border. Here she got out and pretended interest in the jewelry and art of the Mohawks, realizing that much of the crafts were imported from other tribes, some of it as far away as New Mexico. Shortly, as she watched the driver putter about outside, getting bored and starting to come in, she located the ladies' room in the back. As she had hoped, there was a window, through which she climbed, tearing her suit in the process.

She rushed around the back stairs, dodging windows, and was in the cab before the Mountie knew he was being duped. She tore from the sand lot parking area, kicking up a cloud of dirt which the Mountie stood in, outlined in her rearview mirror. It was nearing dusk when she went through the customs gate, where she merely flashed her FBI badge and was waved through.

Thorpe followed the signs that led her from the bridge spanning the enormous St. Lawrence River. They brought her out onto Highway 34, going west toward Massena, New York, but then she was sent on a divergent route that would take her toward the

American side of the dam that she had seen from the Canadian side. But the sign also said she was on the path for the locks.

Tension mounted in her with each mile that brought her closer to the rendezvous with Ovierto. She had taken every precaution, and she believed she was ready for him. She had already made certain concessions to him, concessions he knew nothing about, such as the fact she no longer believed that there was any chance of regaining the remains of her parents. She had made that concession, and it was bound up with her certainty that Ovierto must die at any cost—any cost—including her own life.

She had made arrangements to that end.

She put a hand to her breast, her breathing coming in starts and stops. It only calmed when her fingers wrapped around the snub-nosed .38 beneath her jacket.

All around her was the brilliant blue of a lovely winter's sky. Winter birds took up chase in the branches of the denuded trees, and on each side of the winding road she saw the evidence of an area that had many lovely fishing holes. How she'd love to go fishing. Instead, she was hurtling along toward her death.

Looming ahead, cutting into the countryside like some strange underground laboratory, were the government buildings of the locks, along with the inevitable high fences. One area was turned over to an electrical station. Straight ahead there was a tunnel which went below the locks and under any ship that happened to be in the locks at the time, which surfaced on the other side. Far from there, on the winding, parklike road, the Robert Moses Dam was hidden beyond the trees.

Just short of the tunnel a sign told visitors to turn in, and she did so. The visitor's center was all parking lot and a two-story viewing stand, surrounded by fences and warning signs; below there were a hot dog/hamburger stand, a phone booth, restrooms, and a blackboard listing the incoming and outgoing ships along with their names, time of arrival, cargoes, ports of call, and registry. There were also a handful of the viewing devices she had seen at the dam. Litter from gum wrappers to cigarette packs was given wing by sudden thunderous gusts of wind. From the concrete main deck she could see far and wide, but the island on which the dam was built covered her view of the dam. She did a double take when she realized that one of the huge buildings in front of her was steadily descending and some of the windows that had been over her head were now at eye-level. Then she realized the mammoth structure looming over her, casting its monstrous shadow, was a freighter idled and silent, sitting in the cradle of the locks, being lowered to the level of the seaway by the controls being worked somewhere out of sight.

The superstructure of the great freighter, flying a Canadian flag along with several flags she did not recognize, dwarfed the viewing stand beside her. She now saw men on the ship, some of them waving to the tourists here, but most ignoring the hubbub of the locks, going quietly about their business.

She watched the process of lowering the hulking ship, finding it fascinating. The dimensions of the locks had to be enormous to take such a huge monster into its belly and either lift or lower by virtue of the water level. Now she saw the ship's name, *Bruha*. It was of Puerto Rican origin, she realized. The Canadian leaf had been hoisted to pay a quiet tribute to the Canadians along their route as they'd arrived at the locks. At the aft, an American flag flew, looking like a mainstay rather than an afterthought.

Now getting a little bored with the mechanical show, she did as the other tourists did. She found the blackboard and read about the ship before them. The *Witch,* in English, had been filled with a capacity tonnage of eighty thousand tons of coffee, but was returning now with that much in tons of manganese, iron, aluminum. Thorpe guessed that much of the cargo was actually cocaine, heroin, and other drugs camouflaged as coffee. The ship had already made stops at every major U.S. city along the route—Detroit, Toledo, Chicago, Milwaukee—as well as their Canadian counterparts.

She tried to eat something, but the smell of the burger and her knotted stomach conspired to send it to the trash bin. She returned to the viewing area, wondering if she should stay below or pay the dollar toll to go above. Where did that filthy bastard want her? Her eyes fell on the ship again, and it was astonishingly low, the "building" of before now below her feet. She looked down on the dark men who had moments earlier been looking down on her. They were burnt black from the sun, most of them donning neckerchiefs and looking like Latin swashbucklers. Despite her situation, despite her emotions, she allowed herself a moment's fantasy as she watched one thin young man who looked a bit like Errol Flynn roam the decks below her.

Separating her and everyone else from the ship was a fence that reached up over her head, perhaps eight feet high. It was littered with signs prohibiting anyone's climbing on it. On the other side there was a mere four feet to the edge, a sheer drop. From her

251

vantage point, the ship itself seemed almost to touch the wall of the locks.

Across, on the other side, a few men worked in an area that was restricted to authorized personnel only, and beyond them were the administrative offices which housed the main controls. She was beginning to wonder again what Ovierto was up to, bringing her to this strange place merely to make a drop and exchange. The men working the other side busied themselves now with detaching lines, for the Puerto Rican ship had revved its engines and a large metal gate at the east end of the locks opened for the ship to pass through safely toward the sea hundreds of miles away.

The entire time that the gargantuan ship with its ugly rusted hull had sat in the locks it was helpless, held in check by the lock master at his controls. It was the kind of power that would appeal to the good doctor, like a fast and sharp little sparrow frightening off a giant condor, or holding it in check before its nest.

"Yes, I can see why this place would appeal to you, Ovierto," she said to herself, but an aged man in a guard's uniform, who had been wandering about, startled her when he suddenly said beside her, "What's that, miss?"

For an instant she thought it was one of Ovierto's gophers, if not Ovierto himself. But she calmed when she saw the condition of his teeth, the sunken gums, and the warm blue eyes. "Oh, nothing," she said, "just sort of—"

"Talking to yourself?"

"Yeah, silly, huh?"

"I saw you come up alone. I'm alone myself. When you're alone, who else you goin' to talk to but

252

yourself, huh?" He laughed lightly. "Been a lovely day, and sunset is going to be a nice one. Lovely weather we have up this way. You're not from around here, are you? Didn't think so. The way you dress . . . look 'round at most the visitors here. You can see who's from just around here and who's not, just the way they dress."

"You see anyone else today that looked *different?*"

"Nothing to write home about, no. Well, best tend to my duties."

She nodded and smiled, watching him amble away. But she caught up to him and said, "Sir, would you look very closely across at those men working on the other side of the locks."

"What about 'em?"

"Do you recognize them?"

"Sure."

"I mean, you know *all* of them?"

"McClosky, Walford and Ames Kensington . . . what of it?"

"Are you sure. Take a close look."

"Who are you?" he asked.

"Just a visitor, but I'm supposed to meet someone here and I thought it might be one of those men."

"Hmmmmph." He had tired of her and rushed away. She went back to dawdle at the stand, going up to the second story. Everyone was watching a ship approaching from the other direction, which was about to enter the locks.

253

Chapter Twenty-five

Dr. Maurice Ovierto had taken every precaution, and it did appear that finally he would have Inspector Thorpe within his reach; even more importantly, he would have Pythagoras. With Pythagoras and the power it represented he could one day rule the government. It was that simple.

But he still held a soft spot in his heart for Thorpe, the last of her line, a line he had vowed to see an end to. He'd miss her when she was gone, and he wondered how he would get on without her. But she was getting to be a bit annoying as well.

He would wait until dark at the locks for the arrival of the *Carpathia*—a huge freighter from Britain, trading in iron ore, on its way up to the steel mills of Michigan and Illinois. As the mammoth ship entered and came through the locks, he would conduct his business with Inspector Thorpe. His plans for her amounted to a night's debauchery. She was, after all, quite a beautiful woman, and he was, after all, quite a man.

He had spent countless hours fantasizing about the moments they would one day share, what he would do to her and with her, and how he would drag out her suffering. He had imagined her whine, her plea, her begging for death and mercy. He had imagined the feel of her flesh under his nails—finally under his scalpel. He had even imagined drinking her blood before her eyes.

The fun would start when, before her eyes, he destroyed forever any chance she might have of regaining the bones of her father and mother.

He had paid his porters well to get her this far, and he had kept it anonymous. No one knew what was going on here except Thorpe and him.

He looked over his shoulder at the men who were removing the cold storage crate from their pickup to his van, now shoving it all the way up into his truck.

"This kinda crate don't stay cold long, man," said one of the swarthy, heavyset Mohawks to him. "Whatever you got on ice, you'd better find a freezer soon."

"Never you worry your mind about that. You just worry where you and your friends are going to spend all this." He handed them the second half of their well-earned cash. "You're sure there were no questions at the border crossing?"

"You kidding? We didn't even slow down, man. They know not to mess with Mohawks on our own land, man."

"That's what I thought. And no one followed from Canada?"

"Not a soul. Whatchu so worried for, man? Whatchu got in that thing?"

"No questions asked, remember? That was the deal."

"Sure, sure . . . whatever you want, Mr. Samson."

"Come on!" the others were shouting for their leader. But he was concerned about the future. "Anything you need again, we're here, Mr. Samson. You know how to get in touch."

"Well, there is one thing more you can do—alone, however."

"Alone?"

"Come with me. You will be paid well."

"Sure . . . sure." He returned to the others, and one argued that he'd like to come along, too, but this one made him silent and in a moment, Ovierto and the Indian were on their way toward the locks. Sunset had come on and the night shift at the locks would come on, too, now. Ovierto had already been here at the changing of the guard and he had observed that most of the men working the locks congregated in one building during this time, changing into rubber boots and gear.

The *Carpathia* was chugging toward the locks as Ovierto's van arrived, going to the workman's side of the locks, a place off-limits to the tourists just across the concrete canal of the locks. He tried to imagine which of the dark figures at the observation deck was Donna Thorpe.

"We must hurry," he told the big Indian, who was perhaps in his midthirties, though with such a thick baby face it was hard to say.

"You can't come into the grounds like this, man. They'll have the law after you."

"Don't worry, just do as you're told. Stay here. I'll need you to help me lift this thing when the time comes."

"Whatchu got inside here, man?"

"Damnit, Indian! No fucking questions."

"I don't like jail time, man!"

"Do as you're told and I can promise you no jail." He stuffed several more hundred dollar bills into the Indian's flannel coat.

"All right, but this don't make sense."

"It doesn't have to make sense, damnit. Just follow my instructions."

The man the Indian knew as Samson was gone, and he sat in the rear of the van with the box, which was quickly thawing out in the surrounding sixty-degree temperature. He wondered again what was inside. But for now, he watched the man called Samson go straight to the administrative offices, flashing a badge.

"Damn, he's a cop of some sort."

He began to wonder if he and his friends hadn't just crossed the border with narcotics. He wondered if it had something to do with the lumbering freighter just coming into the arms of the lock. He looked again at Samson, who now seemed to be alone in the office, and it made him wonder about the old man inside. What had happened to him?

Samson rushed toward the other building where the oncoming shift was about to exit. Samson yelled something at them and rushed them all back inside, again flashing a badge. He must have a lot of juice, the Indian decided, as he watched Samson exit the building alone. He thought he saw some strange fog around him like a halo as he opened and closed the door, but now it was gone.

Then the Indian heard a noise coming from the box, a soft, croon that was either animal or human. It made the Indian start and jump from the van, but he was suddenly grabbed by Samson who held a gun to his head. "Help me with the box, now!"

"Sure, sure, but—"

"Shut up and put your back into it."

"All right . . . all right. I didn't see anything, man. I didn't hear anything." The Indian figured it was a police sting, that Samson wanted the box on the ship, and that he had a partner inside. That made some kind of sense out of what at first seemed meaningless.

They carted the cold storage box over to the rail, where the ship was now coming closer, her engines completely cut. The locks had been placed on an automatic sequence. At the moment, the *Carpathia* loomed above them like a monster against the night sky.

No one could see them from the other side, nor could they see anyone on the observation deck. Ovierto thought it perfect for his plans.

He gave a signal to the lock master, the old man now back at his controls. The water in the lock was rushing from beneath the underside of the ship, bringing it slowly, ever so slowly down and down towards them.

Ovierto was taking his goddamned time, Thorpe was beginning to think, when she saw the van move in opposite the viewing stand, just before the large ship entered the long corridor of the locks before her. She watched the man in the van get out after some hesitation and go to the lock master, but her vision was suddenly blocked by the incoming ship. She rushed from the second-story tower to the main observing area, pushing past tourists and visitors. There were signs all along the rail warning her to stand back and not to cross the fence under any circumstances, but if she were to outsmart Ovierto, she knew she'd have to break more than a few rules.

Donna Thorpe rushed through a door in the chain link fence that held the crowd back. People all around gasped at her actions. She paid them no heed, trying to determine how best to get aboard the ship which, for the moment, loomed above her like the Empire State Building. She went the length of the ship, looking for a way aboard. Some member of the crew saw her out a porthole, and he opened a door, waving her off and pleading with her to get back, that what she was doing amounted to suicide.

She raised her badge and hoped he could see it in the dark over the distance. There was an enormous gap between the huge hull of the ship and the cornerstone she stood on.

The crewman put up the palms of his hands to indicate that she should be patient. He then signaled that the ship would soon be moving downward, at which time she might have a chance of getting aboard. He must have excellent eyesight, she decided.

Then the ship began to almost imperceptibly glide downward. Had there been no horizontal lines on the ship, she would not have known it was descending. Somewhere on the other side, on land, Ovierto was preparing for her, but he was expecting her to be where he had last seen her, in the stands, waiting patiently for a message so that she might dutifully follow his dictates now.

She chose instead to surprise the bastard. It wasn't in her nature to sit idly by and let a madman dictate to her. She had come this far under his direction, but the final act would be hers. She felt for the plastique she had taped in the package. All she need do is fire into it when he was near and they would both be dead, hunter and hunted, sent off to eternity in a bloody embrace.

The ship nudged downward . . . downward. On

board, the crewman who had watched her so carefully opened a hatchway and let a ladder fall forward. It jutted out from the ship, braced there, waiting for the ship to lower to her level, all out of sight of Ovierto's prying eyes.

"It's coming due, Ovierto . . . coming due," she muttered to herself, waiting, trying desperately to hold onto a shred of patience.

"Get ready," said the sailor, who seemed fascinated by her now. He had a British accent, and the idea of her jumping into his arms, aboard his ship, had seemed to grip him with a romantic fervor. Too long on shipboard, she imagined; he thought she was some local woman who had gone out of her mind with loneliness in this isolated, cold, northern region. "I'll catch you," he promised.

She looked down to what seemed an abyss.

"Don't look down," he argued.

The aged guard was coming down the chain link fence toward her, agitated, shouting and wildly shaking his hands. The man was out of his element on this side of the fence, and he almost slipped and fell.

"Jump!" said the man on shipboard.

She backed to the fence where some spectator grabbed her, holding her there for the guard. She pulled and tore away, leaving her jacket, exposing the gun. She ran forward and leaped, catching the last rung of the ladder, dangling over the churning water at the huge keel, imagining the whirlpool below her, imagining her body being sucked down into the huge turbines below the water. But she held on, and in an instant she felt a hand grab onto hers.

Donna Thorpe felt the power of the man as he lifted her from the rungs of the metal ladder. She'd hurt herself in the jump, and she felt the warmth of her blood trickling down her left leg, but she ignored this. She came face to face with the man who had helped her, her eyes asking why when suddenly his brute strength was turned against her, twisting her and taking control of her gun.

"You don't understand," she shouted, "I'm FBI, Inspector—"

"Thorpe, yes, I know."

"Who the hell are you?"

"A friend of Ovierto. Damn you! Damn this . . . changes everything. Oh, Christ. No one expected you to board the ship. All you were supposed to do was drop the package." He held her with one hand while he tore through her purse, ripping out what he wanted.

"You'll never get away with this."

"Who's to stop us?"

"Ovierto will kill you before it's over. He's too greedy to—"

"I know what Ovierto is and I know how badly he wants you."

"Who are you?"

"Just another merchant marine."

"Where do you know Ovierto from?"

"Houston. Spent some time in jail with him. Smooth the way he escaped, cutting that guard's throat with his teeth! Now, it's your turn, pretty lady. Too bad, really."

"All right, you've got what you want. Now what?"

"Come on, out on deck where he can see you."

"You actually trust him to cut you in on the deal for the most powerful tool on the face of the Earth?"

"Don't worry about my ass, Fed lady."

He pushed her along the corridor of the ship. One man came out of a hatchway and he hit him so hard with the pistol that he was knocked unconscious.

"How do you hope to escape from here, inside the locks?" she asked.

"All taken care of. Nothing for you to concern yourself with. Now shut up and move. Up, up!"

She was on the ladder ascending to the deck above.

"Higher, go on," he ordered.

"Isn't there anything you want from me before . . . before he gets his hands on me?" she asked in her most sultry voice.

"Huh? Hmmmph!" he laughed slightly. "Guess it wouldn't hurt to take a bite of his apple. He wants you badly, you know, very badly."

"What about you?" She dangled her long leg in his face. Blood stained her slacks and this seemed to excite him further.

"My bunks on the next level. Hold up there," he said. "Guess Ovierto can wait a little longer."

"Good . . . good. You're so strong," she told him as he came up, holding the gun firmly on her. "Which way?" she asked.

He indicated the doorway, a metal hatch through which she had to duck. He shoved her and she fell against the bare bunk inside. Ha was immediately at her, tearing at her clothes, the gun held against her cheek.

"Let me kiss you," she said in his ear. "I want my tongue in your mouth. Now, now!"

He eased the gun away and had shoved his tongue deep within her when he realized that something had fired into his throat, as if a cap had come off her teeth and he'd nearly swallowed it. He caught the capsule in his teeth and she suddenly rammed his jaw and head together, causing him to crush the cyanide between his teeth. His eyes wide, he tried to lift the gun, but the fact that poison was nearly instantaneous, combined with his surprise, rendered him incapable of lifting the weapon to fire. He fell over her, dead. She shoved him away, grabbing the gun and snatching the Pythagoras package from beneath him.

Now she'd find the top deck on her own steam and in control.

Chapter Twenty-six

Robyn Muro had come to her senses but was not fully capable of using her hands and fingers. She tried to wrap them around the flashlight, to check her watch, a process that seemed to take an eternity. She whispered to Riley beside her, but there was no response from him. She began to fear for Paul. She tried rousting him but when she did so, she heard noises from outside the cold box. It was scraping, tearing along the bottom. They were being hoisted out the back of a truck of some sort, she guessed. The time was 7:06 P.M., and suddenly the box was dropped hard on a hard surface.

Outside noises were odd and indistinguishable. She thought she heard the sound of rushing, foaming water, and then it was just lapping water. Over this came the groan of mechanical engines and an occasional human voice in the distance. Someone somewhere had been shouting, but no more.

She wondered where Donna was at this moment. The cold inside the box was beginning to affect her badly now, and she couldn't stop shaking. "Riley, Riley," she whispered, and she pushed at the dead weight against her, but for the moment, at least, it seemed useless.

The shakes were taking hold badly. She felt for the covered needle at her side which would send her back into a state of unfeeling. She dreaded the thought, and feared a second injection. Is that what had happened to Riley? Had he gone to a second injection? And if so, had it been too much for his body and mind to sustain? Had the Benz crap killed Paul Riley? Did she dare inject herself again? She recalled the horror of the loneliness it had created in her, the fearful thoughts that had bordered on hallucinations. At least now she knew there were people just on the other side of the crate, and even the slimy, cold feelings of lying in the damp, frigid water that had condensed inside the storage box were at least feelings. Better than the opposite. Better to freeze to death than to die without feeling, she told herself.

But the frustration was overwhelming, and she wanted to start kicking and screaming and shouting for someone—*anyone*—to pull her free from this hell. Anyone, that is, but Dr. Maurice Ovierto.

So she held on and held on and held on, talking in a whisper to Riley, putting her own numb hand on his, holding it and squeezing in an attempt to regain the feeling in her own hand, but also to reassure him that she was there and that he wasn't alone.

Then she heard *him*—Ovierto. His weight was suddenly on top of the box and he was saying something nearly unintelligible to someone out there. It sounded like they were talking about fish . . . fishing . . . fishing in the area. Then Ovierto suddenly shouted to someone in the distance.

"Stop it there! Hold to this level!"

Hold to what level? Level of what? she asked herself. The letter told Donna to make her way to the locks on the St. Lawrence Seaway. Were they here now? Was Ovierto somehow in charge of the locks? Using a disguise, using Bateman's FBI badge, it was possible.

She tried to think clearly, to work out in her mind exactly why Ovierto had brought Donna here. Below the locks, giant turbines would be sucking in tons of water.

Then it dawned on Robyn, and she realized that doubling for Donna's mother in the frigid coffin was far more dangerous than she'd at first thought. Ovierto intended to send the racked bones of the Thorpes to the bottom of the locks, to be forever lost to the churning waters here as a final defilement of the bodies, all to crush Donna.

Robyn realized that she and Riley could be killed at any moment, no one ever knowing they were inside the crate. She began shoving Riley harder and harder, making too much noise. She then located her gun and grasped it before she realized that since it was solidly frozen and had also been swimming in a pool of water, it might not fire properly. She rubbed the weapon into her body, doing what she could to warm it. She finally tore off the wetsuit gloves and grasped it in both hands. The frozen metal glued itself instantly to her palms.

Then she remembered the crowbar. It, too, would be frozen to the touch. She painfully pried the gun from her skin, couching it in her crotch, and began the search for Riley's crowbar. It must be the other side of him. She rose, and the gun slid into the puddle beside her. From inside the noise seemed enough to raise the dead, but it got no response from Riley, nor the men outside the box.

She fished with her hands, the burning of her palms a constant now, reminding her how one simple slip could end all her pain.

"What was that?" asked someone outside the box, a voice other than the one she was certain had to be Ovierto. Ovierto's voice was tinged with an acidic, crackling sound like an unhealthy motor at the back of his throat constantly trying to ignite.

"Nothing, shut up, kid!" Ovierto replied. "Just get ready to dump over the contents of that crate when I tell you to, and make sure the contents go into the locks."

She knew Ovierto. She knew he had done his research, and that while there'd be filters on the turbines at the bottom of the locks, they'd have holes in them large enough for a human being to be sucked down and pushed out. To recover hers and Riley's remains the entire system would have to be shut down and drained. It was likely the fate he had in mind for Thorpe, too.

She had to do something . . . had to do it soon. But what? And how?

Her gloved fingertips reached the crowbar just as she realized, draped over Riley, that the life had gone from her sleeping partner. The chill in the box became so much colder. Using the light, she saw that he had indeed gone to a second injection. She checked a thermometer needlessly confirming that the temperature inside here was hovering at the freezing point. The seaway water had to be warmer. Poor Riley . . .

"Whataya' got in the box, boss?" she heard the

younger voice overhead, and it made her douse the light.

"You ever hear of casting ashes over the water?"

"Like cremated people, you mean? Sure."

"That's kinda what we've got to do here, kid."

"That ain't no ashes inside there, though. Less you got a regiment of dead men in there all cremated."

"Where is that bitch?" shouted Ovierto.

Robyn's shivering was increasing. The wet suit was not helping much. She worried that soon she'd be uncontrollably kicking the sides of the box, but she dared not take another injection of Boas's nasty concoction.

She tried to concentrate on the sounds from above and to tighten her grip on the crowbar. It went silent above for a moment, and this silence stretched to a while and then to several minutes. She wondered if she dared try her hand at the crowbar. How much noise would it make? Would it alert Ovierto to her presence?

God, she felt alone.

As far as Dr. O was concerned, everything was going as planned, save for one small matter. Where was Thorpe? He could not find her in the gallery of people on the other side as the ship came to the level of the platform of concrete he stood upon. He had heard some disturbance, some crowd noises, but she was nowhere to be seen. And where the hell was Templeton, his contact on board the ship? The one who would go between Ovierto and Thorpe with the goods, bringing Pythagoras to Ovierto's hands? He smelled something in the air that told him things were not right.

He searched through field glasses for any sign of Thorpe. Had she slinked away? Backed out? There were a handful of deck hands milling about on board the ship, some waving at the people in the gallery who watched the ship stop in its descent. Then he saw one of the black-coated crew members coming directly toward him, holding up a package. It was Templeton; the fool had already made contact with Thorpe.

Then he saw that he was not large enough about the shoulders to be Templeton, and he realized it was Donna Thorpe.

"Ready that crate, Indian! Now!" he shouted.

. The heavyset young Indian man was confused suddenly when he found the lid was loose, pried open from the inside. He backed away from the crate, his hands shaking, saying, "You got people inside here! You had us smuggle people into the States, man! Are you crazy?"

"Dump it upright like I told you!"

"Not me, man! I'm through here, through."

Ovierto let him turn before he let fly with a knife that struck the Indian between the shoulder blades and sent him to his knees, where his body hesitated a moment before completely toppling over.

Ovierto then got behind the crate and placed a foot on it, sending it to its side, the top creaking open, water spilling out.

"Hold it, Ovierto!" shouted Donna Thorpe from where she stood on the ship, her gun trained on him.

"The papers, dear, or mommy dearest and daddy

269

dearest are gone, forever lost in the bowels of this place. Do you understand me?" His voice was like knives over stone.

"You go right ahead. So long as you're dead, I'd gladly sacrifice that box of bones."

"You're lying. If you think I'm bluffing . . ."

He tilted the crate forward at a dangerous angle before the locks. The crate would fall between the lock walls and the ship. "Now, just toss over what you have brought me and I'll spare this collection that is so sacred to you."

Donna had him in her sights and was about to pull the trigger when she saw Riley's hand spill from the crate. The flesh was bloated, blue and cold. He was obviously dead, whoever he was, just another of Ovierto's victims. The crate tilted still further and she saw Riley's head, shoulders and torso slide down the stone wall.

"Damnit, no!" she screamed.

Ovierto had not bothered to watch; his eyes were pinned on his prey on board the ship. Across the way, the spectators were aghast at what they were witness to. Some ran for their cars.

"The papers, now! Or the other one goes!"

Donna then saw Robyn Muro carefully feeling her way to the stone edge of the locks, searching for a foothold, her hands making only stiff progress.

"All right, all right!" shouted Donna, trying to buy Robyn some time. "I'm ready to deal."

"That's more like it, my dear," said Ovierto. "I knew you could be reasonable. Throw it over, now!"

Donna hesitated, to make it look good. She knew that the moment he got what he wanted the entire crate and its contents were headed for the deep. Already, the churning waters had claimed Riley's body. "All right, all right," she repeated as she moved closer to the edge. She did a ballplayer's wind up with the dummy package, knowing that she'd have to make her move as soon as the package was airborne. She sent it across just as Robyn found some long spikes in the concrete wall to hold onto, her gun clenched tightly in her teeth. She was wearing a wet suit, and now Donna understood how she had gotten here. It was a foolish attempt that might yet end in her death.

As soon as the package was sailing through the air, Donna braced to fire. Already a bullet from Ovierto pinged into the bulkhead beside her. Someone aboard the ship, in a white woolen sweater, perhaps the Captain, fired a blistering shot from a portal alongside Donna. The bullet slammed into Ovierto, knocking him down. Donna's own shot caught Ovierto's prostrate form in the left arm. Ovierto fired again, killing the man in the white sweater. He then scurried behind the crate, grabbing up the package hurled to him by Donna Thorpe.

"Eat it, you bastard," Donna said to herself, preparing to detonate the plastique Ovierto was holding, but she saw that Robyn was too close. The blast would kill her.

The hesitation was long enough for Ovierto to discover that he had been duped. He howled and threw the package back at Thorpe. It sailed out over the bow and exploded when she fired. At the same instant he stood and kicked out at the crate, sending it over the side; the thing grazed Robyn and almost sent her down.

Thorpe fired again, striking Ovierto in the chest, but it was obvious he was wearing a bulletproof vest. He ran for the lock master's office, shouting for the man to drop the level of the water as fast as possible.

Thorpe drew a bead on him, trying to hit him in the back of the head. She must have come within a hair's breath, and he ducked to the ground as the ship began to descend below ground level.

"That man's a killer, a mass murderer!" Donna shouted to the men on the ship. Get me across! Get me across!"

"We are without power! We can use no engines in the locks," said one man.

"We send a rope over!" suggested one man.

"It's no good. We are going down. Any rope we let out will just be extended and extended. You can't make it."

"The hell I can't! Get the rope out."

"It's madness!"

She lifted her .38 to the man's eyes. "Do it, now!"

As soon as the rope was secured, Donna started across, hand over hand. As she moved closer to the edge, she watched Robyn, who was pulling herself up over the edge. "Be careful!" she shouted to her. "He's wearing a vest!"

She saw Robyn pull herself up and roll onto the concrete floor. The ship's masts were now descending behind Donna, farther and farther away, and the rope she was climbing had gone taut. It was thick and as hard as stone, cutting her hands as she worked her weight along, her arms straining, her muscles threatening to give out.

Robyn disappeared ahead of her. Donna called to

her to wait, but she pushed on, going for the madman. If she could only catch up, they could ensnare the bastard between them and riddle his head with bullets. The thought kept her going, straining against the odds. Behind her she heard the cheers of the men aboard the *Carpathia,* their dead captain at their feet.

"I'm going to get that bastard or die trying," she swore to herself once again.

Chapter Twenty-seven

Robyn Muro was shaky, but now she gripped the gun and held it steady, searching the black, empty spaces of a surreal landscape filled with strange objects, from ventilator shafts that formed giant circles to storage and electrical containers, pulleys, and levers. Inside the administrator's office, the lock master's throat had been slashed where he sat behind the controls. Doing just what Ovierto requested, following his every instruction to the letter, hadn't saved the man from a horrible fate. The body count at the seaway locks was now up to four, counting the man on the ship. Robyn thought for a moment about Riley, wondering if he had family back in D.C., but she had to keep her attention on the silence all around her. Somewhere in the maze of the buildings here lurked the worst killer she had ever faced.

Ovierto was thorough and cunning. He had thought of everything. He had seen blueprints of this place and knew it inside and out. She, on the other hand, didn't know where she was in relation to the outside, nor where to start.

He had cut the lines to the lights. He must be hiding here somewhere. She then heard a door, a large, industrial door, whining with a gust of air as it closed. She raced through a myriad of pipes and conduits and noise and steam. She slammed into the wall beside the door. The fact that she'd made it alive to this point meant the bastard was on the outside again. She slowly opened the whining door, knowing it could be a trap that could ensnare her as quickly as a hammer blow.

She had last seen Donna two-thirds of the way across the rope she was taking over the chasm of the locks. But now, as she came through the door with great caution, she saw Donna again, on her feet, coming towards the back of the building, right at her, and between them there was Ovierto. Donna opened fire at the same instant that Robyn did, Robyn realizing too late, as bullets rained around her, that they were both backdrops for a mirrored, holographic image of Ovierto. Robyn caught one in the shoulder and fell to the concrete, cutting her chin as she did so.

The image remained between them, but Robyn could see through the image to where Donna was slumped to her knees.

"It's not him!" she screamed as Donna looked up at her, blood rushing up over her lips.

Donna was hit. Hit badly by one of Robyn's bullets. Robyn rushed to Donna and took her in her arms.

"Careful, he's still nearby," she croaked, making Robyn search the darkness all around them when she saw a van back from the parking lot and screech away.

"Don't let him get away," said Donna, coughing.

"I can't leave you."

"Get him!"

"You're parents, Donna . . . we have them safe."

"Bury me alongside them . . ."

"Donna!"

". . . in an unmarked grave . . . if Ovierto gets away . . ."

Donna slumped over, her eyes rolling back in her head. Robyn felt the life lift away from her. "Oh, God, oh, Donna, Donna!"

She watched the van in the distance disappearing towards the Robert Moses Dam. She looked around, placed Donna gently down and rushed back to where the lock master's body remained in his chair. There she searched a wall of keys for a vehicle key, finding them numbered. She rushed out to the workman's yard, running into the guard who had tried to stop Donna Thorpe on the other side. He had driven under the bridge below the seaway to get here.

"Whoever that guy is, he's trapped now," said the guard. "There's no way out from that end. It's an island and the dam, and that's it."

"The dam goes across to Canada, though."

"Yeah, but he couldn't . . . wouldn't attempt to . . ."

She raced for the light truck with the number corresponding to the key, jumped in and sped out of the lot, streaking the road with rubber. She pushed it to the floor. Ovierto had a plan of escape, that was certain, and it involved the dam. Had anyone ever attempted crossing the border via the dam? It fit with his grandiose notion of himself. As far as she was concerned, it was a grand place for the bastard to die.

Ahead, in the distance, the dam was lit only by the glow of the orange sodium-vapor lights of the empty parking lot. She saw only the van that

276

Ovierto had used, pulled up just outside the main door. An alarm was blaring nonstop, like a hungry child. She saw a dead guard the other side of the broken glass.

The dam was officially closed to the public. It had come down to her alone against the most awful evil she had ever known.

"For Donna and for Joe," she told herself as she stepped through the broken glass, searching for a way to the dam itself. The place hummed with electricity and there were lights on one floor where the control room was in full operation. Several men were milling about three walls of dials and lights. Huge-faced clocks, set for each time zone, stared down at them. There was a glass partition for the viewing public to watch these men at what appeared to be very boring work. They seemed oblivious to the alarm downstairs or the fact the building had been penetrated by Ovierto and the cop who would destroy him. Apparently alarms went off here frequently.

She searched for and located a floor map. Above her was the observation tower and the only public access to viewing the dam proper. She had no idea how Ovierto intended to get out onto the dam in the dark and make his way across to Canada, but she now knew how she would do it. She'd have to go up to the top floor, four up. Perhaps from above, if she could locate him, she could draw a bead on him and bring him down.

She first found a door that took her into the control room of the dam; the men there were immediately upset by her presence.

"Just call the Canadian authorities. Tell them you have a man on the dam, armed and very dangerous,

277

trying to escape police here to enter their country! Do it, now!"

She knew the Mounties. They would be real pissed off to learn about anyone's trying to use the dam in such a fashion, and they wouldn't hesitate to use their sidearms. But she hoped to get him first. She started away.

"Wait, where are you going?"

"After him!"

The man let her go, trailing behind her up to the observation tower. He unlocked the doors that took her out on a walkway above the dam. She could see the lights of Cornwall on the other side of the seaway, here wide and unencumbered by islands such as that which had made the locks here possible. "I don't see anyone down there."

The spine of the dam here was flat and wide and as long as an airstrip, and every object on its surface looked momentarily like Ovierto, but was not. "Where is he?" she cried as she stared down at the row of giant turbines that kept the enormous generators rolling, sending up a noise from the water like thunder. She imagined how at peace she would be to see Ovierto's body descend into one of those turbines to be chewed to pieces. She realized just how much hate the man had created in her. She realized now how Donna Thorpe had felt for years, how she could use Joe and anyone else she could to get at this creep.

"Try the glasses," said the man beside her, placing a quarter into the viewer. It magnified everything, but for some time she could not see anyone on the dam, only a huge, silent derrick.

"Man's a fool to try to get across that if he doesn't know what he's doing," said the dam expert.

278

"This man is quite mad. He's a murderer."

She located him in the glasses. "There, there he is."

She stepped away from the viewer and prepared to aim her .38 when she heard the rush of wind preceding a helicopter that suddenly moved in as if from nowhere. "Is that a police chopper?" she asked.

"I can't tell," was the response. "Don't see any markings."

"No, no! It's coming in for Ovierto. Damn, damn! He arranged for a thorough escape, timed to the moment. Damn!"

"Could be a Canadian chopper."

"No, too fast." She aimed once more at the speck that was Ovierto. She concentrated as if she were back on the firing range in Chicago. She fired a single shot as the man beside her watched through the viewer.

"Damn, you hit him!" the man shouted.

"Did he stay down?"

"So far, yes."

"Keep him in view."

"What're you going to do?"

The viewing machine rattled, signaling that time was spent on it. "Damn, need a quarter?" said the man, who searched his pockets, having long since lost his calm. He located one and the machine was put instantly back into operation. "Is he still down? Is he down?" she pleaded.

"No . . . no . . . leastways, I can't see him."

"Damnit! The man has nine lives."

"There, he's about ten yards further along."

"Out of range. How can we get down there? What's the fastest way?"

"Follow me."

They hurried to a service door through which they located an elevator that would take them to the surface of the dam. The seconds seemed to stretch on for an eternity while the elevator dropped down and down, and she feared with each passing moment that the deadly O would make his escape.

The doors opened and she told the workman with the tense eyes and the hard hat that she'd take it from here alone.

"It's dangerous unless you know the route," he told her.

She pushed on anyway.

Behind her he continued to follow, saying that, "You'll waste valuable time if you don't follow me."

"The man I'm after will kill you at the blink of an eye," she shouted at him. "Do you want that?"

He stopped cold, gulped and said, "No, no . . . but you need my help."

"All right, but the moment I say down, drop!"

"Good enough."

He led her around the intricate metal and stone maze of the working dam over which they stood. This was no place for visitors, she realized when she had to leap across an open air vent at the bottom of which churned the waters below the dam. The noise of the turbines here was deafening, and they had to use hand signals to communicate. All the while the workman was watching her step, Robyn Muro was watching for Ovierto.

She saw the helicopter hovering above the very center of the dam. It had lowered a rope ladder, and it was a hundred yards from her, perhaps more.

Gunshots rang out, sending Robyn to the concrete floor of the dam. The gravelly surface was rough against her cheek. At the same instant she heard the workman scream and saw that he'd lost his footing, going over the side, into one of the enormous, gaping turbines. She crawled to where she saw him go over and found him hanging by both hands there.

She reached down, holding firm to him, but she wasn't strong enough to pull him up. He swung a leg over the edge and they toppled together, panting.

Robyn looked to see the helicopter lifting upward, Ovierto holding tightly to the rope ladder below, making his way up and up toward the bubble of the machine.

"He's getting away!" she shouted, rushing headlong toward the chopper.

"Be careful!" the man behind her cautioned.

She got into a position on the opposite side of a massive pillar, the chopper and Ovierto clearly in view, but the distance between them increasing with each second. She aimed for Ovierto, whose form was spinning in the wind. Her shot missed. The helicopter was moving off now at a rapid rate. She aimed for the chopper's blade, specifically the rotor at the base of the blades where she knew that there were any number of moving parts the destruction of which could cause it to go down. She fired successive shots at the rotor and watched one after another ping off the blade shaft. She emptied what was left of her bullets into the shaft.

But the helicopter kept moving off, and her last few rounds hadn't a chance of hitting the mark. She slumped into a heap, all her emotions flooding in on her as she watched the blood-thirsty maniac pull himself into the cab, the chopper way out over the St. Lawrence now, going due west. She buried her head in her hands.

Chapter Twenty-eight

"Get me the hell out of here!" a bleeding Ovierto shouted to the pilot of the aircraft. He'd been hit in the arm by Thorpe and in the leg by Robyn Muro's bullet. His ingenious hologram was meant to catch the two of them in a crossfire, to end the careers of both Thorpe and Muro, whom he had recently begun to learn more about. He had no way of knowing for certain, but from appearances, Donna Thorpe was killed due to his last sleight-of-hand, but Muro had survived.

It had taken him some time, during the race from the locks to here, to figure out just how Muro had gotten there, that she had been in the crate all along, somehow surviving the cold. The two women had deceived him and he had deceived them.

One day he would live to see Muro killed, but not like Thorpe. With Muro he'd take his time. Abduct her . . . give it a few days, maybe a week or more to watch her die slowly. He'd think of something fitting to repay the pain she had inflicted on him.

His leg would be stiff for a month or more. He'd have a lingering limp, he decided when he cut the pantsleg open with a knife and saw that the entrance of the wound had been in his kneecap, the bullet exiting just above the pit behind the knee. A limp would mark him, limit his disguises, and he hated the idea of being maimed by a woman.

He silently cursed Robyn Muro and vowed to one day get more than even with her.

She had continued to fire at him while he was dangling in the air like a fucking carnival target, and then she had opted for the chopper, scaring the hell out of the pilot who loped off at such a speed he almost sent Ovierto to the seaway below. But now he had his machine under control—or did he?

The whirlybird began a drunken dance in the air. "What's happening? What's wrong?"

"They must've put one in the rotor shaft, damaged the equilibrium between the blades, Dr. Samson."

"Can you compensate for it?"

"I . . . I don't think so, sir."

"We're going down?"

"Better buckle up, sir."

"We're going down?"

"Yes."

Ovierto had to think fast. The pilot knew his intended destination, the location of his jet. If he should survive the crash, the pilot could talk.

"You're absolutely sure there's no getting us to Long Sault Airport?"

"None . . . not any chance."

They were losing altitude and gyrating in lazy loops, still in the area of the dam, no doubt giving Robyn Muro great pleasure. He thought he saw her jumping up and down atop the dam, but no, just his imagination. It was too far to make her out, but she could see them spiraling down and down toward the trees, the pilot trying to soft-land the thing in the five-foot-high prairie grass banking the wide river.

"At least get us closer to the goddamned Canadian side!" shouted a hurt, frustrated Dr. O, his leg bloody red now, the pain pumping from the wound.

"I'll do what I can," said the pilot, trying desperately to control the uncontrollable. "We're going to hit . . . going to hit!"

Just as the helicopter was coming down into a bay, Ovierto whipped out his bowie knife and reached across the pilot's throat, drawing a deep gash from side to side, turning his shout into a gurgling, sputtering sound like the one his machine was making. The impact of the machine against the water shook the entire bubble, and a tree branch crashed through the glass within inches of Ovierto's eyes. Water was filling the cab. He fought against his seat belt and the weight of the dead pilot over him. He saw the water rising up along the dash, sucking the machine down and down.

"I won't die this way!" he cried out. "I won't die this way!"

The water took him down with the helicopter, the fallen tree following at the end. Beneath the water he struggled to get free, a powerful current pushing him back and down. He cut the restraining belt that held the pilot and kicked madly out at the body, and this effort also sent him out the side and into the current that tumbled him over and over, sucking him like a toy into the maw of the mighty St. Lawrence.

He wondered if he would die here like this,

feeling a great weakness overtaking him.

He fought the desire to simply give in to the power of the water.

But then he remembered Pythagoras and Muro and he wanted to live. . . .

Robyn Muro and the single workman on the dam watched the helicopter spiral into the trees in the distance, and it caused a cheer in them that resounded off the dam. She and the workman made their way carefully back to the safety of the building, which was now abuzz with police who had infiltrated from the lot outside. She shouted that she was a police officer and she flashed her badge. She was still in her wet suit, and they had some difficulty believing her at first.

"We've got to get to the Canadian side about two miles down. A very desperate criminal, a murderer . . . just went into the water in a downed helicopter."

Some of them had watched as the "crazy" pilot had "deliberately" swung into those trees.

"Get me over there, now!"

Even with sirens blaring and going at top speed, it was a good hour up to the bridge, over and down two miles on the other side of the St. Lawrence. Robyn had the local police call ahead to the Canadians, giving them a location fix on the "suspect."

Most of them were relaxed. No one could have survived such a crash, they said, but Robyn knew better; she knew that there was something almost superhuman about Ovierto. He would not readily go to his death, not even plunging toward it in a helicopter out of control. She tried to tell the others this, to convey the sense of evil about this man. She went into some detail about what he had done in Chicago, in Seattle, to Thorpe with her parents, and now this. She only stopped when she realized that the state policemen listening to her were beginning to wonder about her.

She fell silent until they reached the wreckage where some raggedly dressed Canadian in overalls that were torn and dirty had tried to claim the salvage rights to the helicopter since it was on "his" land. He had hooked a tow truck pulley to the damned thing and was cranking it in with great care. The Mounties had simply stood back and watched him do so before they told him he could take not a single thing from the aircraft since it was evidence in a criminal case.

This was what Robyn pushed past when she arrived, going directly for the cab, stepping out into the water up to her knees and peering inside the cab at the dead pilot whose throat was split like a melon, the blood washed away by the river, no sign of Ovierto.

"There was a second man in the chopper! Did you see anyone climb from the water?" she shouted at the salvage man.

"No, no . . . no one."

"If you're lying—" She approached as if she would tear his heart out.

"I saw no one! No one alive!"

She grabbed him by the lapels of the oily jumpsuit he wore and shoved him into the side of a huge green tractor that appeared rusted solid. "Did you see another body, then! Did you? Did you?"

The hefty man swung at her, hitting Robyn Muro in the ribs, to which she responded with a knee to his groin, sending him to his knees as the New York State police officers pulled her off. She felt completely alone, watching all of the local cops staring at her as if she were a monster.

Sam Boas came to her, finding her in a Canadian parka and drinking hot cocoa laced with a local whiskey.

Robyn Muro's distress call had also been heard by Dr. Samuel Boas and the other agents waiting this side of Ottawa. They rushed to the scene in a helicopter, which had promptly been put to work locating the airstrip used by Ovierto, to close off any chance he might have of getting to his airplane and escaping the area entirely. The plane had to be somewhere nearby, but according to the Canadian officer who joined the helicopter crew, there were twenty-one small airstrips in the region. It would take great patience and time to locate a single Beechcraft that didn't "belong."

Meanwhile, Dr. Boas had been dropped at the scene of the helicopter wreckage. He had been monitoring radio transmissions as they had approached, and, on first seeing the crash sight, he cursed their luck. Everything would be much easier if the damned machine had plunged onto the American side, or at least in the center of the river. He had seen what complications could arise between the two countries when extradition orders were put through. And with a man like Ovierto, if the Canadians attempted to hold him for up to six months or a year while they decided, he'd break free to kill again.

Hopefully, he was dead already, a victim of the crash. But somehow Sam Boas didn't imagine that the evil doctor would go so easily. News had it that he had drowned, that the body had not been recovered from the wreckage, only that of the pilot.

Boas's first concern on landing would be to examine the pilot's body and the wreckage closely, to see if it told him anything. Now he was on scene, and Boas saw Robyn coming straight for him—obviously distraught, unattended bruises on her cheek, forehead, and hands—but still alive. She had survived the awful drug and frigid coffin that had killed Riley; she had survived a firefight with Maurice Ovierto, the firefight that had killed Donna Thorpe.

Instinctively, he took her in his arms, but she pulled free, shouting, "Doc, we've got to get these fucking Canadians moving. He's getting away! Ovierto is getting away, and these fuckin' idiots got their fingers up their asses and—"

"Take it easy . . . easy . . ."

"Easy my ass, Sam! He killed Donna! Or rather, he got me to kill her."

"*Whoa* up, slow down." She was on an adrenalin high.

"He's getting away! I know it! I can feel it. He got free of the wreckage. No one saw him. No one saw. He's disappeared."

"He's very likely at the bottom of the river."

"Then tell these assholes to start dredging!"

"We may have to do such operations ourselves, Robyn."

"I can't believe this."

He made her sit down, ordering more of the cocoa from the man who apparently lived in the ramshackle old place on the property. An enterprising man, he had brewed coffee, made cocoa, had broken out some whiskey, and was selling it all at inflated prices. The men and women on scene appreciated his efforts far more than they denounced them.

With Robyn calmed a bit, Boas now went to work overseeing the inspection of both the aircraft and the pilot's body. He immediately noted the throat wound and the severed safety belt. Another victim of the maniac, the pilot had been murdered. The damage to the helicopter was slight. Broken bubble, crushed supports and detached wheel. It was a "soft" landing crash, he felt, soft enough so that both men could have survived. Ovierto had obviously feared that the pilot would be taken alive, questioned, and break under that questioning, so the man was killed.

He returned to Robyn and the clutch of agents who had been with Thorpe since her removal to Nebraska. The other men were offering hesitant congratulations to Robyn for a job well done. "At least you know you put a bullet in him, and you brought down his helicopter," an agent named Pyles was telling her. "That's more'n anyone else, other than Sykes and Thorpe, ever got with him."

Boas then reported to them all the bad news as he saw it, explaining his preliminary findings in the cab of the chopper. "This means that Ovierto was alive at the point of impact, when he knew they were going down. He would have cut the safety belt only if he could not get it unlatched, or if he could not reach it, given the angle of the cab, water

289

flooding in."

"What are you saying, then? He's still alive? I knew it," said Robyn, getting excited again.

He waved her down. "He cut both belts and pushed himself outward in an attempt to save himself, but—"

"Knowing Ovierto, he meant to use the pilot's body as a float, like a goddamned log, to take him down river," she said. "That's it."

"Possibly."

"What do you mean, possible, Doc? Possible, hell! The man's an animal. Deserves to be found hiding in the hole he's lying in and shot dead the way you'd shoot a dangerous snake."

The Mountie in charge of the Canadian investigation joined them, asking Dr. Boas if he would like to share his findings with them.

"He's alive, you asshole! Boas says he's alive," shouted Robyn. "Ovierto is alive and he's making fools of us all, and all you do is sit on your thumbs!"

"We have patrol cars monitoring all along the edge of the river. Highway 12 follows the course of the river, Madam Inspector."

"Muro, Sergeant Muro!" she said.

"Sergeant? Ahhh, I see, then you are not FBI?"

"She is part of the FBI investigation," said Boas.

He nodded and frowned as if he now understood. "You are American police on Canadian soil. We must cooperate, but we must do so with great care. I sympathize with your problem. Many times we must chase bad men across the border. Very often, *your* authorities do not cooperate with us."

Boas told the man about the two Canadian scien-

290

tists who had been poisoned in Atlanta by Ovierto.

The Mountie nodded, obviously remembering the case. "I see, then we have a vested interest, you are saying. I will do all within my limited power. Cornwall is not a large city. We do not have the great resources of Washington D.C., or even Ottawa. But I will see what can be done."

As he walked off, Robyn said to Boas, "You see? You see the fuckin' attitude I've had to deal with?"

"It takes tact, Robyn. More than you have in your state of mind."

"Well pardon me . . . pardon me, but I've just seen four people killed at close range around me."

"I understand."

"Do you? Does anyone? Donna understood . . . but she's gone."

Robyn slumped onto a wooden picnic bench where she had been sitting. Everyone watched her. She was exhausted and frustrated, and the anger rose off her like heat. The fact that Ovierto had slipped through, as she believed, compounded by the snail's pace at which the Canadians were moving, was driving her mad. She was now yelling at Boas to use whatever influence he had, to contact Washington and tell them to contact Ottawa.

"There," Boas said in response, pointing. "Over the river."

A maple leaf was splashed over the side of the Harriman aircraft that was exploring the river and the river's edge all along the possible escape route of the madman. The huge, dark aircraft hovered in place, turned like a helicopter, and then returned down the length of the river in what seemed to be slow motion for its streamlined look. It was a Canadian military plane.

"I contacted them en route."

In the distance a pair of Cornwall Police helicopters also combed the area from the skies. A Coast Guard boat from the American side of the river, followed by a second, was going up and down the river. This went on for several hours, but the search was turning up nothing.

As night turned to dawn, she told Boas about how Riley had died, about how she survived, and how Donna Thorpe had been killed by one of Robyn's own bullets. "It's going to look bad, Sam," she said. "Pyles, some of the others, they heard me threaten her after Joe's death, and now she dies with a bullet from my gun."

"You were lured into a crossfire for Christ's sake. You were almost killed yourself!"

This didn't seem to help. He said softly, "Look, we've ordered everything be left as is, nothing touched, save for the bodies, and I'm going over to the locks now to do my investigation. Why don't you come with me? I'll examine the scene. You can be of great help there. Here, there's nothing for you to do. What do you say?"

"But Ovierto is out there somewhere."

She looked down river. Sam frowned. "I really think we've done all we can here, Robyn. It's over now."

"No, no we haven't. We've got to get divers in here, dredge for the body. We've got to find the body."

"But in this river, with this current, it'd be like looking for the bloody *Titanic*." The river here was spread as wide as a glassy plain, the power of the undercurrent showing up as small ripples in the glass. Seeing the American shore in the distance was like looking at the shore of the Mississippi.

"We've got to try, damnit."

"It could take days, weeks."

"Then it takes weeks, but we do it. We owe that much to Donna. We all owe Donna."

He took a deep breath, placed a firm hand on her shoulders, and said, "All right. All right."

Chapter Twenty-nine

Maurice Ovierto had found a mud hole with a pipe into which he had slithered. He'd tied off the leg to staunch the flow of blood. The wound in his arm had been a mere crease, but the leg wound had developed into a hammering pain and the loss of blood threatened to send him into unconsciousness. Muro's bullet had caused an increase in anxiety which translated to a proportionate increase in the stomach cramps caused by his disease. And he had lain out in the tall prairie grass in the sun too long, having collapsed from exhaustion. The sunlight had baked away at his flesh, and the porphyria was doing its work to scar and pockmark him, not to mention the amount of nerve damage caused by the trauma that she had inflicted on him.

He was suffering, and he didn't like that. He was a wounded animal, unable to think clearly.

But now he had found a hole in which he could regain his strength and control of his mind, in which to think. The first thing he thought about was his medicine. He had lost the small supply he had been carrying, and the rest was aboard the plane with his other things. They would stumble onto the plane even if they were blind, and to go directly to Long Sault Airport was suicide, and yet he needed the drugs.

Where else . . . where else could he get the drugs? A pharmacy? He didn't have steady enough hands to disable an alarm, much less the strength to run from pursuing police. Where else? Where else could he get the drugs?

He must increase his intake of carbohydrates to help combat the attacks of acute intermittent porphyria. If he could get hold of some straight Portagen, the food additive. Then he realized that most any medicine cabinet would have enough drugs for him to create his own homemade variety of the drug he needed, a kind of specialized vitamin supplement.

But he'd have to travel by night, like an animal, and sleep by day in places like this pipe, praying no local cop would think of it as a place where he might create a den.

The water had frightened him. He had always had a morbid fear of drowning, and when the water had gushed in at him where he was semidrenched, caught in the cab of the helicopter, he'd found it difficult to think clearly. He swam out from the machine, instantly taken along by the current, fighting to remain close enough to shore to find footing. Each time he had put his feet down in an attempt to meet the ground, there was no floor, and he was swept inexorably along, snatching at branches that hung out over the river and ripped from these as if he were a toothpick in the rush. He hated the feeling of fear and utter helplessness that had overcome him. To die was one thing, but to become fish fodder in the cold river that'd soon be frozen over disturbed him to his core. He had almost drowned as a child, and the horror of that moment had never left him.

All around him in the darkened pipe he heard noises, the loudest being the drip and movement of the water in the drain pipe, one of thousands that skirted the highways here. The constant sound of the water kept bringing back the terror he'd felt in the river. He couldn't sleep for the sound and its accompanying nightmare, coming as it did in rhythmic waves as he dozed, froze, came awake, dozed, froze, came awake, dozed again, froze again, came awake again, hour after hour in the hole to which Robyn Muro had sent him.

He thought of the revenge he would wreak on her; this thought was sweeter than the memories of the near-drowning, and so he clung to it. He decided he would live to see her suffer as he was now suffering. His face was peeling, burning, and scarred; terrible things were happening to his insides, his stomach, his nerves. His leg throbbed with a fiery pain, as if a jagged knife were lodged there. She'd used some kind of exploding bullet and it had ripped through his leg, severing arteries. He'd be left with a perpetual limp. He'd been maimed by a woman, and he meant to live to see her pay for her cruelty toward him. He dreamed of having her at his mercy, having her in chains on a cold slab below his scalpel. He dreamed and smiled and rested, and in the dreams of revenge he quickly forgot the sound of trickling water and the fear of drowning.

And in the back of his mind, he thought out each step necessary to his survival.

Robyn finally agreed to go with Boas back to the locks to view the scene of Donna Thorpe's death. Donna's body was in the morgue of a hospital in Massena, New York, awaiting transportation back to D.C., where she would join her parents in an unmarked grave, as was her request. Even in death, she felt she must hide from Ovierto's perverted interest in her, and rightly so. Robyn had conveyed her wishes to Boas, who had balked at them, saying, "But if we find Ovierto's body, that will not be necessary."

"Until we find Ovierto's body and it's identified beyond any doubt, doctor, we do as Donna requested."

"Very well," he had conceded.

Now they walked through the firefight with Ovierto, and Robyn explained how everything had happened; how the young Indian man was knifed down by Ovierto, how Riley had been catapulted from the cold container box and into the locks, his body lost forever, she thought. How she had clung to life at the edge of the locks, and how Donna had come on like a maniac herself in close pursuit of Ovierto, just behind her. She explained how they took different directions, Donna to the rear and she to the front of the power plant.

All of the paraphernalia that Ovierto had rigged earlier at the rear of the plant was clearly visible now by daylight. He had set up a three-way imaging mirror using advanced transponders to create an image of himself at the center of the triangle. The ruse had gotten Thorpe killed.

The lock master who had come on in the A.M. had been trying desperately to get Boas and Robyn to listen to him. He said he thought he could possibly get the dead agent's body from the locks.

"Riley?" asked Boas.

"There's maybe a way."

"How?" asked Robyn.

"We throw all our power into filling up the lock to capacity, all at once. It'd work as well as cannons firing off, reversing those turbines so quickly. Everything was shut down after what happened here. I was called in to do the work. There's a chance that—"

"Then do it," ordered Boas.

Robyn exchanged a glance with Boas and they mentally crossed their fingers together. For the next half hour they watched and waited as the lock where the British freighter, *Carpathia*, had sat the night before, as the waters were churned into a cauldron. The level of the water rose and rose and suddenly Robyn saw a man's hand rise to the surface.

A team of men in a boat who had been riding out the manmade storm in the lock cut loose from their safe hold onto the anchoring lines and went out toward Riley, pulling his pale form onto the boat with them, the water lapping up over the side with the body.

Robyn had watched the entire episode wishing to God that it was Maurice Ovierto's body that they were dredging up instead of Riley's, when an idea hit her. She shouted it to Boas. "The water level around the dam could be increased like this, couldn't it! Couldn't it?"

"Well, yeah, I suppose so, but—"

"For Ovierto's body. If it's settled to the bottom a good churning up from the dam might have the same effect as this—"

"And it could send the body just further down river. The search area's already mapped out, and divers are at work out there—*at our request*—along with dredging vessels."

"But the body could be made to rise, if the damned body is out there at all!"

"It'll take all kinds of authorization to—"

"Come on! We'll get it from the American side of the fuckin' damn. We don't wait for Canadian bullshit."

Ovierto awoke with a start, with the drowning dream again, and for good reason. The water in the pipe had risen and was at his chest! Had there been a goddamned downpour outside? The sun was shining. It was three-forty-two by his watch. He was drenched and all manner of debris floated about him. Field mice were scurrying about the upper portions of the pipe. He looked out toward the river side and realized that the grass was gone! *Under water!* Suddenly there was a surge of water covering his vision, filling the pipe, sending him tumbling, coughing, choking. He clawed his way toward the other end of the pipe, pulling hard for the edge, unable to see in the fetid, mud-colored water, holding his breath until he thought his lungs would burst. Further suffering. Terrorizing him with his water fear. She was behind it. She and Thorpe. Thorpe was dead but somehow guiding her hand, telling her he was here, alive in this hole, and so she had filled it with water as if she were wielding a gigantic garden hose! But how? How could she know?

His hands felt the edge of the pipe, and he pulled his drowning, prone body up and up and out, finding his feet and standing in waist-deep water that filled the ditch along the highway. Cars speeding by paid him no mind, not seeing him throwing up and clinging to the roadbed. Thank God, no police cars. But now a beat-up old Dodge pickup came to a screeching halt, sending up rocks all around him.

The driver, a pair of coveralls over his plaid shirt, marched back to him with boots that stank of pig shit and cows. "Mister? Mister? You look like hell caught you by the ass. Mister? You best get in the truck and we'll get you into Cornwall to the hospital."

"Car went off the road," Ovierto managed to gurgle and moan.

"Car? Don't see no car," he said.

"Back a half mile . . . in the ditch . . . in the water!"

"Christ, you mean you been crawlin' half a mile and nobody'd stop to pick you up? Christ . . . world comin' to?"

He stared back, trying to locate the car while at the same time helping Ovierto to his feet and the roadbed.

Gravel slipped beneath Ovierto's feet and the farmer held tighter. Ovierto's good hand was on the blade stuffed in his belt. He could kill the old fool here now, take the truck and try to make it to Long Sault Airport, but cars were passing, one slowing down as if wondering if assistance was needed, and besides, Ovierto didn't have that much strength, *yet*.

"Don't see no car," the old man said.

"It's in the goddamned water!" shouted Ovierto, annoyed. "Get me into your truck."

The older man did so, grumbling about the authorities at the dam. " 'Spose to give residents around fair warning when they're going to open that mother! But they don't . . . they don't . . ."

"Opened the dam . . . yeah . . . that's what she did," Ovierto said to himself as the old man walked around to the other side to get in.

"What'd you say?" he asked, getting in.

"Get going," said Ovierto. "I said, get going."

He cranked up the truck and after a minute's waiting for other cars to pass him, the truck was barreling down the highway, passing a patrol car. The old man waved at the patrol car, saying, "We ought to get you an escort! That leg looks nasty!"

But the patrol car whizzed by, ignoring the old man's wave. "Where you live?" asked Ovierto.

"Back about three or four miles."

"Take me there."

"What? Mister, you need medical attention."

"Take me to your house!" He jabbed the knife into the farmer's ribs.

"Son of a bitch," said the older man.

"Do as I goddamned say!" He punctured the old man's midriff.

"Okay, all right . . . all right!"

"Don't do anything stupid, if you want to live through this day."

"No . . . no, I won't."

"No kindness goes unpunished, old fella. Old as

301

you are, you ought to know that," Ovierto told him with a *tsk, tsk*. Ovierto was beginning to brighten, to feel a bit of cheer, a little hope for his future, which was getting brighter thanks to the Canadian farmer with the pig shit on his feet.

Even with the cooperation of the Canadian authorities, even with the powerful turbines shut down and the undersea doors opened to churn up the seaway for miles upon miles down stream, and even with the rising waters overflowing their banks and flooding the flatlands to the roads on either side, no sign of Ovierto was found. His plane was, however, definitely identified, sitting between two others at Long Sault. Still, they dredged the river for miles below the dam, repeating the process for three days before giving up the search completely. Meanwhile, an APB was circulated to every police agency on both sides of the border. Police were on the alert at every bus depot, train station, airport, and seaport. The net began to tighten when the police began a door-to-door search of every house within a fifty-mile radius of the crash sight.

Boas had seen to it that every pharmacist and doctor in the area was on the lookout for anyone requiring an emergency supply of high-carbohydrate concentrates and drugs to combat acute intermittent porphyria. He also alerted all area asylums to be especially watchful for anyone unfamiliar to the staff, as Ovierto had a habit of charming his way in and out of such places, sometimes with a hostage, such as Rosenthaler. Everyone was on the alert. The newscasts flashed photos of Ovierto in and out of costume, and the headlines warned of his sinister nature, detailing his record of atrocities with the necessary "alleged" before each crime.

In the meantime, the Canadians were calling for a halt to the search, claiming that the madman was somewhere below the St. Lawrence River piloting the *Hellspur* (the ship that had gone down in a terrible gale here the year before and had taken on the status of a legend when the singer Gordon Lightfoot had made a ballad of the incident).

In the meantime, all the efforts to create a net around the phantom that was Dr. O failed one after another. The most important measures simply had taken too much time.

Karl Van Jaecle, an old farmer who ran hogs to and from the Ottawa Market, was found dead with his aged wife inside their farmhouse, discovered not by the police but a young priest who was visiting the wife. The priest called the Cornwall Police, who dispatched cars to the location immediately. They had the scene all to themselves for three hours before they handed it over to the FBI. They had decided to do their own manhunt for the killer.

The moment Boas and Robyn Muro entered the farmhouse they knew it was the work of Ovierto, for he had left a clear message in blood to Robyn. It was smeared on the refrigerator door in the kitchen where he had carved up the old woman. It read:

Was it fun for you, Muro?

"The bastard," she muttered, "the bloody, bloody bastard."

"He's got at least a twelve-hour start on us," Boas said, his voice as rough as a washboard from the days of anxiety.

"He's gotten away . . . far from here now."

"No, there are road blocks everywhere, and we have a description of the truck," said the Mountie in charge. "He's killed Canadian citizens on Canadian soil now, and—"

"And so that makes all the difference!" she shouted. "You're not dealing with a bank robber here. This man's not your ordinary slice-and-dice serial killer, either. He's driven, and he's cunning, Captain . . . more cunning than one of your timber wolves. And he'll kill again and again without respect to borders or who gets in his way. Maybe if your people had cooperated with me a week ago, these poor devils here would be alive!"

The captain shouted at her all the way out the door as Boas rushed her out. "Who do you think you are? He writes a note to you, and that makes you special? I hope it brings you pleasure!"

"Bastard," Robyn muttered to Boas who rushed her to a waiting car.

"It's over here, Muro. It's over. We go back to D.C."

"To do what? Sit and wait for him to dictate our next move?"

"You're off the case, Muro. For you, it's back to Chicago, back to your work there," Boas said.

She looked at him, her eyes trying to penetrate his calm. "Just like that? You want me to forget all this ever happened?"

"It's an FBI matter; always has been, and we—the Bureau—must pick up the pieces. You are not

304

actually one of us."

She was taken up short by his attitude. She slumped in the car which sped toward Ottawa and the airport.

She quietly said, "You've gotten orders from D.C.?"

"That is true, but also, I thought you would like to be at the services being held for Donna Thorpe."

"Yes, of course . . . and we are going to respect her wishes about an anonymous grave site?"

"Well, yes and no."

"What does that mean?"

"It means that she will be buried twice, discreetly and quietly the first time, a show the next."

"But you said—"

"And we've arranged to lure that sick sonofabitch, Ovierto, to a phony wake and burial at Arlington."

She thought about this sad testimonial to Donna Thorpe's life, and it squeezed at her stomach. She didn't want her life to end this way, to be *used* even in death as a lure for a maniac.

"Where'd you get the body?"

"Donated, you might say."

"Riley?"

"No, no, we're not that bloody crude."

"Where then?"

"An unattached female resident of Bellevue Psychiatric, a Jane Doe, already in flight toward D.C."

"So, you guys are taking over from here?"

"That's about the size of it, Robyn. You've got nothing to be ashamed of. You did your level best, and everyone appreciates that, everyone. In fact, if you ever want to enroll in the academy, the Agency could use you. As for now. . . well, we don't need

305

or want another Donna Thorpe-Dr. Ovierto relationship where the crazy bastard's killing people off just to have something to send you. And now the message he left you at that old farmhouse, it's . . . it is as though he's decided to place you in that role, and none of us — you included — wants that."

"I always underestimated you, Sam . . . always thought you took orders."

"I do. We all do."

"No, you put this together, and with the best of intentions, I'm sure, but you could also arrange a temporary status in the Agency for me, if you wanted to, couldn't you? Couldn't you?"

"I'm not going to do that."

"Ovierto has already targeted me as his playmate, Sam. He won't let you do this. He'll find me in Chicago. He only plays if there's an audience that cares, the way Donna cared."

"It's out of my hands, Robyn." The finality of his tone told her that minds were made up and that she was out.

"Then why invite me to her funeral?"

"You're invited to her true funeral, not the bogus one."

She nodded, biting her lip. "Gotcha."

"We all feel you did a brave job, a good job, Robyn, and no one wants to see you become his next psychological victim."

"Funny," she replied, "I think it's too late for that." She sat in silence, the bare December countryside, which was brown and stark here in Canada, where the birch trees proliferated like hair on the head of the globe. The trees stretched on for mile after mile. She thought of how Ovierto had maimed her

306

mind, mutilated her heart and soul by taking the people she most loved and admired. She knew she couldn't just walk away from it.

"How do I get started at this academy of yours?"

Boas looked disappointed in her. "I had thought you were a woman of superior intellect. Why would you—"

"Fine, I know I can expect no help then from you . . . fine."

"I didn't say that I wouldn't help you. If you are determined."

"I am."

"You're sure?"

"I'm sure . . . I'm very sure."

They'd arrived at the Ottawa airport, a Lear jet waiting to take them back to D.C. The flight was dismal and quiet, the absence of Thorpe felt by everyone. In the silence, the others heard a tossing Robyn Muro mutter in her sleep, *"One day . . . I'll get you . . . least expect it . . . I'll be there . . ."*

Chapter Thirty

Maurice Ovierto had triumphed once again over the forces set against him, and he had seen to Thorpe's death, although it had been a terrible waste. Given her mental state, given the trap that had meant to ensnare him, it seemed inevitable, and yet he still hungered to have her on a rack, to flay the skin from her, to do unspeakable torture to her, drain her blood, syphon it into a pint bottle and hold it up to her eyes and let her watch him drain it like red beer. But she was gone now, all but her body remaining. Torturing her body, even if he could dig it from the earth of the largest, most prestigious cemetery in the nation, would gain him little satisfaction. But maybe the mental anguish it would cause to her friend and fellow agent, this Robyn Muro, perhaps that would make the effort worth something? No one had ever grave-robbed from Arlington. Could it be done?

He certainly *missed* the Thorpes. . . .

He wandered about the periphery of the fence now, watching the burial party, listening to the snap and pop of the distant twenty-one gun salute given Thorpe. She deserved all their respect. She had come the closest to stopping him, she and Muro.

He remembered watching them in the restaurant together, seeing their affection for one another, but oddly, Muro wasn't present today. Had she been unable to face it? But how does one stay away from the funeral of a loved one, a colleague, a sister? Was it so painful?

Or was there another reason? He could not fathom the reason. Time and distance constraints? In his casual contact with the Bureau, declaring himself an accountant with the division that took care of such monetary needs as the payment of agents, he had learned that Muro was no agent, and had only been on a kind of lend-lease program with the Chicago PD, like that man, Swisher, who had died for Thorpe's sins. Was there a connection there? Swisher and Muro?

He had made inquiries, discreet and well-targeted, in Chicago, learning that Swisher and Robyn Muro had shared a squad car as partners in various decoy operations, usually in vice and homicide. He wondered about the relationship, and about that which had existed between Thorpe and Muro.

It might take a long time to sort it all out, but it was important to do so, and so he would, eventually.

He had gotten the old man in the back bedroom of the farmhouse, ordering him to tie his wife's hands and legs, forcing her to lie in the bed. As soon as this was done, he stabbed the old man in the heart before her eyes, and told her that if she made any attempt to move that he would do the same to her. She was petrified, and this increased his will to get better and do her.

He had torn the house apart looking for the necessary foods and drugs that he required, stuffing raw potatoes into his mouth, searching for and finding all the starches he could. In the medicinal department, he had located some carbolic acid and camphor. Mixing the two, he created a good germ-combating compound of the tar-based substance. This staunched his bullet wounds, leaving him sweating with the initial pain of applying it, but feeling much better.

He knew he was too weak to move that night and that he needed more substantial green foods filled with carbohydrates to combat the awful porphyria that had gone into a second acute stage. He went in to the old woman and released her bonds, a shotgun in his hands now. He ordered her to cook a huge plate of vegetables for him while he ate sugar straight from the canister.

He ordered her to sit across from him while he ate. She was subdued, but her eyes burned into him with her hatred. He gorged himself like an athlete on a carbohydrate-loading diet, realizing that his escape from the area would be a true endurance struggle. But he was feeling better with each mouthful of the food. He even began to feel like killing the old woman.

He drank down the milk she had secured from the refrigerator. It had come from the farm and tasted unlike any he was used to, neither homogenized nor pasteurized. It seemed almost bitter.

He then told her to fill herself a glass of the milk.

She declined.

He insisted, lifting the gun.

She poured and sat the glass before her.

He told her he was a doctor, and that he was now going to give her a little something harmless to knock her out, and that when she awoke he would be gone, but that she would still have her life.

"Would you like that?"

"Yes . . . yes . . ."

"Here's the sedative," he told her, pouring in what was left of the carbolic acid.

She protested, saying, "That's not a sedative. That's from the vet, to clean wounds outa' the—"

"Christ, woman! I'm a doctor! I know what I'm talking about! So, it cleans small wounds. It can also be used to knock a person out. Now, drink it!"

She swallowed hard, lifted the glass.

"Drink it!" He pointed the gun.

She drank until the glass was half empty.

"More! All of it, all of it. Do as Dr. Ovierto says."

She hesitated but took it up and finished the milk laced with the carbolic acid.

"Now, you old horse, I'm just going to sit here and watch you die," he said, laughing uproariously.

Her eyes widened as she felt the first bite of the poison.

"Depresses the nerves," he said. "That's why it's such a good cleansing agent. Doesn't burn so badly if the nerves are deadened. But from inside? Christ, lady, it's about to stop your lungs from working—"

She lunged for him, but he simply backed off, pulling the shotgun out of her reach, laughing at her pain. "—and, as I was about to say . . ."

311

She climbed from the floor, grabbed a meat cleaver, and came for him.

"As I was about to say, it then stops the blood flow and —"

She collapsed at his feet, the meat cleaver spinning across the ancient linoleum floor.

"And you die," he finished.

But he wasn't finished with the body. He needed some of her blood, if he was to leave his message to Muro. He located and placed on one of her huge linen aprons, dug around for the cleaver she'd proposed using on him, and began to cut a hole in her for the *ink* he required. With the rich stuff in plentiful supply, he dabbled a finger into the bowl of it he had collected. And then he wrote his message.

He returned to the old man after he had cleaned himself up, going for the keys to his truck. He found them, along with clothes that fit him. He had also managed to find enough makeup in the woman's drawer to be of use to him. Finally, he had searched a storage shack for gasoline. He found two five-gallon drums. With what was already in the truck, it'd be enough to get him as far as a gas station that did not have his picture in the window.

But he knew the bodies would be discovered within twenty-four hours, that he'd have to ditch the truck and find another route out. He did this neatly enough, pulling the truck off the road, lifting out one of the now-empty gas cans, and walking along the side of the road for the next town, a place where he was told there was a bridge that went across to the American side. He had lifted Canadian money and wallet from the old man at the pig farm.

Another man in a light truck, a '79 Ford with a King cab that guzzled gas, pulled over to give him a lift. It was what he had been hoping for.

He dispatched the good samaritan with a quick jab to the heart, hauled him out of the truck on the passenger side, and covered him over in the ditch. This man was closer to him in age, so he exchanged wallets with him to further confound the police. At the next town, he crossed the bridge that would take him into America, into Ogdensburg, New York. There were extra men at the toll booths—lawmen. He passed by the Canadian check without incident. When he got to the American checkpoint he saw that the police were checking everyone in earnest.

Cars were being detained, trunks were being popped. Ovierto pulled over into this area, parking the old, black Ford and ambling to the rest rooms. He saw the path out of this lot to the other side of the booths. He was close, but he must be careful.

From the rest room window he stared out at the lot, seeing it empty out, save for his truck and a car. He had seen two cars pull off with several people in each. But the last car seemed to belong to a single woman, traveling alone. He had seen her arguing with the crossing guard as he had sauntered into the rest room. He now saw her going out to her car, apparently cleared to go through.

He slipped back out the rear and went directly to the car, where the woman was just getting in. He shoved in hard atop her, pushing her over and put-

313

ting the knife to her throat, slitting it, cutting off her screams and pushing her to the other side. He started up the ignition and backed out of the parking place calmly. He averted his face and made for the strip of pavement that led to the other side, where only a toll booth remained.

The man in the booth might see the woman. He found a coat in the rear and covered her with it. Paying the man required American currency, and he had to fish in her purse for this, complaining that his wife got to sleep while he got held up at customs. "Slept right through it. So, she can pay for the toll," he finished as he rifled her purse.

"Okay," said the booth attendant. "Enjoy your visit to America."

"You bet . . . you bet . . ."

Ogdensburg had a fairly large airport out of which passenger planes flew, but it would be crawling with cops. He wondered where a smaller airport could be found where he could get a helicopter or a small plane out. He needed a map of the area, and the first place he stopped was at a Texaco station, where he purchased a map while the body of the dead woman was still bleeding onto the carpet and seat of the car. He had parked it out of the way, but some asshole had come in after and pulled in beside him. The man got out and came straight for the station, paying no heed to the dead woman in the car beside him. Ovierto rushed back and saw the blood dripping from the bottom of the door.

It froze him for a moment. But then he nonchalantly returned to the pumps, got a few paper towels, wet them and went to work on the drips that the wind had hardened against the white exterior.

Back inside the car, he shoved the coat below the dead woman's head and throat to catch the blood. In his rearview mirror, he saw a man in another car pulling into the station. The man was waving at Ovierto's car as if he knew it from the license plate. Ovierto calmly lifted a hand, returned the wave, pulled out into traffic, and headed south on U.S. 34.

About eight miles out, on a dirt road, he got rid of the body, but anyone getting into the car or staring too long at the seat would see the blood. He studied the map he had bought, picked out a small airport, and went some twenty miles further south, where he saw the international sign for airport. He pulled in and found the guy in charge. He had seen no helicopters so he asked if he might rent a plane to take up for the afternoon.

He was told that he'd have to leave some ID and a Visa or MasterCard. Fortunately, MasterCard did a great business in Canada. He used the dead man's card and a twenty and a ten for the hours of flight in advance.

"You going to want to file a flight plan, Mr. *Annnnnreeee?*"

"I just thought I'd circle about the area . . . not going anywhere. Maybe check out the river, that sort of thing."

"Just don't go too far into Canada," said the slim flight instructor. "I mean those dudes get real pissed off if they pick you up on any of their radar. Figure you for a goddamned cargo of drugs. Trust me."

"Sure, no problem."

"Well, just bein' friendly. You aren't from around here. I know most of the flyers around here."

"I'm on vacation . . . with the wife . . . up here to visit the in-laws. Had to get away from that mob."

"Best place to hide," said the man with a smile. "Straight up."

"You got that right."

"Come on." He led him out to a battered old plane, but it had a full tank of petrol and from here he could be to Detroit before this fool realized that he had lost his plane.

Detroit wasn't his favorite city, but from Detroit he had been able to get to his safe retreat in the heartland.

But he hadn't long remained content in the old farmhouse in Missouri. Each hour that clicked by reminded him that Robyn Muro hadn't heard from him since Canada. So, he'd come to D.C. to find her at the grave site when he had learned of the burial plans for her friend. But Muro wasn't here.

He moved calmly from the cemetery gate so as to garner no undue attention. The streets were busy with milling tourists; a clutch of them were getting off a bus in front of him. He wandered into them for cover, looking over his shoulder to see if anyone was watching him. Then he saw some men in an office window. They had high-powered lenses and they had been tracking him. He tried to remain calm. In his disguise, they had no way of knowing it was him. He wondered if Muro was with the surveillance team. But he could see no evidence of this.

316

He had to know of her whereabouts. He must know where to send his *gifts*.

As for Pythagoras, he had no further illusions of their ever parting with the secret of such power. So, he'd have to go on killing, and killing, and killing until one day he was killed. He saw no other end to it.

He had to get to a phone, find out where Muro was.

Epilogue

Boas hadn't made the bogus burial either. He had instead seen Muro off at Washington National Airport. He stood tall and decrepit all at once, as he waved her off.

In her seat, heading for Chicago, Robyn Muro thought about what Sam Boas had told her, and she wondered if it was the truth—as unbelievable as it was—or if it was meant to simply keep her from ever talking about Pythagoras again.

Sam had sworn it was the truth when he said, "That project has been a worse drain on the American economy than Star Wars, and has proved just as useless! Pythagoras was scrapped a year ago, but a handful of scientists, Oliguerri the worst of them, wouldn't let it go. They kept hammering at it and talking too much about it in the process."

"What are you saying, Sam? That Pythagoras still does not work, not even with what Oliguerri left?"

"Exactly . . . all a dream, Robyn, a foolhardy dream."

"A dream to heal people."

"That was Oliguerri's dream, Hogarth's and the others."

318

"But the Pentagon's dreams were a little skewed toward another kind of end?"

"Those Pentagon dreams are dead as well."

"You wouldn't lie to me, would you, Sam?"

"Not about this."

"What about Ovierto? He doesn't consider it dead, but maybe if you could somehow convince him. Go public with the botched project, the cost to the taxpayers, all of it . . . then perhaps."

"We've considered all of that. Problem is, and this I support with all that I know about Ovierto . . . the man doesn't really care about Pythagoras. He had created an idea of himself actually capable of putting it to work for him, but he's like a dog chasing a car. If he caught it, what would he do with it?"

"Then why not give it to him?"

"It would change nothing, don't you see?"

"He'd go on as he has been."

"Without stop."

"Is he right to blame Pythagoras on his own mental state?"

"Yes, there was an accident. Others lost their lives. He . . . he was considered at the time . . . *lucky.*"

They had parted on that note, both of them witnesses to Dr. Maurice Ovierto's incredible "luck."

And though they had heard nothing from Ovierto in all this time, Robyn sensed that the silence would not long go undisturbed. She feared not knowing how or when he would come at her again. She feared she had not heard the last from him.

She planned a quick visit to Chicago, to set

things right with Chief Noone and the department, put her life there in order, prepare for a move to D.C., where in a month she would become an FBI cadet. With her time in at the police academy, and the time she had logged on the force in Chicago, she had been assured that she would move up in the Agency quickly.

But she knew that "quickly" would not be soon enough, before Dr. O struck again.